SCARS

SCARS

—

C. M. Newlands

ISBN 1944196935
ISBN 9781944196936
Library of Congress Control Number: 2016912465
SloWriters Publishing LLC, Tampa, FL

eISBN 978-1-944196-94-3

**Dedicated to everyone
that has felt the painful, life altering effects
of substance addiction.**

Acknowledgements

———

*Thank you to my mother, Mary, who taught me I could
accomplish anything with hard work and dedication. You led
by example, showing me how to conquer any obstacle.
You will always have my love and admiration.*

*To my amazing daughter, Annalee, you are the light of my life and
I love you so very much. I cherish all of your supportive words
and thank you for always being so proud of the things I do.
We will always be stuck like glue.*

*To my one true love and best friend, Ed, thank you for believing in
me whole heartedly. Your support and encouragement are priceless.
You have filled my world with smiles, love, and laughter.
I love you honey, then, now, and forever.*

*Thank you to my friend, Kim. You have always been super sup-
portive, even when offering a needed, sobering dose, of reality.
Your friendship is unparalleled.*

EPILOGUE

—————

"HEY, YOU GUYS LOOKIN'?" HE asked, with a gesture of his head motioning them over towards him.

Barely visible beyond his outline, Derrick Bishop was leaning on a building and hidden by the shadows that fell on the street from the surrounding structures. The two men appeared to be in their early twenties, and began to approach as he moved into the light. It could be seen that he was dirty, unkempt with matted hair, and wearing stain covered clothing that showed signs of age.

Seemingly unaffected by his appearance, one of them said, "What ya got?"

Stepping into the adjacent alley, Derrick said, "Weed or oxy, I'll make you a good deal."

The men looked at each other, and then one asked, "What type of deal?"

Quickly reaching into his pocket, Derrick pulled out a few bags displaying them in the dimness cast by the streetlight on the corner.

"My dime bags are full, not like some others where you only get half, and with the oxy, the more you buy I can throw in some extra as samples."

The taller of the two men asked, "What are we talking—" trailing off leaving it open ended.

Derrick answered, "The weed will cost ya ten and the oxy is five a pop."

Just then, a blinding spotlight cut through the darkness, and the whining of a siren from deeper in the alley rose above the sounds of the neighborhood.

Over a loudspeaker he heard, "Turn and put your hands on the wall, you're under arrest."

As Derrick began to turn, he said, "You're fuckin' cops, I shoulda known...I thought I smelled bacon."

Without hesitation, the officer closest to Derrick nudged him in the direction he was moving, while placing a foot in front of him, causing him to fall forward and smash his face against the brick wall.

Bursting into laughter, the other officer said, in a mocking tone, "Oh...Poor, smelly, homeless, drugie, did you get hurt?"

Derrick's forehead was split open just above his eyebrow and blood trickled down the side of his face. A third officer, which seemed to be in charge, appeared from the blackness of the alleyway.

"Knock it off you two, cuff 'em and get him back to the station." Then as they walked away, he called out, "Stop the bleeding before you put him in the car, God knows what diseases he has."

Illuminated by the flashing red lights of a squad car that now blocked the alley, the officers opened a first aid kit. Then the one that tripped him uncuffed Derrick's right hand long enough for him to wipe the abrasion and put a bandage on it. Within minutes, he was cleaned up and being carted off for booking by a uniformed officer that had come in to assist. Looking out the window, and watching the neighborhood go by until they entered the downtown area, Derrick thought about his previous arrests. He didn't feel terribly concerned about this one, after all, the others didn't have any lasting effect on him and this time would be no different, or would it?

ENTERS AN ANGRY MAN

As THEY TURNED OFF THE main road and onto the long driveway, Derrick Bishop caught his first glimpse of what would be his home for the next twelve months. The large stone sign stood at the entryway to greet all that entered, *Conversions Recovery Center.* He was just one among many, since they opened their doors in the 1980's, that was an unwilling participant. Truth was, he would rather be almost anywhere else, almost that is. His choices were CRC or the local jail. After spending the last few weeks since his arrest, in jail, inpatient rehab was the better of the two.

Pulling up in front of the building that sat towards the back of the parking area, they stopped and his probation officer turned and said, "This is where you get out."

Glancing side to side, then turning and looking at the grounds, he could see three large buildings that bordered the parking lot and a smaller shed type structure in the distance. The building they headed into was cold and sterile in nature with the signage on the door indicating it contained the administrative offices, the intake department, and the infirmary. It also boasted that they were the highest rated inpatient substance abuse facility in the eastern United States.

Probation Officer Randolph signed in at the reception desk, and said, "I'm PO Randolph and I'm here to drop off Derrick Bishop."

The receptionist smiled and motioned towards the door to the left while saying, "I'll buzz ya."

When they heard the buzz of the door, the probation officer pushed it open and waved Derrick in while following behind him. Inside was a small room with a desk, three chairs, and another door opposite the one they had entered through. A chipper woman came in with a folder and introduced herself as Dee. She explained they needed to go over some things and then Derrick would sign all the required paperwork.

First, she explained that Derrick would initial for each form he was given as she went over them and without speaking Derrick nodded with a grunt. The first form she presented was a list of rules and consequences. As she read each rule, Derrick felt like he was in elementary school. He nodded without saying a word, while sitting slumped down in his chair with his arms crossed. The consequences were even more childlike to him than the rules, ranging from a lost privilege to discharge from the program. After it was explained, Derrick was given a copy to keep with a folder to hold his paperwork. Then she continued on with a map of the facility and grounds, insurance information, and a list of items not permitted in Conversions. Lastly, she gave him a sheet explaining the phases and corresponding privileges. Glancing down as it was handed to him, phase one made Derrick laugh.

Phase One Privileges-Living at Conversions Recovery Center and receiving treatment, food, and shelter.

Wanting to ask where they got off saying food and shelter were privileges, he contained himself feeling irritated and barely listening. Then Derrick wondered how they really thought being at CRC was a privilege because he considered it a punishment. He was choosing to remain quiet, partially because he knew he would get himself into trouble, and partially because he was angry about being mandated to an inpatient program. Derrick decided upon arrival that it would be easier to nod, grunt, and just get through his mandated time without incident.

Finally, after all the paperwork for the program was completed, his probation officer pulled out his conditional release form. It stated that Derrick was agreeing to inpatient treatment for a period of twelve months with monitoring by probation in lieu of incarceration. After the terms were reviewed, Derrick was asked to sign it, as well as Dee being the representative of the facility. Before handing them each their copy, Probation Officer Randolph signed approving Derrick's transfer into CRC and they were told the original would be filed with the court. Before leaving, the probation officer reminded him if he left the program before the year was up he would be returned to jail to complete his sentence.

Derrick rolled his eyes, and said, "I know, you told me lots of times."

The probation officer wished him good luck and said he'd be stopping in from time to time to check on him.

Showing overt displeasure, Derrick said, "Yeah...great...see ya."

Then Dee made a call, and was heard saying, "Bishop is admitted and ready for you."

She hung up and told Derrick to go through the far door in the room, take off his pants, and open his bag on the table.

"Take off my pants, are you crazy? Why do I need to do that?" he asked, with a sense of outrage.

In a rote manner, Dee explained that his primary counselor had to check to make sure he wasn't bringing in any substances or items that weren't permitted.

"You've gotta be kiddin' me!" he said as he grabbed his bag and went through the door.

Inside the second room, Derrick did as instructed and waited while pacing and looking at the posters promoting sobriety that were hanging on the walls. Within a few minutes, another door opened and a tall broad man who appeared to be in his fifties entered. He had a goatee that was showing some gray, long hair that was pulled back into a ponytail, and he was wearing khakis with a golf shirt that had the CRC logo on the left breast pocket.

"Hi, I'm your primary counselor Justin. I need to check you and your things to make sure you're starting off in compliance."

Derrick, still showing attitude, said, "Whatever man…I got no say in any of this."

Justin laughed as he started going through the duffle bag, feeling all the clothing items.

"I am glad you get it already, you make my job easier."

Even though it annoyed Derrick, he said nothing, but Justin was aware it did because he heard, "Pssssttt" as Derrick dropped into the chair by the door.

They finished up, Derrick was handed his jeans, and told that next he would be visiting the infirmary department to fill out medical history forms and get a quick physical.

Walking down the hall, Justin explaining he would be back to take Derrick to his room when the medical was done. In the infirmary he met with the staff nurse and completed the required paperwork. After that, she recorded his height, weight, and blood pressure. Then she listened to his heart, checked his ears, and looked down his throat. Before clearing him for admission, she reviewed his TB testing and blood work that was done in jail, and forwarded ahead of him, which was a requirement prior to being given an admission date. The whole process took about twenty minutes, and almost on cue, Justin was back to escort him to his room.

As they left the main building, Justin explained the facility consisted of the administration building, which they just left, the residence, and the commons building. Commons was where treatment groups and recreational activities occurred, but Justin clarified individual treatment sessions were usually held in the counselor's offices, located on the first floor of the residence. He also pointed out the maintenance shed in the back of the main building, stating it wasn't an area utilized by the residents. As they walked, Justin explained that on campus they use terms for things or shortened names. The campus terms used for the buildings were Admin., Residence, and Commons and he was assured that he would pick up the campus jargon in no time.

Derrick was told each resident was assigned chores and the schedule changed at the first of the month. With the day of admission and birth-days, being the only days residents didn't have scheduled chores, Justin joked that since Derrick's birthday wasn't until January, he should enjoy the rest of his day off. Although he was unhappy about being at CRC, Derrick found himself laughing a little.

They entered the residence and went directly to the second floor, as Derrick's room was 216. The room was small and sparse, containing two twin size beds, two nightstands each with a lamp, and two chests of drawers located on opposite sides of the room. One bed was made and the other had a pile of linens, a blanket, and a pillow on it. The chest of drawers nearest the made bed had a few framed pictures and an alarm clock on top. There was a small window on the far side of the room and the curtains were beige with blue and burgundy specks. Even though it was nondescript, as Derrick surveyed his surroundings, he thought it was better than a jail cell.

After dropping his duffle on the unmade bed, Justin gave Derrick a printed schedule that listed his chores, group meetings, and individual sessions on it. He also explained Derrick was assigned the same chores as his roommate to assist in familiarizing him with the program. Just then, a guy came in and looked startled jumping slightly when he saw them.

"I knew I was getting a roommate today, but I didn't realize you were here already." Extending his hand to Derrick, he said, "Hey man, I'm PJ… how you doin'?"

The men shook hands, and Derrick said, "I'll be better in twelve month, but I'm hangin' in there."

PJ laughed, "I was there too. It'll change for ya…just give it time."

Glad to see the two talking, Justin excused himself saying, "I'll see both of you tomorrow."

As he left the room, Justin told Derrick if he had any questions PJ would steer him in the right direction. PJ responded by saying goodbye, but Derrick just ignored him and sat on the bed. Although he always appreciated a challenge, Justin found himself shaking his head at how resistant Derrick was, especially since they hadn't even began treatment. As he thought about the next twelve months, he expected the process with Derrick was going to be anything but easy.

Trying to go through everything Derrick needed to know, PJ explained some of the rules and how things worked at CRC. Half listening, Derrick just grunted as he looked out the window to the property behind the house where a saw a small garden was planted. The daisies were in bloom and it made him think of her. He began to drift in his thoughts to the first date they had, and before he knew it, he didn't hear PJ speaking as he was consumed by his memories.

Recalling how nervous he had been, he remembered that they met at a party of a mutual friend, talked for hours, and planned to go out the following weekend.

Holding the bouquet of daisies he had for her, he knocked, cleared his throat, and cracked his neck. When the door opened she took his breath away, she was radiant and her smile seemed to ignite something in his heart. They said their hellos and she gave him a peck on the cheek when he handed her the flowers. With a smile she thanked him, while placing them in vase and making awkward small talk. Just then he blurted out more then he intended.

"I've been thinking about you all week."

She turned and smiled.

"I've been thinking about you too. Talking to you at the party last week was great and I was really looking forward to seeing you again."

Derrick was relieved that she didn't get weird with the eagerness of his disclosure and within a few minutes she placed the flowers on the table, gathered her things, and they headed out.

"Derrick, are you listening?" PJ asked, pulling him back to the confines of the small room in CRC.

Looking away from the window he turned, shrugged, and said, "I was thinking about somethin'…sorry."

Getting ready to leave, PJ turned towards the door.

"I was telling you I have an individual now, I'll be back in about an hour and can show you around then."

Disinterested, Derrick agreed just because he knew he should and then he started to unpack his bag.

In the way of possessions, he didn't have much since he'd been on the streets for the past three years. Slowly things were stolen, lost, or even sold for drug money. In jail he was given uniforms to wear so it didn't matter what he did or didn't have. When he agreed to go inpatient, they were able to secure a stipend to buy street clothing. It didn't buy much, just enough to get through, but that was all Derrick really needed. The losses suffered on the streets extended beyond clothing, his photos and sentimental items were gone as well. All Derrick had from his past were memories, some good and some not, but regardless they stuck with him through every up and down.

After making his bed, he laid back and started to read some of the paperwork the intake lady, Dee, had given him. He also looked at his chore and treatment schedule noticing the next day he had an individual session with Justin in the afternoon and breakfast detail from seven to ten in the morning. The more he read, the more Derrick thought how much he hated being at CRC and how he would be much happier out on the street getting high. As he laid there staring up, he began to think about her again and how just seeing her made him feel warm inside.

Suddenly he felt angry and he told himself he shouldn't be thinking about her because it didn't matter anymore. In one quick motion, he got up and punched the wall behind his bed leaving a hole. As soon as he did it, Derrick realized it was a bad choice and knew it wasn't going to be overlooked. Almost instantly, two staff members were in his room looking at him and the hole left from his outburst.

They asked what happened, and he said, "I got pissed and hit it."

Following procedure, they examined his hand, which appeared un-injured, and asked if he needed to go to the medical department. He said he didn't and the men spoke with him for a few minutes while he re-mained calm and responded to their questions with short answers, like yeah, nah, I don't know, and whatever. Before leaving, it was explained by the staff that an incident report had to be written and filed with his counselor.

"Like I give a fuck…write whatever ya want," he yelled as they walked out.

A few minutes later PJ returned.

"Oh guy, what the hell did you do?" he asked, as he looked at the hole in the wall.

Derrick mumbled, "I'm an ass…what can I tell ya."

Shaking his head, PJ explained that there were likely to be consequences. Uneffected, Derrick indicated he didn't care, laid on the bed, and rolled over to face the wall.

As promised, PJ tried to go over the schedules and things, but Derrick wouldn't engage.

Offering to show him around, PJ said, "We have about forty minutes before dinner, let's go for a walk and I'll give you a tour."

Derrick was silent and didn't answer at first, but PJ repeated the offer.

"Not now, I'm tired." he barked, while still facing the wall.

Feeling annoyed, PJ turned to leave.

"Ya know, if you don't do what ya need to they'll bounce ya from the program. I don't know if you're a remand or a walk-in, but you came in for a reason…ya wanna discharge before you even get started?"

PJ left and closed the door behind him leaving Derrick alone in the room.

Within minutes, he started to think about what PJ said and realized that even though he didn't want to be at CRC, he had to pretend at least a little, or they would ship him back to lock up. Feeling somewhat foolish, he decided to go downstairs to look for his roommate. As he stood, Derrick took a deep breath and looked at the hole in the wall he created. Hoping he wouldn't be in too much trouble, he thought to himself, *Well, I guess it can only get better from here.*

Wandering around the first floor he saw some offices, a dining area, a kitchen, and a TV room. PJ was out on the front porch with two other men. As Derrick approached he was introduced to them, thinking how PJ presented them was odd.

"Guys this is Derrick, he's my new roommate. Derrick this is Pat, third floor, phase two and Jerry, third floor, phase three."

Derrick said hello and stood listening as they finished up their conversation. Jerry was telling them about his job and Pat was explaining that he was scheduled to begin working with job placement. Pat was excited, stating once he began the job search he would advance to phase three. It all sounded foreign to Derrick, so he decided to listen and ask PJ questions when they were alone.

A few minutes later, they heard a buzz and the men said, almost in a chant tone, "That's dinner!"

Heading into the dining area, Derrick could see the meal was being served in a buffet style. Men, who were probably residents, were setting up the trays which offered three hot choices as well as salad and rolls. On another table, beyond the dinner choices, were cookies and brownies for dessert. As they waited in line, PJ explained that every week it was the same menu. He went on to state, that since it was Monday, the choices were ravioli, meatballs, and baked chicken with roasted potatoes.

The line moved quickly as the workers filled the trays. Once they had their food, they sat with a group of guys that PJ seemed to be friendly with and Derrick was introduced to each. There were so many, that the names just seemed to blend together. He sat quietly while they ate and he listened to the chatter around him. Derrick wanted to get a feeling for his new temporary home, so what better way than listening to people talk about it. They spoke about chores, recreational activities, and their respective phases. As he listened, he gained a lot of information about his new living arrangement. The food was a lot better than what he'd been getting in jail for the last six weeks and Derrick enjoyed every last bite, even going back for seconds. Finishing up, the guys decided to shoot pool in Commons. Derrick was told the recreation hall wasn't permitted for people in phase one, so PJ stayed behind with him while the others went on. While chatting, they headed to the TV room which PJ called the lounge.

Once they were out of ear shot of the others, Derrick said, "Hey, I'm sorry if I was actin' like a prick earlier. I was just pissed off and…well…ya know what happened."

PJ laughed, and said, "Well guy, you were actin' like a prick, but I get it 'cause I felt the same way when I came in."

That seemed to release the tension between them and the mood was lightened. While sitting and talking, Derrick learned PJ came to CRC ten months earlier, was close to being discharged, and had been working for the last five weeks. As the conversation continued PJ smiled when he mentioned he was married and had a two year old daughter. Then he inquired about Derrick's family.

Derrick just shook his head, "Naaaa…I got nobody, it's just me."

Respecting his privacy, PJ nodded and asked about what he was doing before coming to the center. Derrick explained that he had been in jail because he got caught dealing to an uncover cop. Since it wasn't his first drug related charge, the Judge said it was either inpatient with probation monitoring or jail.

Shaking his head and tossing his hands up slightly, he said, "I figured rehab would be better than jail, so the choice was easy.

With a chuckle and a shrug of the shoulders, PJ responded, "Well, on most days anyway."

The men smiled, and to Derrick it seemed maybe things might not be as bad as he expected because at least he had a cool roommate.

After a while, Derrick asked about the earlier conversation out on the porch and why the men were introduced with their floor and phase information. Having forgotten earlier that most people wouldn't understand the system, PJ apologized and stated that on campus that's how people refer to each other. He explained that if a staff member asks who you are, those are the details they expected as a response.

Giving him an example, PJ said, "So if they ask your name, you would say Derrick, second floor, phase one."

Thinking it was odd, Derrick asked why they did it that way and PJ explained that each piece of information gave staff something they needed to know. Then he tried to clarify it by breaking it down.

"The phase lets staff know if you are doing something you're permitted to do whereas the floor would tell them if you are in the right place at the right time. Some activities are scheduled by floor."

Comfortable Derrick understood the procedure, PJ headed on and Derrick followed. As they walked, PJ pointed out, that once staff got to know him it would be unlikely he would be asked for that information, although, he would still give it when introducing himself or another resident.

Once back upstairs, PJ showed him the bathrooms and shower rooms. There were two of each on the second floor and residents were assigned to them based on their bedroom. Derrick learned showers were not permitted after 9:00 p.m. or before 6:00 a.m because it could be disruptive to those on the floor trying to sleep. Understanding the shower rule, Derrick asked about being in the other areas of the house. PJ explained residents had to be in their rooms by 11:00 p.m. unless they were attending a special event that ended later.

Feeling tired from the long day, Derrick decided to take a shower and turn in so he would be well rested to work breakfast in the morning. He wasn't sure what it entailed, but knew he had to be up and downstairs fairly early. After taking a few things out of his drawer, he realized that coming from jail he didn't have toiletries, so he asked PJ about soap and towels. Quickly standing up, PJ said he forgot to show him that part and they walked to their assigned shower room.

Inside, there was a rack with piles of towels and cloths across from a wall of cubbies. Each of the cubbies had a plastic basket in it which was labled with a name sticker. Derrick was shown his, which contained soap, shampoo, a toothbrush, toothpaste, and deodorant. Reassuring him was all new, PJ mentioned it had been put there earlier in day and he would be given replacements as needed by asking in the office on the first floor. After making sure he didn't need anything else, PJ stepped towards the door and Derrick thanked him.

Entering the first stall, Derrick stood under the hot water enjoying the relaxation of the shower as it had been so long since he had that luxury. During the six weeks he spent in jail, the shower was not a place that he could let his guard down, and prior to that, being mostly on the streets, showers were a rare indulgence. Derrick recapped the events of the day, and thought if he could get through without too much mumbo jumbo crap in his head, he'd be just fine. He didn't really buy into the whole therapy thing and believed if he wanted to stop using he would. Full of denial, Derrick convinced himself that he just never really wanted to stop.

When he returned to his room, PJ was already in bed and as Derrick entered he reminded him of their assigned morning chore to work breakfast. Pointing up towards the dresser, he also said he set the alarm for six. As Derrick closed the door PJ turned off his lamp. Before laying down, Derrick went to place his things in his drawer stopping momentarily by the window. Looking down at the daisies, they could barely be seen in the dark. With the moon casting a slight glow, he could just make out some white. After drawing in a long breath, he made his way to the bed and snuggled down pulling up the covers and feeling very tired. He would never admit it to anyone, but Derrick realized he'd been anxious about coming to Conversions. As a result, he was awake most of the night before, so within minutes he fell asleep.

Month 1

WHEN THE ALARM WENT OFF the next morning, Derrick was startled. With a yawn and a stretch, he realized was well rested, having slept much better than he had in a long time.

As he got up to turn off the buzzer, PJ said, "Good morning, hope ya slept well."

Not adjusted to sharing a room with PJ yet, he knew it would take some time to learn his ways, but it was already apparent PJ was more of a morning person than Derrick. Mindful of the time, he dismissed the thought of rolling over for a few more minutes of sleep and stretch once more before sitting up.

Full of energy, PJ urged him to not waste time stating they had breakfast duty starting in an hour. Then he turned on the radio portion of the alarm clock and began to softly sing along with the song that was playing. They each quietly went about their business of getting ready and dressing for the day. Then it was down to the first floor, arriving in the kitchen a few minutes early so they could eat before they started their work. Several other men were there to work as well. Derrick was introduced, but feeling anxious, so to him they were all just a blurr. PJ gave him a quick rundown on what was expected, explaining their job was to fill trays as they emptied and cart away bins of dirty dishes as they filled. After PJ familiarized him with where things were, they started setting out the food.

Within minutes the dining hall was full. The chatter of the men and clanking of dishes was loud and the pace was fast, leaving Derrick feeling overwhelmed and unable to keep up with the demand. With an encouraging manner, PJ nudged him along when he saw Derrick was falling behind and before he knew it the shift was over. Being slightly younger than Derrick, PJ teased him a little when they were back in the room.

"Hey you're movin' like an old guy...I think you're not use to hard work."

Derrick nodded, and said, "It's been a while since I've done much of any work."

Having a few hours before his individual session with Justin, Derrick decided to lie down and nap for a while. Once he laid down, it felt like he'd been run over by a truck with every muscle being fatigued from the morning chore. Almost instantly he was out and slept for about an hour.

Feeling apprehensive, Derrick reported to Justin's office a few minutes early and stood in the hallway waiting for his appointment. Right on time the door opened and Justin stuck his head out.

"Hey Derrick, come in."

Reluctantly he stepped in, sat in the chair closest to the door, and crossed his arms while saying nothing. Justin sat next to him and picked up a folder which he scanned before looking up at Derrick.

"I was just looking over your intake paperwork that they completed with you at the jail."

Derrick just looked at him and again said nothing, so Justin continued, "It seems it's been a long time since you've had any stability in your life."

Knowing it was true, and not having anything to offer, Derrick just shrugged.

Justin smirked, and said, "Okay man, if this is how it's gonna be let's lay it out. I get paid if you talk to me or not. I wanna help you, but it's up to you if you're gonna let me. You can shut me out...but we're still gonna meet."

Feeling angry, Derrick just nodded, and said, "Got it."

Justin was unwilling to give up, so he just shook his head before saying, "I guess they forgot to tell you that redecorating isn't permitted."

Knowing what he meant, Derrick shrugged again and Justin asked why he punched the wall.

Derrick thought it was fairly obvious, saying, "I was mad."

After several attempts by Justin to get more details by asking different questions, Derrick said, "I was just thinking' about someone and felt pissed."

Not willing to let it end there, Justin asked for specifics, and he said, "A girl I used to know."

Sensing the defensive nature of Derrick, Justin asked several questions to help determine how important this girl would be in the recovery process, but Derrick wasn't willing to share anything.

Needing to clarify what happened, Justin then asked, "Do you love her?"

Squirming in his chair, Derrick replied, "I told you man...I used to know her...I'm not with her anymore."

Studying Derrick's response, Justin nodded, and said, "Yeah, I know that you said that, but just 'cause you're not with her, doesn't mean you don't love 'er."

Staring back at Justin, with slightly squinted eyes, Derrick sat in silence and glenched fists that were resting on his thighs. As he appeared tense and rigid, Justin knew they probably were at an impasse for the session and indicated their time was up.

When Derrick got up to leave, Justin said, "Ya know, if you love her and don't deal with those feelings, they'll eat ya up inside."

Without commenting, Derrick turned and kicked the trash can next to the door as he left, sending the can and its contents scattering across the floor.

Later that night, PJ asked if he wanted to go down and watch a movie in the lounge, but Derrick decided to stay behind. Instead, he sat and watched the shadows dance on the wall as the sunset, and thought about what Justin said earlier. He knew he loved her, but it wasn't something he'd admit to anyone. Hell, he had a hard enough time admitting it to himself. After all he put her through he knew it was over, but his love for her never faded and just then his mind began to drift.

"What happened to you last night, you said you were coming by and you never showed." she said with annoyance in her voice, as he walked up to her while she was getting into the car.

Derrick didn't exactly know what she was talking about.

"Why are you mad?" he asked.

"Are you kidding me! We were texting and you said you would come over in a while. I asked what time and you never answered the text, then you never showed up."

Thinking about the previous night, Derrick finally realized what she was talking about, recalling that he was smoking his nightly "relax after work joint" when they were texting. Full of dread he realized he must have lost track of the conversation forgetting all about it. Knowing she had good cause to be angry, he scrambled in his mind, What can I tell her?

"Baby I'm sorry. I had a rough day...I...I fell asleep...I woke up and it was late...I...I...didn't wanna call you 'cause I figured you were sleepin'."

She shook her head.

"I don't know, this crap is happening a lot lately. If you're seeing someone else or getting tired of me just say it."

As Derrick remembered that day, he recalled feeling shaken because he didn't want to lose her.

"No, no, no, I promise, nothing like that-I-I was just tired."

Reluctantly, she accepted his answer and they kissed. As she meant the world to him, Derrick breathed a sigh of relief, knowing he would have to be more careful going forward.

Thinking back now, he could see how she might have thought he wasn't interested in her. Those things were happening often in those days and his excuses were just that, excuses, so they held little credibility. There are only so many times someone can say they fell asleep on another, without causing questions about what it meant. In retrospect, he knew letting her think he had been falling asleep that often, when talking to her, was definitely sending the message he wasn't interested.

In the years that had since passed, Derrick carried guilt about how he treated her and the things he did to conceal his addiction. She was the one person that loved him in his entirety and he knew she would have done anything for him. Without thought, she ranked his happiness and well being right next to hers and he didn't cherish her the way she deserved to be cherished. When Derrick thought about her, and his guilty feelings rose up, he would always run to using so he could forget. Tonight, being inpatient, that wasn't an option. After deep contemplation, he decided to take a walk downstairs and see if he could find a distraction.

As he hit the bottom landing in the stairway, he saw a light on in Justin's office, so he looked in and found Justin sitting at his desk doing paperwork.

"Hey, you got a minute?"

Looking up, Justin replied, "Sure, come in."

Derrick stepped in, and said, "I do love 'er. I feel guilty about things I did to her-But-I do love 'er."

Justin rubbed his chin and smiled before saying, "You wanna close the door and talk a while?"

"Naaa-I don't think I can tonight, but I saw your light on so-I don't know-I just thought I would stop by."

Surprised at the unexpected visit, Justin said goodnight and told him they could pick it up the following day in their individual session. Derrick made his way to the lounge and quietly slipped in, finding a seat near the door. Trying to change his thoughts he watched TV for a while, but it didn't really help. He decided to get some sleep as he had to be up early, and working in the dining hall was harder than he had expected.

The next day started with breakfast detail, and this time it went a little smoother because Derrick knew what to expect. In the afternoon, he had an early sobriety group and then an individual session with Justin. As he read over the schedule, he noticed, during his first week, that each day seemed to have one more thing then the last. Knowing center life was a lot to process, he figured they were breaking him in slowly to get him use to the program.

The early sobriety group consisted of six guys and Justin who was running it. This was the first time he was in the Commons building and the meeting room was plain with chairs in a circle. There was a small table against the wall and a bulletin board hanging above it that had some flyers posted. Next to the door there was a sign that read,

No Profanity and Always Be Respectful.
What is said in group stays in group.

Derrick didn't expect to be saying anything, so he sat planning to just listen as the meeting opened. Before starting, Justin introduced Derrick and then had the men go around and say their name, phase, and how long theyhad been at CRC. The early sobriety group was for residents that were in the program three months or less. Derrick listened as they each talked about difficulties they were finding in their new sober life. Then it was Derrick's turn.

"I know you've only been here a few days Derrick, but has anything been a challenge?" Justin asked.

Shaking his head from side to side, and trying to offer as little as possible, he said, "No, I got this, no problem."

Then one of the guys, named Leo, made a disapproving sound and shook his head causing Derrick to feel offended.

Without thinking, he sat forward, and said, "What's your problem?"

In an argumentative manner, Leo answered, "You say got no problem being here? Yea right... you're not bein' honest."

Derrick stood up ready to fight.

"How am I not being honest?"

Leo looked up, and they locked eyes as he said, "You just walk in the door and you say you got this, like you're not thinkin' about getting high. If that's true, then man, you don't need to be here...we all think about it."

Dumbfounded at the truth of the statement, Derrick retreated and sat back down while looking at Leo for a minute. Knowing the group dynamic was one of the most powerful things in recovery, Justin just sat watching and waited to see how it was going to unfold.

In a low deep voice, Derrick said, "Yea I think about it...but I can't use 'cause I'm here so...no problem."

Leo started to responded and both men were glaring at each other. Justin knew it needed to stop, popping in and ending the group for the day by mentioning some ongoing tasks he had the members working on during their down time. As they shuffled out, Derrick was reminded he had an individual session scheduled in a half hour. With a silent nod at Justin, he following the group as they headed back to the residence.

Arriving for his individual session on time, Derrick sat in the same seat as the day before, the one closest to the door. Still processing the conflict that occurred earlier, Justin asked what Derrick thought of the group. Trying to avoid conversation as much as possible, he shrugged, saying it was just a group. Without wasting time, Justin suggested they talk about the girl that Derrick said he still loved.

"So I was glad you came back last night, you said you love her, what's her name?"

In an automatic manner, Derrick just shook his head, and said, "Her name isn't important, I told you...we're not together anymore."

With a frown and crinkled brow, Justin was confused. Wanting to open communication, he explained it would be easier to talk about her if he had her name, but Derrick stuck to his position. With a blank expression, he simply stated he wasn't offering up her name.

Finally giving in, and realizing it wasn't important, Justin said, "Okay, tell me about her."

In a quiet manner at first, he described her as beautiful, loving, and caring with an open heart.

Derrick's face seemed to brighten as he continued to speak of her, and with a soft smile, he said, "She was fun loving, funny, and could always make me smile and laugh."

Justin appreciated thim sharing the way he felt about her, stating, "It sounds like she is very special."

Looking off into the distance, through the window adjacent to Justin's desk, and with a sense of longing, Derrick just nodded, but didn't say anything. Knowing there would be a wealth of counseling sessions around the woman with no name, Justin asked what the guilt was about. With his expression turning more stern, his lips puckered slightly while his brow tightened and Derrick was quiet for a few minutes.

Then in a very hesitant tone, Derrick said, "I acted like an ass...the drugs got in the way. I would poof 'cause I was getting' high...she started to think I lost interest or I was seein' someone." He stopped, holding one finger on each side of the bridge of his nose and drew in a deep breath. Then he continued, "I would make up half assed excuses 'cause she didn't know I was using." Then he sighed and looked out the window again for a few minutes, "When we split she still had no way to know... she thought I just didn't want 'er anymore."

Justin could see the pain in Derrick's eyes, so he just sat quietly and gave him time to recover.

"Like I told you...we're done, I never stopped loving her but...well...I might as well have, 'cause to her it felt like I did."

Knowing the topic was difficult, Justin thanked Derrick for sharing and said he realized it wasn't an easy thing to talk about. He told Derrick they would probably work on some of those feelings as time went on.

In a statement of avoidance, Derrick said, "Whatever...I can't change what I did."

Time was up, and Derrick stood to leave when Justin said, "I know how you feel, I hurt a woman that was special to me with my drug addiction. I felt guilty about it just like you, but I was able to come to terms with it. I'll help you get there too."

Not having thought about Justin being in recovery, Derrick was surprised and wasn't sure what to say, so he just nodded and thanked him.

Lost in the pain from the memories of how the relationship ended, he went to dinner and spent the rest of the evening just mindlessly going through the motions. Derrick considered Justin's disclosure about his own addiction and was intrigued to learn more, wondering if Justin had been a resident at CRC. Seeming somewhat older than Derrick, he assumed Justin had a wife and kids. There was a picture of him, with what looked like a family, on the desk in his office. After thinking a while, he figured as time went on he would learn more a because he and his counselor would get to know each other.

As the evening slipped away, he continued to think about her and what he and Justin talked about. Derrick thought about why he wouldn't tell Justin her name, but the fact was saying her name killed him. With a heart full of pain, he couldn't sit through a conversation about her and run the risk of hearing it over and over again. Realizing it might seem odd to some, he knew it was how it had to be. For him it was better that way, because it masked his feelings and kept her from being real. If they talked about her, while using her name, then it would be like she was still part of his life and Derrick couldn't invite the pain of a repeated reminder that she wasn't his anymore.

That night, PJ was exceptionally upbeat and Derrick asked if something was going on.

As he fluttered around the room, while putting his laundry away, PJ said, "As of tomorrow I have only two months left here." It was apparent he was thrilled with being so close to completion and kept talking. "I'll finally go back home to my wife and little girl." He picked up a picture from on top of his chest of drawers and held it out. "Her name is Brianna and she's just turning three."

Derrick asked a few questions about his family and learned that PJ visited every weekend having earned overnight passes. He was permitted to go Saturday and returned to CRC on Sunday evening.

"I can't wait til I can go and stay…it kills me every week to say goodbye."

Congratulating his roommate on doing so well and being so close to finishing, Derrick thought about how completion for him was so far off. Still unsure of his surroundings, Derrick wasn't convinced he would make it the twelve months, but decided he would just take each day as it came and see what happened.

Then he started to think about himself, and when he would get to the point that he could have an overnight pass, realizing he had no one to spend an overnight with. Suddenly he felt angry again, but contained it. Instead of letting it show, he decided to step away by taking a shower and getting ready for bed. As he collected his clean clothes from the drawer, he glanced down to the flowers below. Full of sadness, he knew he could never go back, but the thoughts of her was so vivid. When he looked at the garden it made his heartache wanting to be near her.

As he stood in the shower, full of doubt about the changes the center wanted him to make, Derrick began to contemplate ways to slip away and get high. Thinking about the length of the driveway, he wondered if he could make it to the street before being seen by a staff member. With the mesmerizing effect of the water running over him, Derrick was hypnotized into a daydream of making it to his old neighborhood. He began to think about who might have something to share, and the cravings became overwhelming.

As he was getting dressed, he decided to try to slip out the front door. Realizing the sun had set, he knew it was the best time to try and get away because the low light would provide more opportunities to move towards the gate without being notice. With his desire to use growing stronger, Derrick rapidly dried off and dressed. Within minutes, he quietly crept down the stairs where he found two staff members standing outside the main office by the front door. Quickly his mind shifted to the dining hall, which would be empty and dark since it was long after the dinner service. In there was a door that exited to the property behind the house, which didn't have any lights like those on the front porch.

As expected, there was no one in that area and Derrick slowly unlocked the door. He slipped out gingerly and then closed it behind him. Scanning the area outside, he looked in both directions. It was dark and he began to walk down the stairs. Full of vigor, he was motivated by the plan of the moment, which was to sneak to the wooded area and then trek undetected through the brush to the main road. Engulfed in darkness, he didn't see the ground had a slight dip and Derrick stumbled forward landing in the flower garden face first on the daisies.

Full of frustration, and consumed by his addiction, he began hitting the plants and ripping them up. Without thought, he was throwing them in every direction while yelling curse words. After a minute, he sat up and was completely overwhelmed by his feelings. Thoughts of his love, and the daisies he gave her so long ago, rushed in, leaving him conflicted between running and staying. Derrick's heart began to race and he was immobilized by his internal conflict.

Then he heard a voice from the darkness say, "Who's there?"

Standing and cleaning himself off, Derrick retreated to his days on the streets when excuses were often needed without time for thought. He said his name and blurted out that he was looking for his watch which was missing. As he fumbled to explain, his mind raced trying to formulate a believable story because falling into the flowers wasn't worth going back to jail. Although he was straining to get his words out, he continued by saying he was in the yard earlier and thought maybe it had fallen off.

The staff member spoke and sounded skeptical, saying, "You shouldn't be out here at night without approval, get back inside."

Hearing the voice as familiar, Derrick realized it was Justin. Feeling somewhat embarrassed, he apologized and went back into the door from which he exited and locked it behind him.

The next couple of weeks seemed to go by quickly. Justin mentioned the night in the daisies during an individual, but didn't push it too much when Derrick repeated the explanation of the lost watch. Unsure if he was picking up on something, or if it was his guilt for trying to leave, Derrick felt Justin somehow knew it was just a cover up story. Not wanting to bring attention to his failed getaway plan, he decided to leave it alone. Feeling somewhat lucky, he was relieved he was only caught being outside and not trying to escape.

Taking the stumble into the garden as a sign, Derrick decided to try and resist any other urges to elope from the center. Before long, he was managing his chores while getting to groups and individuals sessions when he was supposed to. It all seemed to just fall into a rhythm and he was adjusting to CRC life. Full of remorse, he thought about her every day, almost all day, and Justin would bring her up in their individual sessions at least once a week.

CRC was geared to have you prioritize sobriety, but his mind was consumed by her and his heart was filled with the love he silently carried all this time. During the years he spent on the street he missed her, but he wasn't talking about her all the time and getting high helped him escape thoughts of her when they crept in. These day, he often found his mind wondering if there might be a chance to win her back if he completed treatment and reclaimed his place in society. It was probably unobtainable, so he wouldn't say what he was thinking to Justin, and although it sounded crazy, Derrick was beginning to think that was what he'd try to do.

About three weeks after entering CRC, Parole Officer Randolph popped in to check on Derrick. Not expecting his PO, he was apprehensive when he heard his thunderous voice booming in the hallway one day.

"Hey Bishop, you gotta minute?"

When Derrick turned and saw him, he immediately wondered if his parole officer was were there due to a problem and his mind leaped to the night in the flower garden while he thought, *What if they figured out what I was trying to do.* Being sure he hadn't broken any house rules, he tried to calm himself down. His release from jail was subject to the approval of probation, so that's immediately where his mind jumped.

Feeling uneasy, he walked down and met him in Justin's office who was also there.

PO Randolph said, "Your counselor says you punched a hole in the wall."

Derrick's stomach flipped, and with a nod he said, "Yeah, I did."

In an authoritative voice, PO Randolph asked, "Did it make ya feel better?"

Derrick smirked a little while saying, "It kinda did."

Both smiling, Justin and the parole officer looked at each other.

"Well that's your one free pass, don't do that shit again."

Feeling like a weight had been lifted, Derrick smiled, and simply said, "I won't."

Then PO Randolph said he was told that Derrick seemed to be adjusting well to the routine at CRC and he was pleased with the progress that had been reported. Feeling slightly proud, Derrick thanked him and agreed that he'd become more comfortable at the center. As they finished up, he told Derrick he wouldn't be by until the following month unless there were problems, than it would be sooner. Understanding what was expected, Derrick promised there wouldn't be any issues.

As he was leaving, his parole officer called out, "Bishop we're gonna leave the hole in your wall as a reminder that you used your free pass."

Grateful for the understanding they showed him, Derrick smiled and nodded, then said, "Got it."

At the next individual session, Justin asked about Derrick's family and it was apparent he was immediately guarded.

With a tensing of his shoulders, Derrick said, "I don't have family, it's just me."

Reading his body language, Justin realized Derrick wasn't going to easily disclose, so he had to ask specific questions.

"Do you have any brothers or sisters?"

Shaking his head no, Derrick said he was an only child. Then Justin asked about his parents and he turned and looked out the window.

After a few minutes, Justin asked again.

With slight hesitation, Derrick finally said, "I never knew my dad and I don't know about my mom."

That didn't sound quite right to Justin, so he questioned, "What do you mean, you don't know about your mom?"

Becoming visibly uncomfortable, Derrick hesitated again, then said, "I walked out when I was eighteen. When I went back six months later, she was gone. They must've moved...I hadn't talked to her since."

Sitting for a moment motionless, in silence, Justin looked at the pain on Derrick's face.

"You said they must have moved, who are they?"

With a quick reply, he uttered, "My mom and my stepfather."

By his reaction, Justin realized the family issue was significant and asked him to tell more about them.

"Nothing to tell, they were there, then they were gone," he said.

Unwilling to leave it without further detail, Justin asked why he walked out at eighteen. In an unexpected stream of talking, Derrick drifted into thought and started recalling the night he left. Justin sat and listened as he described the argument that day.

"Just eighteen...I was finishing up high school and wanted to go to college, but there wasn't any money so I was gonna work for a while, then go. We had nothing, but I was gonna to do better...have better... show everyone I was better than all that shit they did. I'd been workin' and savin' all senior year when I came home one night after work. I re-member it was a Friday 'cause I just got paid. I went in my drawer, where I had my stash, to put away my money and it was all gone...all I saved... like nine hundred dollars."

Derrick looked angry and clenched his fists for a moment, before continuing. "I ran into the living room, "Who took my money?" I was mad. My step father looked at me, and said, "We needed to pay the rent." I stared at him, "Why didn't you use your money?" I asked. "You know your mama, she likes her gin. I guess she over did it this month 'cause we ran short." He was laughing, I felt so angry and started to yell,

"Mama, do you know he took my money to pay the rent." She was just sittin' there with her bottle, "We couldn't let them put us out…stop your whining." she said."

Stopping to make eye contact with Justin, he noticed he had a scowl on his face and was leaning forward waiting to hear more.

Then Derrick continued, "Next thing I know I'm packing my clothes and yelling, "You people are fucked up. Takin' my money 'cause you to busy sittin' on your asses g'tting' drunk…I'm outta here." Then my step father jumped up and pushed me against the wall and yelled in my face, "Watch your mouth boy!" I pushed back, "You put your hands on me for the last time, you're a fuckin' asshole." and I punched him in the mouth and left. I was lucky that I had a friend I could stay with until I graduated, like a month later."

Finishing the portion of the story that was emotionally charged, Derrick's expression softened slightly and he continued, "After graduation I worked full time and eventually met this guy that had a trucking company. He brought me in and slowly I learned how to work on diesel engines. I went back to the apartment about six months after the fight, but they were gone. They'd been evicted about a month after I left. The landlord said at the time he evicted 'em, they hadn't paid rent in about six months. I guess my money didn't go to the landlord like they said."

Justin was starting to develop an insight into how Derrick ended up addicted and homeless, so he decided to just sit, listen, and watch without commenting. It was obviously a painful memory for Derrick and Justin thanked him for sharing. They talked a little more about his childhood and it seemed the incident Derrick described, with his mother and stepfather when he left home, was fairly consistent with how things were throughout his life. As the session was winding down, Justin asked Derrick if he was okay. Although he said he was, Justin was concerned and reminded him that if he felt the need to talk, even after hours, he could go to any staff member or they could call him at home.

Derrick thanked him and admitted he felt somewhat drained, but said he thought he would be fine.

After returning to his room, he kept running that incident of leaving home, so many years earlier, through his mind. That night, he woke up what seemed to be every hour, so the next morning he found himself nearly as tired as he was when he turned in. Derrick hadn't thought about the last time he saw his mother in a really long time and now that he did, it seemed he couldn't stop thinking about it.

As his first month at CRC was nearly over, Derrick was starting to think maybe coming to the center was a good thing. Sometimes he had days he hated being there, but he was also starting to remember what normal life was like. Life seemed much easier while having a place to live, three meals a day without digging in the trash, and people that cared about how well he was doing and were willing to help if he needed it. As he became more comfortable, he would sometimes think to himself, *I could get use to this, I never want to live in a box again.*

With his newly developing positive outlook, Derrick was feeling pretty good, and then it hit him that it was the day before her birthday. With the thoughts of her so close to the surface, he started to wonder about how she was doing. Flashing back, he remembered when they were together and how he called her at the crack of dawn because he wanted to be the first to wish her Happy Birthday.

In a loud silly voice, he sang over the phone while she giggled and laughed and he could tell it made her happy. Later that evening, when they were sitting arm in arm, she told him he had given her the best gift ever because he had started and ended her day with love.

With this memory, Derrick suddenly found himself in a bad mood and feeling like he was wasting his time at CRC. Full of emotions, he wanted nothing more than to to get high. Missing her always made him want to use and escape, and this time was no different.

As scheduled, he went to his early sobriety group and Justin could tell by the look on his face that he wasn't doing well. After opening the group, he asked Derrick how he was feeling.

Full of anger, Derrick answered, "I'm feeling like I can't do this...like none of it matters, and like I'm less of a person."

Concerned about him, Justin asked if anything happened to make him feel that way, but he said it hadn't. Knowing times of doubt were often part of recovery, Justin started talking about focusing, working through the difficult times, and using the resources available. To reassure him, he was also told that everyone in recovery has days they feel discouraged.

Having heard these accounts from others in while in groups, Derrick nodded, and then said, "Yeah, I know."

Even though it was true, it didn't make it any easier.

The other group members chimed in and offered examples of when they each felt discouraged. Half listening, Derrick just nodded and looked at the floor.

Being aware that Derrick was in a fragile state, Justin wanted to get him to a more stable place, so he asked, "What do you think is the most important thing you need to hold it together?"

Not really caring about anything they asked or said, Derrick shrugged while still looking at the floor.

Justin asked again, but still received no answer, so he announced, "I'm gonna keep asking until you give me something."

Concerned that this was a moment that could lead Derrick in either direction, he asked the same question again.

This time Derrick mumbled, in a low tone, "Faith."

Relieved, Justin felt as if he had finally made the needed connection.

With a smile, he replied, "Say it again for us all to hear."

Feeling vulnerable, Derrick looked Justin in the eyes and repeated it louder, "Faith."

Justin was thrilled at his answer because it seemed Derrick was starting to come around. Maybe he was gaining some insight, so he told him to hold onto his faith and he would get through anything. Believing spirituality played a large role in helping the men through the rough patches, Justin emphasized to Derrick that between his faith and the center, he couldn't be held back. Still feeling somber, Derrick nodded and said nothing, just hoping the conversation would shift away from him.

The group went on and some of the others talked about things they were finding difficult. Derrick just listened, while slumped back in his chair and tapping his foot. Still in a negative place, he was eager to be done for the day.

After they wrapped up and were funneling out the door, Justin called out to him, and then with a fist bump said, "Derrick hold on to your faith and you'll be just fine."

Derrick meekly smiled, and softly said, "I will."

MONTH 2

———

ABOUT FIVE WEEKS AFTER ARRIVING at CRC, during an individual session with Justin, Derrick was surprised when he was congratulated on being advanced to phase two. Having never asked how long each phase was, Derrick assumed the program divided evenly over the three phases. For a year program, he thought each phase would be four months.

Justin explained that phase one was the shortest, usually lasting about four to five weeks. A resident was advanced to phase two once they showed they acclimated to the program and were starting to make progress in their sobriety. Phase two would be the longest, and a resident would advance to phase three once they were ready to work with job placement. That was typically when they had about three to four months left at CRC.

Derrick was thrilled, and knew that with an advancement in phase he would be given some additional privileges like being permitted to go to Commons for evening recreation. Feeling very happy, he thanked Justin and smiled. It was one of the few times, thus far, that Justin had seen him look genuinely happy.

Then Justin held out his hand to give him something, and said, "I got this for you to help you keep going."

With a narrowing of his brow, Derrick reached out. It was a silver cross on a neck chain.

With surprise, he took a deep breath and studdered slightly, "Thank you…I don't exactly know what to say."

Giving a smile, Justin said, "You don't have to say anything. I hope you like it."

To Derrick, being given a gift was moving. In fact, getting a gift was a rare occurrence, so it meant a great deal to him. When he was with her, she gave him gifts, but that had been one of the few times in his life that he'd been on the receiving end of gift giving. Immediately he put the cross on, and shook Justin's hand.

Sensing Derrick's appreciation, Justin said, "It can be a reminder to hold on to your faith."

With a nodded and a smile, Derrick held the cross between his thumb and pointer finger.

Then he told him, "I will never forget."

The rest of the afternoon, Derrick found himself reaching up to fiddle with the cross and spending a lot of time thinking about his last five weeks at CRC. With his advancement in phase, he started to believe that he could complete the program. While reflecting, he realized he liked Justin who seemed like he truly cared about Derrick. He believed his counselor was invested in him being successful. Excited to see what the phase change meant, Derrick took out the paperwork they gave him when he entered and looked up the privileges came with phase two.

Phase Two Privileges- All those privileges in phase one, access to Commons for evening recreation, participation in off sight group recreational trips, and off grounds passes to be determined on an individual basis.

As he read it over, Derrick was pleased with himself and eager to get off the grounds, but knew he had to take it one step at a time. He was sure he would have to wait a while, but knew Justin would tell him when he could have a pass. Feeling encouraged, he laid back on his bed and dangled the cross in front of his face while thinking to himself, *Faith will get me through.*

Just then, PJ came in from work and Derrick told him he'd been phase advanced.

"Alright, see you're makin' progress," PJ said, with a smile.

In the last five weeks, he had come to like PJ and would miss him when he completed and left the center.

Eager to get out of the residence, Derrick said, "I can go to Commons now, maybe we can shoot some pool later."

Knowing the challenge of being confined to the residence, PJ smiled and agreed saying it sounded like fun.

"Hey, what ya got around your neck?" PJ asked, pointing at Derrick's cross.

Smiling, Derrick held it up.

"It's a cross to keep me focused on what's goin' to get me through the rough times."

PJ nodded, "I know you'll get it done. I got a good feelin' about you."

Later that evening, they walked over to Commons to play pool. The recreation room was down the hallway past the group meeting rooms. When they arrived, there were a few guys already at the pool table. Music was on, a group was playing cards, and others were talking by the ping pong table.

Derrick perused the room. He knew it was there, but in the daytime it was closed and locked so he had never seen the inside before. As his eyes wandered, he saw a shelf with checkers and chess games as well as a TV with a video game hooked up to it. On the far side, there was a small sitting area and a full bookshelf in the corner. In certain sections there were area rugs and the room was painted a medium shade of blue. Scenic pictures were on the walls and the curtains were stripes that tied all the colors together. It was a pleasant room and less institutional then most of the others at CRC.

Upon entering, Derrick and PJ put their names on the board for the pool table so they would be next. While they were waiting, they joined the group talking in the far corner and PJ announced Derrick as the newbie to phase two. The others congratulated him and teased that the recreation room was the big time.

Enjoying the accolades, he smiled and said, "I'm just happy to get out of the lounge in the residence. After five weeks I was getting a little twitchy."

Before long, it was their turn at the table and they played doubles against the guys that won the previous game. Derrick had been fairly good at pool, in the past, when he was still functional and would hang out with friends on Friday or Saturday nights. After the first few shots, he had the feel again and held his own in the game. As they laughed and had a good time, Derrick thought how good it felt to just be out enjoying the company of other guys. In the midst of his fun, a brief flash of sadness washed over him as he realized it had been so very long since he'd been able to do so.

They finished up the game and PJ said he was going to head back because he had work the next day. Knowing he could return any night, Derrick decided to head back with him and as they walked they talked a bit.

"How'd it feel being sorta normal?" PJ asked.

At first Derrick hesitated, then he said, "Felt good...I'd forgotten."

PJ patted him on the back.

"Brother, we all did. This place gives you a chance to remember and to feel good about it. If you make up your mind, it only gets better from here."

That night Derrick reflected on the day and his friend's words. Deep in thought, he decided he wanted to feel good, be *normal*, and do regular everyday things, but most of all he wanted a chance to have her. As he reflected, he accepted that it was a long shot and his mind rested on the thought, if not with her, he would try to find something similar to what they had. As his memories focused on her, and how she was with him, he smiled and reached down to touch the cross. Then he put it to his lips and kissed it. While settling into bed, Derrick rolled over and for the first time in a long time he felt hopeful.

Time at the center seemed to pass quickly, it was a new month and with it came new chores. Derrick was assigned laundry duty in the morning, which was in the basement of the residence. Each resident washed their own clothes, but sheets, towels, and aprons from the kitchen, were community property and washed daily. With an early start, he ate breakfast at 7:00 a.m., and then head down to begin laundry duty at 7:30 a.m.

In addition to the assigned chores, his schedule included early recovery group which met three days a week and three individual sessions a week with Justin. Derrick found there was a lot of down time which he was beginning to find difficult. Either he was thinking about her, or thinking about how to get away and use. Now that he was starting to see a life beyond his addiction, he realized he had to occupy his time better. The recreation room was only open in the evening, so the hours in between treatment and chores were void of distractions.

At about seven weeks in CRC, during an individual session, Derrick mentioned to Justin that he needed more things to fill his time. He told him his thoughts were working against him and what he was trying to accomplish. Justin smiled, leaned back in his chair, and rubbed his chin as if he were sizing Derrick up.

"Well…hmmm…I'm impressed that you're identifying a need to help further your recovery. Let me think about what we can work out," Justin told him.

Eager to be busy, Derrick agreed and said, "I'll even do extra chores, anything would be good as long as I'm busy."

Impressed with the request, Justin smiled and nodded.

"You realize this is a sign of growth."

With a shrug, Derrick said, "Call it whatever…I just need to get something else goin'."

Two days later, after the early recovery group, Derrick was told to stop by Justin's office at about 3:00 p.m. When he arrived, Justin explained to him that he'd been trying to find something that could fill his time better. He didn't want to just stick him with extra chores, especially since he was identifying a need and asking for something to do.

After a few minutes of making sure Derrick was still looking for additional responsibilities, Justin explained he had asked the different CRC departments if any of them were in need of a helper of sorts. The maintenance department, which is made up of just two men, indicated they were trying to tackle some repairs and could use an extra set of hands. Justin explained it wasn't housekeeping, but light carpentry. Since he knew Derrick was a mechanic, he figured he might enjoy working with his hands.

Feeling ambitious, Derrick said, "Sounds like something I could be good at."

After they chatted about the tasks that maintanence was responsible for, he was told they would work around his treatment and chore schedule. Directing Derrick to the maintenance department, Justin said he should go out to the shed behind the Admin. Building, as they had a small office there and were expecting him.

Excited, Derrick felt like he was being given a reward and was eager to be working with his hands again. Once he left Justin's office, he headed directly to the shed and as he entered he saw an older man sitting at a desk writing something in a book. The office was dark and dingy, with shelves that had various tools and building supplies scattered on them. In the corner were power tools and lawn equiptment and a faint smell of gasoline filled the stale air.

The man didn't hear him enter, so he said, "My name is Derrick Bishop…Justin told me to come in to talk to you about helpin' out."

Slightly startled at first, The man looked up, and said "We were expecting you. My name is Sal. I'm glad you can give us some time." Then he reached out and shook Derrick's hand.

They talked for a few minutes and he asked Derrick about any prior experience he had. Hoping experience didn't matter, Derrick explained that he was a diesel mechanic, but didn't have any real experience with construction. Sal assured him that what they would be doing wasn't difficult and that he would teach Derrick whatever he needed to know.

Then Sal told him the other employee in the maintenance department was Calvin and that they worked Monday through Friday from 9:00 a.m. to 5:30 p.m. Derrick was asked about his schedule, and they agreed that based on his availablilty, each day they'd decide the hours for the following day. While shaking his hand, Derrick thanked Sal for the opportunity.

Looking surprised, and with a laugh, Sal declared, "A helping hand, it is me that needs to thank you."

On the way back in, Derrick stopped at Justin's door.

"Hey, I just met with Sal. I'm starting tomorrow at 11:00 a.m. I'll work two hours before lunch. Thanks man."

Justin waved his hand, and said, "No need to thank me. I am proud of you for seeking out new sober opportunities."

Full of energy, Derrick waved back at him while saying, "I'll let you know tomorrow how it went."

As he disappeared from the doorway, Justin could hear how thrilled he was by the tone in his voice, and he felt good about Derrick's motivation.

The next morning, excited to start his day, Derrick quickly grabbed a bite in the dining hall and headed down to laundry room. As usual, he and the other two guys on duty made small talk while discussing baseball and the heat wave they were having. Derrick's mind wasn't really on the conversation, as he was anxious to get to the shed and see what they'd have him working on. When the others complained about the heat, his mind flashed to the past and he thought about her a few times, remembering the summer they were together. They went to the town pool and she splashed him while laughing like a playful kid. Standing there smiling, he thought recalled how they always seemed to have fun when they were together, it was like nothing else mattered.

In record time, he finished up the laundry and immediately went out to the shed, where he found Calvin and introduced himself.

Calvin pointed towards the main road, and stated, "The fence by the entrance was damaged when a car crashed into it during a rainstorm. We'll be heading out to replace several sections."

Feeling intimidated by the task, Derrick told him he had never installed fencing, but was good with his hands. Seeing he was anxious about the job, Calvin told him not to worry reassuring him that any help he could give would be fine. Then he explained Sal would be meeting them at the fence because he took the truck into town to pick up the supplies. After looking him up and down, Calvin handed him coveralls so he wouldn't damage his clothing. They climbed onto the golf cart that maintenance used to get around the grounds, and headed towards the edge of the property.

As they approached, they saw Sal. He had already started to take down the damaged portion and it seemed like four sections were either entirely down or damaged. They immediately joined in by laying the broken fence pieces in a pile. When all the debris was cleared away, they unloaded the new sections from the truck. Sal and Calvin seemed to know exactly what to do, so Derrick watched as they worked and followed their lead. Knowing this was all new to him, Sal was very good at explaining the process as they worked on each step, and Derrick was appreciative of his instruction. Before long, the four replacement sections were installed and the fence looked good. Before heading back to the maintenance shed, they cleaned up the area and loaded the broken pieces and tools onto the truck.

As they arrived, Sal asked, "Do you have any time tomorrow? The fence will need to be painted."

Having enjoyed the work, Derrick smiled, and said, "I have time either before lunch or after three."

Then, to Derrick's surprise, Sal asked, "Do you think you can handle the painting alone, or would you prefer one of us to help with it?"

Feeling slightly honored that they would trust him to work independently, Derrick declined help, saying he would be fine working on it alone. As they unloaded the truck and golf cart, Sal explained the rest of the fence had only been painted about two months prior, so once painted the new sections should blend in.

Derrick got back to the residence at about 1:00 p.m. He headed in to grab lunch and a quick shower, finishing just in time for his 2:00

pm individual session with Justin. Coming off a morning of hard work, Derrick walked into the office with less enthusiasm than usual.

"Wow, you look like a tired man," Justin said, with a smile.

Feeling the effects of physical labor, he chuckled saying, "I am a little, but it kinda feels good."

Knowing what he meant, Justin nodded and replied, "I get it."

Before they started the session, Derrick thanked him again, outlining how they had worked on the fenced and that Sal explained each step so he would learn. Sitting back, Justin listened and just took it in, enjoying seeing Derrick excited about something positive.

Then he asked Derrick, "Where do you see yourself when you complete?"

Still with his mind on the fence, Derrick wasn't exactly sure how to answer.

"What do you mean?"

Trying to focus him back on treatment, Justin explained that it was obvious Derrick enjoyed being productive, so he was wondering how he saw his life upon completion of CRC and returning into the world. Not really ever thinking that far ahead before, Derrick just sat and thought for a while.

After pondering the question, he said, "I see myself working, probably as a mechanic. I'll have an apartment and all the things I need to live. I'll have a sponsor, go to meetings, and live a drug free life."

Pleased with his answer, Justin nodded.

"That's a good start. Will you be doing it all alone?"

Feeling a flush on his cheeks, Derrick just looked at him and paused for a few minutes.

"I'd love to have her back in my life...I don't know if that'll be possible."

Drilling deeper, Justin asked, "What would that be like?"

Derrick hated these conversations and was starting to feel uncomfortable, but he knew if Justin was asking it was important.

"It would be like it was before the drugs got in the way. We'd laugh, smile, talk, and it would be nice...just be together, even if we were just sitting watchin' TV."

Cocking his head to the side, Justin asked, "Does it have to be her?"

Breaking a sweat, Derrick's face flushed again. He didn't like to think of others because he was holding on to a dream of winning her back.

"Well...ummm...for now that's how I like to see it. The dream of getting her back carries me forward."

Knowing he still loved her, Justin said he understood, but explained he was concerned if it didn't happen, it could set him back. With a deep breath, Derrick looked down and didn't say anything at first.

Then he said, in a forceful tone, "Maybe it could, but...I owe it to myself to try. I owe it to her to see. I treated her bad...I owe it to both of us to see if I can make up for the things I did...make up for how I made her feel." He paused for a few moments, and then continued. "If she tells me to go to hell, well...I know I deserve it. I'd rather feel bad 'cause I tried and failed instead of livin' my whole life tortured by the what if question."

Validating his response, Justin told him he knew it was difficult for him to talk about her, but stated it needed to be done before he went out and faced whatever was to come. Knowing he was right, Derrick said he understood, even though he always felt emotionally drained after they discussed the past.

As the session ended, and Derrick was almost out the door, he heard Justin say, "Keep faith."

Derrick responded, "Always" as he kept walking.

That night, he took out a piece of paper and began to write a list of things he'd tell her if he had the chance.

The list read:

* *I'm sorry for the things I did.*
* *I was using drugs and it affected my judgment.*

- *I'm clean now and I see all I did that wasn't right.*
- *I love you and I always have.*
- *I know you felt like all that happened was because my feelings changed, but I was wrong to let you feel that way.*
- *If you're willing I would like a chance to try again.*

Reading his list over several times, Derrick realized it was simplistic, but those were the basics that he wanted her to know. Contemplating what to do with it, he decided to keep the list in his drawer and add to it if something else came to mind.

Thinking about her made him wish he had her picture, but he only had his memories of how she looked. As his mind moved through the time they spent together, he started to wonder if his drug use increased because he was running from the feelings he had for her. His stomach flipped, as he recalled being so in love, how he'd never felt that way for anyone else, and how he was often scared that he would get hurt. Although he knew she had no tolerance for drug use, he went from the occasional pot smoking to almost daily use, and then he added pills to the mix. Thinking of it now, he wondered if it could have been because he was scared. Feeling perplexed, Derrick realized maybe it would come out in treatment, as Justin seemed to have a way of zooming in on the reasons he acted the way he did.

The next day, Derrick set out to paint the fence as promised. When he arrived at the maintenance shed, Calvin already had the golf cart loaded up with the paint and the other needed supplies.

Before sending him on his way, he asked, "You sure you don't want me to help you?"

Still happy to be trusted, Derrick just shook his head, and said, "I got it."

Without wasting time, he got started right away and was enjoying the quietness of the day while he became lost in his thoughts. CRC is located along a main thorough fare. Lacking neighbors on either side, and with the facility occupying such a large amount of acreage, it has the feel of a remote location. Trees flank the central area where the buildings are located and the campus is set back at the end of a long driveway. With the location being as it is, standing up by the fence gave him a sense of freedom and isolation from the center.

As Derrick painted, he found himself thinking about a future, that was so called *normal,* with basic issues and problems, but was drug free. He began to remember the pain he caused her and how he saw it on her face several times when she felt dismissed or unimportant to him. Unskilled at relationships, he recalled saying over and over how much he loved her, or that he was going through stuff. At the time, Derrick felt she was unreasonable because she didn't just accept he was struggling with something. Now, with a new perspective, he realized it was unrealistic to ask her to blindly accept that his actions weren't a reflection of his feelings for her. Since entering CRC, he had gained clarity and understood how his actions didn't match his words.

Mindlessly painting, Derrick was thinking about ways he might be able to get her to see it was all him, and his poor choices, in hope that she would forgive him. Feeling confident in his newly developed insights, he was sure he would never make the mistake of dismissing the feelings of someone he loved again. Yet, although he carried that belief with confidence, he still needed a chance to prove it to her.

Just then, his mind jumped to the thought of leaving. He looked back towards the center, there wasn't anyone in sight, and he realized if he left they probably wouldn't know for hours. Full of desire to use, he began to contemplate walking down the road and heading back to his old stomping ground. His heart raced and his stomach flipped, he could just walk off and he was just about to, when her face flashed in his mind. Standing and looking at CRC, he placed his hands on the fence, leaned forward, and hung his head.

As he looked at the ground, while taking deep breaths and trying not to cry, his cross broke free from the confinement of the coveralls and began to swing in his view. Reaching up, he held it in his hands, while tears streamed down his face.

Feeling weak and conflicted, he softly said, "Faith is what I need."

After a few moments, Derrick straightened, took a deep breath, and composed himself, while tucking the cross back into his shirt. Unsure what brought on the urge to leave and get high, he tried to put it out of his mind and continued with his work.

Regaing his composure, he looked up at the center and saw Justin in the distance standing on the porch with another resident. Immediately, he was filled with a guilt similar to that a child feels when they get caught breaking the rules, and Derrick wondered if Justin saw him struggling. Trying not to stare, he continued with his work. Sure he was being scrutinized, worry flooded his mind, until he saw Justin turn and go back into the residence. With a sigh of relief, he reassured himself that his thoughts of leaving were not suspected, because if they had been, he would have been retrieved from the openness provided by the work at the road.

Derrick assessed his paint job, to make sure he hadn't miss any spots, cleaned up, and made his way back to the shed. When he arrived, he told Sal he thought the fence might need a second coat since it was raw wood, and quickly soaked up the paint.

Glad to have the help, Sal asked if he had time to put on a second coat the following day. Pausing for a moment, Derrick was thinking in his mind that being alone by the road was testing his commitment, and he didn't ever want to be torn like that again. Unwilling to disclose his earlier struggle, because he didn't want to stop working with Sal and Calvin, he stated he was available to start about 11:00 a.m. As he hung his coveralls, they agreed, that if the weather permitted, he would tackle the second coat the following day. With just an hour to clean up before his early recovery group, he scurried back to the residence, ate lunch, and changed his clothes.

In group the men were talking about significant relationships and how they affected their recovery. One of the residents explained he and his wife would use together, which was how they originally met, and it followed throughout their relationship. He described trying to get clean before, but when one of them relapsed so would the other. They both entered treatment, him at CRC, and his wife was in an outpatient program. Now he hoped they would be able to stay together and support each other in their sobriety.

Each of the members had spoken except Derrick, but Justin wasn't planning to push him, knowing the turmoil he felt from his former relationship, as well as his family history.

Then, Leo said, "Derrick you didn't share. How'd your use impact your relationships?"

With an immediate change in his expression, Derrick looked out the window, and then looked back with a stoic face.

"My use pushed my one true love right out of my life, and I'll probably never have a chance to make her see it wasn't about her or my feelings for her."

Everyone, including Leo, who would often try to irritate Derrick, was silent.

Feeling the tension, Justin decided it was time to wrap up the group meeting, telling the men the next time they would talk about relapse triggers.

On the way out, Leo said, "Hey Derrick, sorry man...I didn't know."

With a nodded, Derrick said, "I know."

Before he was able to leave, Justin asked Derrick if he was okay. Needing to show he was strong, he said he was fine, when he really was in pain and trying to keep it to himself. Derrick Bishop was accustomed to carrying his pain alone and often found it difficult to volunteer those feelings when asked.

The rest of the month was filled with chores, group meetings, individual sessions, and working with maintenance. Derrick enjoyed his evening recreation time and made some friends in Commons. He'd gotten fairly good at pool, and would sometimes play cards as a fill in player when one of the regulars couldn't play. With the passing of time, Derrick was becoming comfortable in his surroundings and every now and then would think about how nice it was to be off the streets.

At the end of the month, PJ completed and left CRC, and although Derrick was happy for him, he also felt the loss. His roommate was good company and had shown him friendship by being very helpful, so he would be truly missed. For his last night, the center had a get together in the dining hall so the housemates and staff could say goodbye. Feeling connected to PJ, Derrick tried not to show emotion when he wished him well and thanked him for all his help.

Appreciating the changes he'd seen in Derrick, PJ said, "You're gonna complete and if you have goals, a focus, and know what's important, you'll go out into the world and be great."

With a smile, Derrick replied, "I'll keep your words in mind when I doubt myself."

Shaking his head, PJ told him doubt had no place in his mind, and reminded him to keep positive thoughts.

MONTH 3

———

As Derrick started his third month at CRC, he had become very comfortable and was working with Sal and Calvin four to five days a week. In addition, he had his group meetings and individual sessions, which seemed to be going fairly well, and of course he also had his regular chores. Since PJ left, Derrick had the bedroom to himself which was nice at times, but he sometimes missed the chats they had. Recreation in Commons was something he looked forward to and would walk over a few times a week. The guys seemed to enjoy his company, he felt like he had made some friends, and he had a sense of belonging.

Friends to Derrick, were people that knew his name and that he shared a few laughs with, but he rarely shared much about himself with them. That was where his comfort level was when interacting with others, and although he knew that was how he was, he wasn't sure why. He also knew he shared more about himself with her, then he ever had with anyone else.

Never really quite sure how it happened with her, he was glad it did, because it had added a connectedness he felt only when they were together. Derrick realized he felt the way he did about her, in part, due to how comfortable he was in allowing himself to be vulnerable with her. It just always seemed to feel natural when they were together and he didn't have to try. His defenses just came down.

During an individual session early in the month, Justin asked him to talk about his life when he was growing up, and Derrick hesitated, sighed, and as he often did when the past came up, looked uncomfortable.

Justin could see the reluctance, so he asked, "What's so difficult to say?"

With a blank look, Derrick responded, "I don't know how to really describe it. It just…It just was."

It sounded genuine, so Justin leaned back in the chair and studied Derrick's expression. After careful consideration, he realized that Derrick really didn't have any idea how to describe his childhood. With that he knew he would need to ask specific questions.

"Tell me about your family, who lived in your house?" he asked.

In an uncomfortable tone, Derrick said, "I never knew my father, he and my mom weren't married. He saw me when I was born, but…he never stayed around. It was just me and my mom until I was about nine, when my stepfather moved in. At first he just lived with us, but then the government assistance people wanted him to pay or move out, so they got married so he could be on her case."

Then Justin asked if there were any differences in his mother after the stepfather moved in, and Derrick explained before he was there his mother went out a lot. After a short pause, he mentioned he was with his grandmother sometimes, but other times his mother left him alone to go out, even though he was young.

Continuing to recall his youth, he went on to say, "She drank a lot and well…my stepfather did too and once he moved in they were always home. I'd spend a lot of time out with friends so I didn't have to be there."

"You mentioned being with your grandmother some, tell me about her and how that went."

With a visible change, Derrick's expression turned sad and Justin could tell he was thinking.

Then, he said, with a crack in his voice, "My nana passed away when I was about eleven."

Seeing his pain, Justin said he was sorry to hear that and asked what happened to his grandmother. Full of emotion, Derrick explained she had a heart attack and he was the one that called the ambulance. With eyes full of tears, he recalled he was at her house when she bent over and couldn't speak or breathe very well, so he grabbed the phone and called for help. She died before reaching the hospital.

Feeling how traumatic that had to be, Justin said, "I imagine that must've been very hard for you, you were just a boy and many adults struggle with those types of situations."

Now crying, Derrick just nodded.

"If you're up to it, I would like to hear about the type of person your nana was."

His face brightened slightly, and Derrick cleared his throat.

"She was wonderful...she loved me...she made me feel safe."

Hearing the positive feelings he had for her in his words, Justin said, "Sounds like she was a great nana."

Nodding slightly, Derrick agreed with Justin, and smiled. Wanting to learn more, Justin inquired about what type of relationship they had. Wiping his tears away, and without hesitation, Derrick described spending a great deal of time at her house and how she'd make occasions special by making sure he had a cake on his birthday or gifts on Christmas.

Looking for a full understanding, Justin asked, "What was your mom doing when your nana was making sure those things were special?"

In a baffled manner, Derrick looked at him and cocked his head to the side slightly.

"She was just taking care of her business," he said.

The session concluded, and Justin told Derrick he wanted to talk about other things from his childhood at their next session. Although it was comfortable, Derrick agreed.

As Derrick stood to leave the office, Justin said, "Hey Derrick, sounds like you were blessed to have such a good nana."

Content with the pleasant memories of his grandmother, Derrick smiled, and said, "I know."

Later in the evening, Derrick couldn't stop thinking about that day his nana had the heart attack. As he visualized her gasping and holding her chest, tears began to roll down his cheeks, and he thought, *If only I had known how to help her.* Truth be told, Derrick always felt responsible for her passing, as he believed he didn't responded appropriately, because he didn't give her aspirin or CPR. Full of guilt, he didn't accept he was just a boy when it happened and no one would have expected him to know those things. Thinking of his nana, and that day, always made his heart ache, so he had tried to avoid those thoughts as much as possible.

Settling in for the evening, he realized he hadn't told anyone of that day since it happened, except for her, and now he shared it with Justin. Like it was yesterday, Derrick remembered when he told her.

She reached out and took his hand, then told him, "You were just a child, you couldn't know how to treat her heart attack. You were awesome just knowing to call for help."

Looking at him with a loving gaze, she put her arms around him and kissed his forehead, then his cheek, and then his lips.

Derrick remembered how, in that moment, he felt safe, which was a safety he hadn't felt since he'd been with his grandmother. In her presence, he could always sense the love she had for him and it made him love her even more.

The next day, the center was having an open house for other service providers that would referred or mandate men to CRC. Having made a great deal of progress, Derrick was asked to share his experiences while functioning as a tour guide. To him it was a sign of the trust they had in him, so he agreed and felt honored to be selected.

In the morning, when they were getting organized, Justin said to him, "Do us a favor, when you show them bedrooms steer clear of yours. We don't need to explain that hole in your wall."

He winked as he walked away, and Derrick just laughed, but realized his counselor was right because he didn't want to explain the hole.

At 11:00 a.m. visitors started to arrive and the office staff introduced the first group to Derrick, while explaining he would be their guide and would answer any questions they had. The group consisted of one man and two women from an outpatient treatment program. Derrick started by sharing how he came to Conversions Recovery Center, and explained he was there as an alternative to a jail sentence, how long he had been at CRC, and that he was in phase two of the program.

They started the tour on the first floor, where he showed them the lounge, dining hall, and counselor's offices. Throughout the tour of the residence, he outlined the chores and how each resident was assigned duties that rotate on a monthly basis. Then he took them upstairs to the second and third floors to see the bedrooms. Derrick explained that usually there are two men per room and he showed the group the bathrooms and shower areas. Before moving on, he asked if they had any questions. They all smiled and said he'd answered everything in his explanation as they toured.

As they returned to the first floor, he motioned to the door and said he was going to take them to the Commons building. On the walk over, Derrick spoke about what they would see in the Commons. He gave them details about the recreation hall and the meeting rooms used for groups. Explaining the program, he reviewed the types of groups in each of the phases and mentioned going to recreation was a privilege earned once a resident was advanced to phase two. The visitors were given handbooks by the office staff when they arrived, and Derrick pointed out that all the information about the program was contained in it should they forget or want to clarify something after they left.

The recreation room was open for the visitors even though it was during the day. Derrick explained it was normally locked until 6:30 p.m., emphasizing once it was open a staff member would be present until it closed at 10:30 p.m. He also discussed that recreation activities were sometimes held off grounds. Elaborating, he stated residents would be permitted to go depending on an assessment, by their primary counselor, on how stable they were in their recovery at the time. Derrick shared that the next off grounds trip would be the following weekend, when they were scheduled to attend a baseball game.

During this portion of the tour, Derrick was asked many questions and he felt secure that he was answering them thoroughly and accurately. There were staff members scattered about, to assist the residents if they were given a question they were unsure of, but Derrick didn't feel the need to approach any of them for assistance.

The next stop was the Admin. building, which was relatively quick as they walked past the offices and took a brief look at the infirmary. Derrick explained that when someone was enrolling at CRC, the admissions process took place in Admin. They asked a few questions about the admissions procedure and Derrick answered based on his own experience. As he concluded the tour, he asked if they had any questions, and they said they didn't commending him on being so thorough. Then Derrick reminded the group that lunch was being served in the dining hall, and escorted them back to the residence.

After entering the dining hall, Derrick read the menu offerings to the group and pointed to the schedule, mentioning that in about twenty minutes there would be a presentation by staff. They thanked him, went through the buffet line, and found seats. Derrick joined the other residents near the side of the room and Justin asked how it went. Confident he did as expected, he reported it went well and that he felt he answered all their questions appropriately.

They stood quietly, as several staff members, including the program director, spoke about CRC and all it had to offer the men that enroll. After the closing speech, the people Derrick escorted on the tour stopped, before leaving, and wished him continued success in his recovery. Derrick felt a sense of pride, which was an unfamiliar feeling, because he hadn't felt proud of himself since he worked as a mechanic so many years earlier.

As the week moved forward, Derrick was dreading his next individual session with Justin because he didn't want to discuss any more of his childhood. He had been thinking a lot about the death of his grandmother since their last session and it brought some of those old feelings, that had been previously squashed, back to the surface. Those feelings always made his desire to get high stronger and he didn't know what to expect if they were to delve deeper into his past. Uncomfortable at the thought, he knew he didn't want to find out.

Thursday came and that meant he would be meeting with Justin at 3:30 p.m. Having felt anxious all day, he realized he had no choice, Derrick decided he would just tell Justin he wasn't comfortable talking about issues from his childhood. With careful consideration, he was going to tell him they'd need to discuss something else, which is exactly what he did.

"Really, you think we can just bypass that whole portion of your life because you don't like talking about it?" Justin asked, as he looked at Derrick with surprise.

Derrick felt like he should know what to say, but was somewhat confused by Justin's question.

"Umm…well yeah, I figure if it is something that makes me feel bad, it can't be good for my recovery…right?" Derrick asked, as he cringed slightly and waited for an answer.

Feeling slightly amused, Justin just laughed and Derrick wasn't sure what that meant.

"You just answered your own question. You're right, it isn't good for your recovery. Really…isn't that why we need to talk about it? Don't you think those types of feelings played a part in your addiction issues?"

Stunned, Derrick just looked at him. He knew he was addicted, but he never made the connection.

After a moment, he nodded, and said, "I never thought about it before but… I…well…I guess I see what you mean now."

They settled down, and Derrick was asked to talk a little about his friends because he mentioned he stayed out a lot. Always enjoying the time with his friends, he was glad to talk about them. After taking a minute to think about it, he explained he had a good core group of friends, they'd hang out all the time, and it was almost like family. Derrick also said he was known in all the neighborhoods, even if he wasn't exactly part of those other groups. Knowing Derrick was often closed off and glossed over things, Justin asked him to clarify what he meant by a core group.

"Well, they were the people I spent most of my time with…we had some good times…would laugh. Also we had each other's back if needed."

Frowning slightly, Justin asked, "Did you ever need any help from them?"

Making a somewhat disapproving face, Derrick said, "No...not really. I always kept my business to myself. That one friend let me stay at his house when I left home."

Justin leaned back, and Derrick had learned that when Justin leaned back he was thinking about what was just said. Having seen this before, Derrick knew he was likely looking to make a point with the next thing.

"Your friends were there for you, but you never shared anything with them and you dealt with everything yourself?" he asked, with a sound of confusion in his voice.

What he said was accurate, so Derrick nodded, and agreed.

With a deep breath, Justin fiddled with the pen in his hand, and then said, "Just trying to make sure I understand. How did you know they were there for you, if you never shared anything or let them help you with anything?"

Growing slightly uncomfortable, Derrick ran his hand over his face, then leaned forward putting his elbows on his knees.

"'Cause I would be there for them, so I knew they'd be there for me."

Not understanding Derrick's thinking, Justin explained that in theory that would make sense, but asked why he never opened up to them if he believed they would be there for him.

Derrick threw his hands up, "I don't know...that's just not how I do things," he said, with slight annoyance in his voice.

Understanding that Derrick wasn't seeing how this point connected, he suggested that maybe holding everything in, and trying to shoulder his own problems, as well as everyone else's, might have contributed to his drug use and eventually addiction. Processing what was said, Derrick looked at the floor, and then at Justin.

"Never gave it any thought...I just used when I felt like I wanted too...then later when I felt like I needed too."

Silence fell over them for a minute, as the men just looked at each other and pondered what was just said. Then, Justin asked if there was ever anyone he was comfortable enough with to open up to about his life.

Derrick looked at him very intensely, and said, "You know there was, I opened up to her...maybe not with everything...but with a lot."

"Why her?" Justin asked.

Wishing the session was over, Derrick shook his head, and looked uncomfortable.

Then he stood up and rubbed his forehead, and in a low voice said, "I don't know...why not her. I guess I felt safe with her...I knew she wasn't judgin' me. I knew she loved me no matter what...I just told her things... I don't know why." He was in a ramble and got louder as he went on. Then he just stopped, shrugged, and looked at Justin, "Man you're the counselor, so why don't you counsel. I don't know...you tell me."

Justin smirked, and said, "Well, I think you enjoyed the company of your friends and if you got in a fight they would've jumped in to protect you, but emotionally there wasn't a connection. It sounds like, from everything I've heard, you haven't made too many emotional connections in your life and when you did you ended up being hurt. Why you allowed yourself to connect with her, deeper than others, is probably because she made you feel safe."

Justin paused and let Derrick process what was said, as he could tell he was thinking.

Then he continued, "Isn't it interesting that when you allowed yourself to be connected your drug use increased, which eventually resulted in the relationship ending. Might you have been trying to avoid the emotional intimacy because you realized you were starting to feel vulnerable?"

Anger washed over his face, and Derrick yelled, "Are you saying I did it to end the relationship 'cause I was scared?"

Knowing he hit a nerve, Justin answered, "I am asking if it might be possible, even if you didn't realize at the time."

In one quick motion, Derrick got up and tossed the table next to the couch.

"Man you know I love her...why would I do that?"

Not surprised at the outburst, Justin told him to calm down, and explained that maybe he should just think about it as a possibility because if he understood why he did the things he did, there would be less chance of him making the same mistakes. Within minutes Derrick settled down, picked up the table and items that were on it, and apologized.

Having come to understand Derrick, Justin replied, "No worries, this shit isn't easy to deal with, we're good."

The session ended and Derrick was asked to think about what they discussed so they could recap everything in the next session.

Feeling tense, he agreed, and Justin said, "Just remember no punching walls. If you get the urge when you're thinking, get up and walk it off."

The mood lightened and he laughed, then in a more serious tone Derrick told him not to worry about it, because one hole in the wall was enough.

As the week came to an end, Derrick gave the individual session with Justin some deep thought. He began to realized that he had always kept things to himself, except with her of course, and he wondered why he didn't show much of himself to his friends. Thinking of his time at CRC, he realized he was still like that, being most comfortable keeping things to himself, but couldn't really figure out why. Having grown weary of the subject, he finally decided to stop thinking about it and convinced himself that Justin would make sure he figured it out, because he was sure they weren't done with the topic.

That Sunday, CRC had an off grounds trip to the afternoon baseball game. Permitted to attend, Derrick was excited for a few reasons. He had always been a baseball fan and it had been a long time since he watched a game, let alone having gone to one. Also, he was excited because this would be the first time he was off the grounds since entering Conversions. Eager to go, he got up early to get ready. Then sat on the porch, enjoying the peace and quiet of the Sunday morning, while he waited to leave.

At 10:00 a.m. each counselor was scheduled to hold a group with their residents that were attending the game. Anxious to get it over with, he arrived early because he knew once it was done, they would be boarding the buses. Justin started a few minutes after ten, explaining the meeting was to go over some ground rules and that he would conclude with each of them signing a contract that listed the rules and acknowledged that they understood what was expected.

The first rule was that they were not to leave the group unless their counselor gave them permission to do so. Justin explained each group would be sitting together, so if he didn't know where someone was, they were considered to be breaking the rules. Next, they talked about possibly being exposed to alcohol while at the game, and that under no circumstances were they to consume any. Justin also explained they each would be subjected to a breathalyzer when they returned to the center, and blowing numbers would result in a discharge from the program. He spent a good deal of time on this and emphasized there would be no exceptions to the rule. The last rule was that they were to conduct themselves in a polite and controlled manner. It was outlined that foul language, arguing, or being disrespectful to others would not be tolerated.

After he finished, Justin asked if anyone had questions or if anything was unclear. There weren't any questions, so they all signed the contracts and turned them in. Before the meeting broke, Justin mentioned he would be buying hotdogs and sodas at the game, and they would get them as a group to make things easier. They boarded the bus and waited for some of the other groups to join them. As they left, Derrick felt as excited as he was the first time he attended a baseball game.

Having always been a baseball fan, he would watch the games on TV, but never attended one, until he went to one with her. As a surprise, she bought him tickets and they went with her cousin and her cousin's boyfriend. Derrick remembered how cute she looked in her ball cap, while eating a hot dog, and doing the wave. At the time, he thought that she was adorable and now, remembering her child like enthusiasm, he smiled all over again.

Then he recalled the silly bets they would make over baseball games each week.

Before sitting down to watch a game she asked, "What's the bet tonight?"

Derrick would tell her whatever she wanted, and usually she would pick the stakes, but from time to time she would put it back to him. Sitting on the bus, deep in thought, he smiled thinking about the time they bet the loser had to sing to the winner. He recalled how badly she sung and how he loved her for doing it. Although she was a little embarrassed, she was a good sport about it and sang her heart out.

It didn't matter who she picked, or who he picked, she rarely won a baseball bet. One time he felt bad that she kept losing, so he picked the underdog and she still lost.

"Why do you keep asking me to bet when you keep losing?" he asked before the game started and was overwhelmed by her answer.

She smiled, and said, "Because it makes it fun, we trash talk each other and… well…I don't really like baseball. I think it's boring, but I watch it because you like it. The silly bets give me something to do."

Derrick just looked at her and was speechless at first. The fact was he'd never had someone care enough about him, to sit through something they didn't like, because it was important to him. Instinctually he got up, put his arms around her, and kissed her.

Then he looked at her, and said, "I love you."

Looking in his eyes, she smiled, and said she loved him too.

In his reminiscing, he suddenly remembered that was the first time he spoke those words, and he felt like he could weep from the memory of the love lost.

While he was thinking, he was holding his cross in his fingers and running them over it. When he looked up, the bus was pulling into the stadium, and the men grew noisy as they approached. The weather was clear and warm, and the home team was favored to win, so the group was excited. Derrick was out in the world, so win or lose, to him it was a good day, and he planned to savor every moment.

During the game, the men all acted appropriately, while the energy of the crowd in the stadium was electrifying. Derrick just took it all in, while singing along with the songs, yelling out answers for the trivia games that came on the scoreboard jumbo screen, and doing the wave when it came his way. He laughed at the silly videos that were shown and stretched for a few foul balls that were hit into their section, all the while thinking this was how life was supposed to be.

As promised, they were bought hot dogs and sodas, and then later, Justin got peanuts and popcorn for the group to share. A few times the guys would nudge each other to look at a cute girl going by. Derrick felt like a *regular guy,* hanging out on a Sunday afternoon, and thought about how lucky he was to have been placed at CRC instead of being in jail. With the feelings of normalcy, he began to recognize the importance of working the program so he could be a *regular guy* for the rest of his life.

The home team won, and the guys were thrilled, because it was the perfect ending to a perfect day. On the way back, the bus was filled with loud chatter about the triple play that was the turning point in the game. They also talked about the pretty women they saw and how Justin spilled his soda when the guy behind him fell forward while tripping. Upon returning to the center, they were processed in through the front office, and none of the men blew numbers when breathalyzered. Still talking about the events of the day, they moved upstairs and to their rooms as a boisterous mob, with their chatter echoing in the hallway as they went.

Derrick settled in, and although he had fun, he was glad to be alone in his room and away from group. After grabbing a shower, he relaxed for the night, while his mind recapped the day, as well as the memories the day brought forward. He thought to himself, *I miss her. We had a great thing before*—. Then he stopped himself from thinking the rest, the day had been good and he wasn't about to ruin it with negative thoughts.

Having grown sleepy, he rolled over, pulled his cross up, kissed it, and closed his eyes.

As the month came to an end, Derrick and Justin continued to discuss childhood memories during their individual sessions.

After several sessions that focused on his youth, Justin asked, "Do you think that your relationship with your mother, and her not being there for you, then losing your grandmother, made you feel like you had to protect yourself emotionally?"

Derrick looked dumbfounded by his question, and then began to cry. Giving him a few minutes, Justin waited, but he kept crying and didn't say a word.

After a while, Justin asked, "Are you okay?"

Looking up, Derrick said, "I've been thinking about it since it came up. I knew I keep it all to myself...but...I...I didn't know why. I couldn't figure it...I just didn't see it played a...what you said... I think it might be part of it."

Handing him the tissue box, Justin nodded, and said, "Take a minute 'cause this is rough stuff."

Although Derrick felt like a fool for crying, he couldn't stop it once it started. After a few minutes, the tears tapered off and he composed himself. They talked for a while and Derrick began to recognize he was hurt by the lack of a relationship with his mother and the loss of his grandmother, who had been the key adult in his life when he was young.

As the session ended, Justin said, "Just somethin' to think about, maybe we should consider trying to find your mother, so you can confront the feelings you have about her. Just think about it, we'll discuss it more."

Instantly feeling defensive at the thought, Derrick wanted to yell, but stopped himself, and said "We can think about it."

MONTH 4

As September rolled in, the summer came to a close and the oppressive heat of August began to fade. Derrick always liked autumn, with the changing of the leaves and cooler weather. It was an especially good time when he was on the streets, because the temperature was comfortable. Winter was so cold and finding a sheltered place to sleep wasn't always easy. Summer was often hot and humid, and in the springtime it rained so much that he usually walked around in soaked clothing. To Derrick, the fall provided comfortable weather and conditions, that weren't too harsh for someone that had to lay their head down where ever they happened to be when night fell.

During his individual sessions, Justin was fixated on childhood and how it related to Derrick's problems in adulthood. He hadn't really thought about it too much before, but now Derrick began to see that maybe he did close himself off because he was hurt as a child by his mother and the passing of his grandmother. Although open to what Justin thought, he still didn't exactly understand how closing himself off led him to drug addiction. Knowing it was important because Justin was focused on it, he was trying to work through it so he could understand.

"So we talked about many different experiences from your childhood. You told me about your nana, your mother, your stepfather, and your friends. Do you see any connection between the experiences you had and your need to conceal your true self and feelings from people?" Justin asked.

Derrick drew in a deep breath, and then said, "I didn't see it, but it makes sense so...I think you might be right."

That answer was good enough for Justin, because as long as Derrick was seeing possibilities, they had something to work with.

"Okay, do you see a connection in keeping everything to yourself and turning to drugs?" he asked, while peering at Derrick.

"Well... I know what you want me to say but... honestly I... I don't see what that has to do with anything," Derrick said, as he looked like he was straining to find an answer.

Knowing the answers didn't always come easily, Justin smiled and thanked him for being honest in his response. Then he began to ask questions about how Derrick dealt with certain types of situations before getting sober.

"So if you were stressed about something, what would you do?"

Derrick answered, "Drink or get high."

Then Justin asked, "If you were angry about something or someone, what would you do?"

"I'd probably drink or get high."

Justin nodded, then said, "Okay, and if you were hurt by something or someone what would happen?"

"I would have gotten drunk or high."

With a scrunch if his brow before asking the next question, Justin said, "Well, let's say you were happy or excited about something, would you reward yourself or celebrate?"

Nodding, Derrick simply said, "Yeah, probably."

In a sarcastic manner, Justin put both hands in the air, with palms up about shoulder height, and said, "And how would you have done that?"

Pulling his lips tight, Derrick took a breath, and said, "I would've used or drank to celebrate."

Trying to make a point, Justin paused and just looked at him for a minute.

"I'm giving you time to let it sink in, sorta just letting it percolate in your brain." With an embarrassed look, Derrick stared back at Justin.

After a few moments, Justin said, "So tell me, did you see a pattern?"

As it had become obvious, Derrick answered, "I see a pattern... I used or got drunk for any situation in my life. I get it...I know I had a problem. What does that have to do with keeping things to myself?"

With a squint of his eyes, and a crooked smile, Justin said, "Fair question...so let's do the same thing, but with someone you know that wasn't a drug addict. Think of someone you know well enough to answer how they would've acted."

Derrick indicated he had someone in mind, he was thinking of her of course. Then Justin began the same series of questions.

When he asked about what the person would do when stressed, Derrick said she would have complained, talked, or maybe went for a run. Next he asked about getting angry, Derrick chuckled slightly, remembering her ranting when she was mad about things, because he always thought it was cute. He told Justin she would have vented, clarifying if she didn't vent to the person that made her angry, then she would vent to him about the person. Hammering him with questions, one right after the other, he asked what would happen if his sample person felt hurt. Recalling the past, Derrick indicated she would have cried or verbalized those feelings. Then the last question about celebrating was asked, Derrick stated she would share a happy time with someone she cared about.

Sitting back in his chair, Justin said, "Okay, I'm gonna let it settle in, you can percolate again."

With his mind working, Derrick looked at the floor, and then out the window, and they were silent. Justin said nothing, because he needed it to come from Derrick or it wouldn't have the right effect. Patiently he waited, sitting with his fingers laced and hands in front of his mouth, as he leaned back in his chair.

"Okay... maybe because I held it all in it ate at me, then maybe it came out in a negative way...kinda like... a self-destruct mode. I mean... umm...if I got high or drunk I forgot how I was feeling and then I didn't feel it anymore. Does that make sense?"

Thrilled with the answer Justin leaned forward, and said, "Friend that makes perfect sense. Does your brain hurt 'cause that wasn't easy for you?"

Knowing how difficult that process was, Justin smiled, and smacked Derrick on his knee.

Full on insight, Derrick went on to say he never realized other people, non-addict people, just dealt with life situations, but now he sees he hid from them by getting high or drunk.

Clapping softly, Justin said, "I think you've got it. You are starting to see it."

Then he asked Derrick, what would have to be different, in order to prevent the same things from happening, in the future. With hesitation, Derrick said he would need to be more open about things and not try to deal with everything himself.

Agreeing with him, Justin nodded and told Derrick he needed one or two people he could share things with, including his thoughts, feelings, and reactions, so he wouldn't shoulder it all himself.

"I know what you're saying makes sense, but I also know that's gonna to be so hard for me."

Understanding the challenges Derrick faced, Justin answered, "I know... baby steps...you'll get there."

Deep in thought, Derrick said, "She could've been one of those people... she was the closest to that type of person I ever had."

Knowing how Derrick often fixated on the past, Justin could see he felt sad by the look on his face. With reassurance, he again told him they would get there, and that he would help him along the way.

The session ended, and Justin told him if he needed to talk, even if it wasn't during a scheduled session, he should come in. Derrick agreed, saying he just needed to think about things. As he was leaving, Justin again suggested that Derrick consider finding his mother, so he could confront her about his feelings and his childhood.

Exhausted from the emotions of the session, Derrick shrugged, and said, "I don't know... maybe... I've gotta think about it."

Feeling very solemn, Derrick went to his room and closed the door. He sat on his bed and began to think about her and when the drugs started to get out of control. Full of emotion, he recalled how she would be upset about how he was acting, and would say he seemed disinterested or that she felt dismissed by his actions. Derrick would always profess his love for her, because the fact was, he did love her. He loved her very much, and that never changed.

Then he thought about how she would almost plead with him trying to help.

"Just tell me what's wrong. I'll help you. I only want what's best for you."

With his standard answer, he said, "Nothin' to tell, I'm just going through somethin'."

Wanting to help, she asked what it was with the assurance that, no matter what, she would be there for him, but Derrick just pushed her aside telling her it wasn't anything that had to do with her.

Reliving that time in his mind, he began to visualize her face and how she was not only angry, but also feeling hurt that there wasn't enough trust between them for him to confide in her. With his newly developed understanding, Derrick began to see how that, in itself, was enough to kill the relationship.

Then his mind flashed to one incident, when she said, *"If you keep pushing someone away, eventually they'll go. Be sure that's what you want, because sometimes after it happens, you're left with a hole that can't easily be filled."*

Having become irritated, he thought to himself, What more could she want? I told her I loved her and that should be enough.

Full of intolerance, he yelled, "I'm not pushin' you away. Your problem is you won't respect that I won't tell you what it is."

Sitting in the solitude of his room, with the memory running throught his mind, he began to feel like a fool for not embracing her as a person that would hold his problems, as gently as she would have held her own. Tears softly trickled down his face and he started to ask questions in his mind, *What have I done? How could I have not seen it?* In that moment, full of regret, he vowed to himself to do whatever he could to ensure that he never treated anyone like that again.

After dinner that night he was going to walk to Commons for recreation, but he didn't feel like engaging in small talk with the guys.

Instead, he just sat out on a bench, on the porch, looking at nothing and staring into the distance.

So far away in his thoughts, he hadn't realized Justin sat down on the bench next to him, and he was startled when Justin said, "I know today's session was rough on you. Nobody ever said your journey would be easy, but I do know the rougher it is now, the smoother it will be later."

Appearing statuesque, Derrick didn't even look at him, and sat quiet for a moment.

As Justin was about to leave, he heard, "I think I should do it...find my mother. I don't know about seeing her, but... let's try to find her, then figure it out from there."

Believing this was an important step to his success, Justin validated his decision and asked him to write down everything he knew about her before their next session.

Turning and looking at him, Derrick said, "I can't say I know much... but...I'll give you what I remember."

Over the next few days, Derrick thought a great deal about his mother and if something came to mind he'd write it down. The list didn't look like a lot to him, and he wasn't sure if some of it would be helpful, but if it came to mind he wrote it down.

Evelyn Louise Bishop (Elcott)
Married Henry Elcott
Born May 3, 1950 (not sure)
One sister-Jennifer
Graduated high school
Was born here and grew up here
Last address I knew her at-9 Juniper Drive, Apt. C
Her mother-Eloise Bishop
Her father-Jordan Bishop

Derrick was prepared for his next individual session with list in hand, and as he entered the office, he gave it to Justin.

"This is what I know that might help us find her."

They spoke a few minutes about ideas on how to start the process and decided they'd start with the internet. They were hopeful an address, or phone number, would show up for either his mother or stepfather, Henry. Justin suggested they end the session about twenty minutes early, so they could dedicate that time to trying to find Derrick's mother. Derrick agreed, and they planned to continue that pattern until something turned up that would allow them to move forward in locating her.

As the session started, they briefly spoke about the feelings the last session brought out and, Derrick shared that he'd thought a lot about her and how she wanted him to share what he was going through. He also disclosed that he now understood she just wanted to hold his hand and help him through whatever was troubling him. With a frown and a deep breath, he mentioned how the more she inquired, the more he pulled away.

"I thought she was wrong because she wouldn't leave me be, but… I see now what she was trying to do would've been the normal way people that care about each other act when one of them is havin' hard times."

Having seen the emotions he was experiencing in this part of the process, Justin was pleased that Derrick connected what came out in session, to a real situation in his life. He had come to CRC so battered by his life experiences, and so shut down, that early on Justin was concerned he wouldn't be able to find the man that was hidden away deep inside. Now, here he was a few months later, stringing together the pieces that would make him whole again.

With them both eager to see what they could find online, they wasted no time, and went to Justin's desk to type Evelyn's name into the search engine.

A list of results popped up, and they scanned the page to decide which to click on first.

About halfway down, there was an obituary, and Derrick pointed to the screen asking, "Do ya think she's dead?" as his voice cracked.

Justin clicked on it and read it aloud, while Derrick was reading it silently. It was for Henry Elcott and she was listed as his widow. They learned that Henry died two years earlier from sclerosis of the liver. No locating information was noted, but she was alive at the time. Picking up a pen, Justin wrote deceased next to Henry's name on the list, with the date he died.

They returned to the screen with the search results, and found a site that claimed to show addresses and phone numbers. When they clicked on it, up popped her name with two local addresses.

With another click of the mouse, Justin printed the page, and said, "Well that's a start, maybe she's at one of them, or maybe she isn't, but we won't know until we try and see."

Slightly confused, and a little concerned, Derrick asked what he meant by, *Try and see.* Sensing his apprehension, Justin carefully explained the only way to know would be to go to the addresses and knock.

Seeing a fearful expression flash on Derrick's face, he immediately chimed in saying, "Not until you're ready. It's just a start."

Feeling relieved, Derrick nodded and let out a deep breath, while standing up and stretching his shoulders. Able to tell he was tense, Justin asked him to talk about what he was feeling.

Seeming uneasy, Derrick paced a little and then stopped by the window, leaned on the wall, and looked out.

"Well...I know this doesn't sound nice...but... Henry being dead... that doesn't really make me feel all that bad. I thought, when I first read it, good for you, ya son of a bitch, ya got what ya had comin'."

Based on what he'd learned in their sessions, Justin understood why Derrick felt that way. He assured Derrick his feelings were to be expected, and said that just because he didn't feel bad, that didn't make him a bad person. It simply showed that there were only negative feelings where Henry was concerned. Then he reminded him that he was only a boy when Henry came into his life and Henry did some inexcusable things.

Derrick, still looking out the window, almost in a trance, continued, "I remember shortly after he moved in I was eating dinner one night. I fixed it myself 'cause my mother was sleepin'…just a ham and cheese sandwich. He came in and had been drinking and started to yell that I was eatin' his cheese…I was only nine and hungry… I just made a sandwich." Derrick's voice was real low, and almost shaking in a tremor, "I didn't know what to do. Then he picked it up and threw it on the floor and ground his heel into it. He was real angry, and said, "How'd you like to eat it now ya little bastard," as I just stood there and watched."

Derrick, still looking out the window, was wiping tears from his cheeks.

Seeing the magnitude of the disclosure, Justin asked, "What happened next?"

"My mother woke up and came into the kitchen. She saw the sandwich on the floor and told me to clean it up. I tried to tell her what happened, and she said, "Derrick, don't make a big deal out of things, no one wants to hear you complainin' all the time," and she went into the living room with Henry."

Justin leaned back in his chair, and asked him to think about what his mother said and how he handles problems now as an adult. Instantly in awe of what was Justin suggesting, Derrick looked at him with a sense of amazement on his face.

"Wow, I guess you're right…I never thought about that. She would say things like that all the time now that I think back."

Tilting his head slightly, Justin said, "We're all a collection of events and experiences that make us react, and retreat, based on what we've learned."

Liking that line, Derrick smiled mulling it over a minute, then he nodded, and told Justin he was a smart guy.

Before they broke, Justin suggested that he could try to confirm if Derrick's mother was at either of the addresses without Derrick knowing when he was going, This would prevent Derrick from being anxious each time they made an attempt. Aware of Derrick's reservations, he promised he wouldn't let on who he was, or mention what he found, until he was sure Derrick was ready to know. With reluctance, Derrick agreed, knowing Justin's motivation was to help him get where he needed to be to maintain his sobriety beyond the walls of CRC.

As they broke, Justin said, "I know you got it, so hang on to it, and you will be fine." Looking back at him, Derrick was confused, and Justin said, "Faith my friend, hang on to your faith."

As always, Derrick smiled, and said, "I think about that every day."

With a jump from his chair, Justin high fived him as he left the office, and Derrick felt good about all they were accomplishing.

While writing up his session notes, Justin thought of young Derrick, and how humiliated he must have been by the actions of his stepfather. Then he began to consider how it must have made it so much worse, when his mother dismissed him, and went to be with the man that treated him in that manner. Justin's heart broke a little when he thought about the little boy, that just wanted his mother to make him feel important and put him first, if not all the time, at least in that moment. The more he learned, the more he was sure that Derrick needed to confront his mother to put all those negative feelings to rest.

As the month progressed, the sessions between Derrick and Justin focused primarily on Derrick's childhood with him sharing many experiences that were similar to the one that involved the sandwich. Henry always did something mean, and then his mother would dismiss Derrick and his feelings, while returning to her husband. The more Derrick remembered, the more he saw a correlation to how he would deal with any emotions he had now. He always kept his emotions in, and told himself,

I"m being strong, I'm a man and men deal with things on their own. With the progress he was making, Derrick began to see that hiding yourself from those you care about, and who care about you, isn't a sign of strength, but of weakness. Now he understood it was a reflection of being too afraid to be hurt again.

One night, after several sessions that focused on Henry, Derrick leapt from bed while gasping for air. The feeling was intense, and it took a few moments for him to settle down. Sitting on the side of the bed, his heart was racing, and he was clenching his left forearm with his right hand. Beads of sweat were on his forehead and he felt a flush wash over him. Still holding his arm, he lifted his shoulder to wipe the dripping sweat away from the side of his face, and he noticed he was shaking slightly.

As he began to recall the dream that jerked him from his slumber, he became aware of the thunderstorm that was raging outside, with the room becoming illuminated by flashes from the lightning. Feeling paralyzed, Derrick took quick shallow breaths, as his mind retreated to the memory that resurfaced in his dream.

Ahh...no...stop... please! He screamed, as he squirmed, and tried to break free of Henry's tight grasp on his arm. Mama, I didn't do anything wrong. Mama help me, please.

Sitting in the dark, his heart was racing again, but he couldn't stop thinking, the memories were so strong. His arm began to burn, like the wounds were fresh, and he ran his hand over it as he flinched, while his mind recalled the incident.

Henry, I promise I'll be a good boy. I'll do whatever you say. Ohh... please... ahh...stop!

Cigar smoke filled the air in the small bedroom, and he could smell the whiskey on Henry, as he rambled on barely understandable. As the young boy pulled and fought, with tears pouring from the pain, he continued to scream.

What did I do? I was just sleeping. Just tell me what I did wrong!

Derrick began to visualize how his mother walked in the hallway, past his bedroom door, and paused a moment to look in. Then without any reaction, she continued on without saying a word.

Knowing it was now just a dream, and holding his arm tightly with the other hand, Derrick began to speak softly to himself, "It's in the past. It was a long time ago."

In the flashes of light from the storm he could see his arm and took his hand away. As he looked down, the memories were so vivid, that he believed he saw fresh burns and jumped to his feet. Trying to calm himself down, Derrick moved to the window, placing one hand on either side, and leaning forward with his head resting on the cool glass. In the next flash, he lifted his head while looking up at his arm, and realized all he was seeing were the marks left behind from that night so many years before.

Trying to gain his composure, he reassured himself that he was safe and alone in the room by saying, "That isn't your life anymore, the scars can't hurt you."

With a deep breath and a stretch, he settled back into bed and listened to the storm, while trying to think about the possibilities of the future. After what he had just experienced, Derrick felt confident the problems he encountered in life were likely a result of all he had endured. Now, more than ever, he was convinced that Justin's guidance was moving him in the direction necessary to prevent his past from creating future problems.

Within that same week, just as discussed, Justin began the process of trying to find out if Evelyn Bishop Elcott was at one of the addresses they found online. He went to the first, which was not far from CRC, making several attempts, at different times of day. Then one evening, on the way home, a woman about fifty, or so, answered the door and Justin explained he was trying to locate Evelyn.

The woman looked him up and down, and asked, "Why you tryin' to find her for?"

Not disclosing the real reason, Justin shared a cover story which stated he knew her husband before he passed, and wanted to speak with her about Henry.

She looked at him with a scrutinizing look, and said, "Evelyn don't stay here anymore, she moved on 'bout nine months ago."

Hoping for a lead, Justin asked if she had any information about where Evelyn was currently living.

Without hesitation, she nodded, and pointed, "She's down in the junction, not sure where exactly, but somewhere down there."

The junction was an area of town, close to the train depot, that was drug invested, and crime ridden. Pleased to have an idea of where to look, Justin thanked her. He returned to the car and looked at the computer print out. The second address was in the junction, so it was likely to be where he would find Evelyn.

A few days later, he decided to stop by the address in the junction before heading into work. That particular day, his shift began midday and late morning was generally a safe time to venture into that part of town. Justin had chosen to try the other address first, in hopes of not having to make the visit to the portion of town he always tried to avoid, but in this case, the trip was necessary.

Arriving at the home about 11:15 a.m., Justin noticed the streets were relatively quiet. Across the way, a few guys were sitting on the steps drinking forties, and he heard some voices coming from behind the house next door. Although he wasn't wearing his CRC shirt, he was certainly conspicuous. People in the junction seemed to just know those that didn't come from there, and as he knocked on the door, he could feel the stare of eyes on his back from the few that were within sight.

Almost instantly, he heard a harsh voice yell, "Who is it?"

Just then, a Caucasian woman, appearing to be in her sixties, opened the door. She looked weathered, her face was full of wrinkles, and dark circles were under her eyes. With a quick scan, Justin noticed her hair was a mess and she wore a loose tee shirt, making it obvious she wasn't wearing a bra underneath. In her hand she held a glass, and when she moved, he could hear ice tinkle as it tapped the sides.

"So answer me!" she said. "What do you want?"

Her voice was gritty, like sand paper, and the smell of alcohol and cigarettes filled his senses.

Realizing information might not come easily from her, Justin said in a very polite professional manner, "Good morning ma'am, I'm looking for Evelyn Elcott."

The woman took a swig from her glass, and growled, "Evelyn doesn't know any dumb ass losers like you."

Even though her statement surprised Justin, he also found a little humor in it, but did his best to maintain his composure.

"I don't know Mrs. Elcott, I knew her husband."

She studied him for a minute, then said, "I'm Evelyn, you say you knew my husband, what was his name?"

Using his cover story, Justin began to explain how he knew Henry, but she cut him off, and said, "I don't know you and I knew everyone he knew."

Having accomplished his goal, Justin knew it was time to disengage. He found out where she was and that was all he needed. Now it was time to get her to close the door so he could leave without getting into a hole of lies.

"See Mrs. Elcott, I own one of the bars downtown, and at the time Henry passed, he had a very large tab that was never paid off."

Pointing at him, she laughed, "Join the line of people waitin' to get paid, go to hell asshole" she said, while slamming the door in his face.

On the drive to the center, Justin considered Evelyn's presentation, and he realized that if Derrick encountered her in that condition, it could do more harm than good. Evelyn's actions were harsh, so he had to make sure Derrick was emotionally ready to be exposed to that before he struck out to confront her.

Upon arrival at the center, he saw Derrick helping Calvin cut up some branches that had fallen during the storm they had a few days prior. Before going to his office, he walked over to them and they greeted him, making small talk for a few minutes. As he looked at Derrick, and saw all the good traits he had, he thought it was a wonder he ever even made it to adulthood with all he had to overcome as a child. Justin had a great deal of respect for Derrick. He felt connected to him and was going to do his best to make sure he was successful, and equipt with all he would need to reclaim his life when he left CRC.

Month 5

———

With the air turning brisk, and the leaves beginning to change, Derrick found his mind thinking about how much she enjoyed fall and the activities she made him endure. Whenever he thought about the pumpkin picking excursion she dragged him on, he couldn't help but smile.

Derrick had never been pumpkin picking in his life and thought it was silly, but she wanted to go so they packed a picnic lunch and headed out to the farmland in search of pumpkins. It was a bright sunny October day, the air was still, and they talked and laughed while driving, as the neighborhoods gave way to open fields.

As they approached the pumpkin patch, he could see crowds and a sea of cars. She sat up looking around and he was tickled by how excited she seemed to be. Within minutes, they found a parking space and decided to have lunch first. The temperature was comfortable, so he dropped the tailgate for them to sit as she pulled out the cooler with sandwiches, potato salad, and cold soda. As they ate they talked, but Derrick found himself watching the families that were walking by. Mothers, fathers, and kids were laughing and smiling, while holding hands and enjoying family time, and he felt envious having never experienced that type of day.

Then he looked over at her sitting there, sporting a ponytail with sunglasses on and big smile, he knew she was happy to be out pumpkin picking. More importantly, he knew she was happy to be sharing it with him. Derrick watched her and his heart was full of love thinking that the day with her could be the first, of many, on the road to a family day filled with kids. He believed her to be his future and in that moment, nothing else mattered but being with her forever.

They walked out into the field and she was like a child excited to find the best, biggest, most perfectly shaped pumpkin. Finally, she settled on two and pouted that he didn't pick any. Derrick was thrilled to see how she was enjoying herself and that was all he needed, but with her urging him to select a pumpkin, he finally did.

"Ohhhhhh, that's a good one," she said. "It will make a good jack-o-lantern."

With a double take, he looked at her, and thought to himself, You mean we aren't done, picking one isn't enough. They walked back to the farm stand, paid, and she asked to go into the corn maze. Having never been in one before, Derrick didn't know the appeal of such, but it was her day, so he agreed.

They wandered around trying to find their way out, and she held his hand and would giggle when they found they were in a dead end. It was fun and Derrick started to enjoy the corn maze as well. He would steal kisses when they got into a remote area, outside of the view of other participants, and then she would run on in a teasing manner. After wandering about for quite a while, they finally found the exit and Derrick was glad she talking him into giving it a chance.

They climbed back into the pickup to start home, and she said, "This was the best pumpkin picking day ever." Derrick asked why, and she looked at him, and smiled, "Because I was with you."

His heart fluttered, and then he smiled back, and said, "Babe, I never did this stuff before, but now I'm glad I did. I had a great time and it was because of you."

Thinking back, Derrick realized that those types of experiences, are the moments that give people something to hold on to when the world gets crazy, stressful, and busy. Still now, as he sees the changing of the leaves, he is reminded of the specialness of that day, and it makes him feel connected to her, even after the passing of so much time. Derrick felt lonely when his memories showed him the times he once enjoyed, he felt lonely when he was reminded of how much she loved him, and he felt lonely when the experiences of childhood were relived in his mind.

In fact, Derrick Bishop spent much of his life feeling lonely, with the exception of that one year with her, when he truly had a partner in life.

Several weeks passed since he and Justin found the addresses for his mother and Derrick hadn't inquired if Justin made attempts to find out if either were current. Knowing that the face to face was going to be difficult for Derrick, Justin decided to let his visit with Evelyn go unmentioned until there was more progress in their sessions.

One afternoon as group concluded, Derrick decided to ask, "Those addresses...did ya have a chance to follow up on 'em?"

Justin just looked at him for a minute. He didn't want to lie, but he wasn't convinced that Derrick was ready to hear about the condition in which he found Evelyn, so he hesitiated.

Knowing he had to share what he knew, he said, "Yeah, I did have chance to check them out."

Feeling immediately tense, Derrick pulled his lips together tight, and gave a slow nod, all the while keeping eye contact with Justin. He was thinking, and debating, if he should ask the outcome because he knew if they found her, they would have to take additional steps to confront her.

"Well...did you find 'er?" he bluntly asked.

Justin rubbed his chin, then his eyes, and took a breath.

Before he could answer, Derrick said, "Ya did didn't ya?"

"Well yeah...I did."

Turning to look out the window, Derrick felt like Justin's body language was sending a bad vibe, but he had to know what happened.

"What did ya tell 'er? What did she say?"

Before disclosing what he knew, Justin explained he wanted to make sure Derrick really wanted the answer.

The desire to get it over with took hold, Derrick looked at him, and said, "I know it isn't gonna to be easy, but I wanna to move past it...I wanna to be normal...I want a wife and kids...I want her back if I can get 'er. If I don't face this, I'll never get where I need to be."

With that statement, Justin felt more comfortable that Derrick was prepared to confront his mother, or at least hear about her. Then they would take it one step at a time, facing each hurdle as Derrick was ready.

"I found your mother at the address in the junction."

Letting him absorb the information, Justin just left it at that and waited for Derrick to ask for more.

With a serious expression, he looked at Justin, raised his chin slightly, and asked, "Did you tell 'er about me? You said ya wouldn't."

Having been true to his word, Justin explained that he pretended to be a debt collector and said Henry owed him money before he died.

Rubbing his forehead, Derrick asked, "How'd she act? What was it like?"

With pity in his eyes, Justin looked at him, and hesitated. Overcome by a rush of emotions, Derrick put his hand to his eyes and pressed one finger to each side of his nose in an attempt to stop tears from falling.

Then without opening them, he said, "She wasn't good...was she drunk?"

Confirming what he thought, Justin answered, "She was drinking for sure and was cantankerous and disheveled. She cursed at me and slammed the door, but remember, she thought I was there to collect a debt."

Then with a look of determination, Derrick said, "Okay, we know where she is, what's next?"

Concerned it might be too fast, Justin asked if he was sure he wanted to go forward, but Derrick said he knew he needed to, and insisted they take the next step. Before moving on, they talked about how seeing his mother would bring up many feelings that have been pushed down for so many years. They also decided to make the process easier, Derrick should write down some things he wanted to say. Then they could prepare before he actually went down to the junction to speak with her.

The conversation ended, and Justin told Derrick they'd move at a pace that was comfortable for him.

With a roll of the eyes, Derrick said, "None of this is comfortable to me, but... neither is being a homeless drug addict so...this is the better option."

Feeling proud of his attitude, Justin patted him on the shoulder, and said, "I will be here for you every step, I got your back."

Although he was reassuring him, Justin knew it wasn't going to be an easy stage in his recovery. Derrick was correct in saying it had to be done, so they would try to anticipate any struggle, and plan for it accordingly. Having seen Derrick come so far, Justin didn't want to do anything that could cause a set back in his recovery.

As evening set in, Derrick began to think about what he wanted to say to his mother. Having never really considered the possibility of seeing her again, nonetheless telling her all he thought about her and her parenting, he struggled with the task of forming clear thoughts. While staring at the blank paper, he wondered if he should put specific incidents or general feelings. Realizing the list might take time to complete, he decided he would carry the paper with him and add things as he thought of them. Unsure of what exactly should be included, Derrick knew he and Justin could talk about the list, and fine tune it during his sessions, if they needed to. As he began to write, Derrick felt emotions building in him as he remembered his childhood.

- *You never acted like you loved me or even cared about me.*
- *You picked Henry over me and made me feel dismissed.*
- *Because you were drunk all the time I didn't feel like I had a mother.*
- *You never listened to me even when something was wrong.*
- *I had to take care of myself even when I was really little.*

After about a half hour of working on his list with flashes of childhood memories bouncing into his thoughts, Derrick was emotionally drained. He decided he couldn't think about it anymore and would put it away for now, so he folded the list and placed it in his wallet. Even though he was at the center, he put his wallet in his pocket each day just like he did when he was homeless. Even though it was usually empty, it somehow gave Derrick a sense of normalcy.

That evening, Derrick walked over to the Commons to hang with the guys for a while. He wasn't very talkative, but just sitting and listening to them talk, about their issues, families, and sports, helped distract him from thinking about his mother and his childhood. For a long time he sat playing video games, while nodding and grunting in response to things his friends said. After a while, someone asked if he was okay.

As usual he wasn't going to disclosed his true self, and said, "I'm just tired and happy to be listening to everyone else talk."

After few hours passed, he walked back to the residence, and went upstairs to his room. As he settled in, he expected to be uneasy and anticipated having a hard time falling asleep, but within minutes he was out. That night he slept soundly and woke the next morning before his alarm rang. Derrick stretched, rubbed his eyes, and laid looking at the ceiling, as his mind began to reflect on his time at CRC. He was only in his fifth month, and was in jail for about six weeks prior, but his time living on the streets seemed like a lifetime ago.

Derrick began to think about his mother living in the junction and wondered how close, or far, they had been. He'd spent a good deal of time in that area of town because it was the area that drugs were most accessible, and the cops rarely bothered the homeless. In fact, the junction was where he was when he was arrested the last time.

The memory of the arrest was somewhat cloudy because he was high at the time, but he was able to recall he was selling marijuana and oxy for TiTi and sold to an undercover cop. TiTi had a sweet deal going, he would get guys living on the street to work for him. and only gave them small amounts to sell at a time so they wouldn't steal it. Then. when they sold what they had been given, they would bring him the money and he would give them a small amount more to sell. At the end of the day they were paid in product, but just enough for a day or two. They would vanish for a few days, but would come back for more when they were looking for another fix.

For about six months before he was picked up, Derrick worked that deal with TiTi and it kept his habit going strong. If you wanted to move product, the junction was where you worked. There was a steady flow of buyers, if you sold you got paid, and it was all about getting paid. Now Derrick wondered if he had seen his mother, or if she had seen him. and they never even realized it.

Derrick was feeling ambivalent about speaking to her and telling her how he felt for all those years. Growing up, he always just wanted his mother to make him feel loved. In the years since he'd seen her, he carried a secret hope that she would come to him one day and say she was wrong and that she was lucky to have him as her son. In fact, there was a time he would have done anything to please her just to feel her approval and acceptance. Although Derrick never truly expected that to happen, by putting his displeasure out there, he was sure it never would.

In his next individual session, Derrick showed Justin the list he'd put together. Justin liked all that he wrote, stating the list made good points. Then he asked if he was planning on just listing them, or if he would elaborate by giving examples. Unsure, Derrick shrugged and indicated he hadn't thought about it with that much detail. They discussed the different scenarios as they might play out, and realized that his mother probably wouldn't welcome the opportunity to hear about her shortcomings as a parent. Together they decided it would be better if he was able to give details, but were cognizant that the interaction might not allow for it. Focusing on the best case scenario, they decided to rehearse it out with examples, in the event that Derrick had an opportunity to use them. From the top down, they worked on each listed item, taking one at a time so it wouldn't be too overwhelming.

The first item listed was, *You never acted like you loved me or even cared about me.* Justin pointed out that was a big statement and Derrick could probably rattle off item after item, so they'd have to try and formulate a few sentences that gave the idea of what he meant.

Derrick thought for a minute, and then said, "She never hugged me or kissed me. I remember falling and cutting my knee, I was small and she didn't even look at it. I would be at my nana's sometimes for days at a time and I wouldn't even hear from her. When I was with Nana, she wouldn't check on me or call to talk to me. When I was with her, she wouldn't put me to bed and never talked to me. Also, she let Henry hurt me and didn't protect me." Justin told him to write down all that he said and read it over. They needed to make sure it was what he wanted to share with his mother.

After he reviewed what he wrote, he made a few additional notations, then said, "I can give specific examples, but like you said that's a big statement."

Agreeing to leave that one with what was written, they knew they could revisit it if they decided too.

They moved on to the next item, *You picked Henry over me and made me feel dismissed.*

When he read this one aloud, Derrick just shook his head and said, "Man, you don't know how bad it was. It was like...well...like I didn't exist and once she was with Henry, it was even worse than before he came 'round."

Justin referenced the situation with the ham and cheese sandwich, and Derrick indicated that was only one little thing.

"Henry would berate me or hurt me...she'd walk by and said nothing and if I showed any reaction...mad or sad...she'd tell me to suck it up and not be a baby. Then she and Henry would always go off and I was left sittin' there all alone."

Justin told him that what he just shared would be a great way to explain it to his mother, and then maybe the sandwich story could be used to illustrate the point.

Agreeing, Derrick wrote it down and read it to himself. Then he noted next to it, *The Sandwich Story*, and since it was burned into his memory, there was no need to write it in detail.

Then Derrick asked, "Don't you think a mother that cared would've stopped that shit?"

Nodding, Justin paused, and then said, "Well yeah I do, but… remember… her addiction took hold of her, just like yours did to you."

With a questioning expression, Derrick squinted his eyes slightly. He never really connected the two, but Justin was right. His mother was an alcoholic and her addiction had to have some influence on how she acted.

They broke for the day and agreed to finish working on the list in their next session. Justin told him he'd done a good job and the session was productive. Feeling comfortable with what they had covered, Derrick thanked him for his help.

Before leaving, he turned back, and said, "I always hated 'er for the things she did, but….well…. you made a good point. She was addicted… just like I was."

Derrick was evolving as he gained insight, and Justin was pleased with the man he saw coming to the surface.

Over the next few days, Derrick would often think of his mother and times she was passed out, or could hardly walk. Rambling through his thoughts of the past, he remembered the incident when the police came to the house in the middle of the night because she fell on the steps outside and had to be taken by ambulance to the hospital. Thinking back, he recalled how his nana tried to shelter him from that life and how, when she was still alive, he always had a safe place to escape the comings and goings of his mother. After she passed, there was no escaping it. As a child desperate to be loved, Derrick often tried to take care of his mother, and thought if he did, she would appreciate and love him. After Henry moved in, there wasn't a place for him in her life, not even as her helper. It was very clear to Derrick, that once she had Henry, she had no use for him.

Even though he was still angry for all he was exposed to, he was beginning to see how his mother's actions were beyond a simple choice to act in a certain way. Her addiction likely dictated much of what she did, and his sessions with Justin helped him realize addiction pushes out even the best of intentions. Now that he was gaining insight into the things he did before coming to CRC, he saw her actions somewhat differently than he had before. From the last session, he was developing an understanding of her focus being the alcohol instead of him. When she was under the influence nothing else mattered, just like when he was using and dismissed the one he loved.

In the few days that followed, Derrick's mood was solemn while attending his group sessions and he contributing minimally. Justin was the leader of the making sober choices group. He understood what Derrick was going through and gave him some slack however, the other group he was scheduled for each week was restoring positive connections, which was led by Sam. It was a group that spoke about past relationships and trying to make amends for things done when the resident was actively using. Derrick was often on the quiet side in this group, but would occasionally talk about her and things that he did which he now regretted. This week he was in no condition to speak, but Sam kept pushing. Finally, Derrick stood up and threw his chair against the wall.

"Are you fuckin' deaf or just dumb? I said I have nothin' to say today! You're a real prick Sam...why couldn't ya just leave me alone!"

Everyone, including Sam, just sat stunned by his reaction.

After a minute, Leo began to laugh under his breath. and Sam said, "Derrick, why don't you head back to the residence and we'll talk after the group breaks. I'll come find you."

Derrick said, "Whatever!" and slammed the door behind him as he left.

While sitting in his room, looking at the hole he left behind the last time he lost his temper, Derrick began to wonder if his reaction in group would get him sent back to lock up. Feeling worried, he paced and began to consider sneaking out, as his mind kept telling him if he was going back to jail, he could get high one last time before they caught him.

Talking himself in and out of eloping from the center, he began to realize his urge to use was because of the stress he was feeling. After careful consideration, Derrick knew running back to his poor choices would make him feel better only for the moment. If nothing else, Derrick had learned that over the long haul, using drugs had caused him more pain that pleasure. Full of worry, he sat alone holding his cross in his hand and trying to calm down. Mentally he was rehearsing what he should say when he was called into the office as he sat there feeling pensive.

About an hour later, another resident showed up at his door, and said, "Justin wants to see you in his office."

Full of dread, Derrick didn't say anything. Having just expected to meet with Sam, he thought to himself, *Great now I have to listen to his shit too.* Less that eager, he entered the office and saw Sam with Justin. They closed the door behind him and asked him to sit down. Derrick's heightened sense of anger, combined with worry, was obvious in his body language as he sat in the chair closest to the door.

Sam started by saying, "Justin explained to me some of what you've been going through. I see how pushing you to talk about the past in the group setting, with all you're focusing on, might have been upsetting. I should've respected your request to just listen to the others today. Since I didn't know what was going on, I wanted you to be part of the discussion, but either way, you always participate, so I should've realized there was something there. I'm sorry."

Derrick felt his posture relax slightly, and then he said, "Okay, ya didn't know. We're good."

Glad it resolved without incident, Justin jumped in by saying, "Even though Sam didn't know what was going on, the way you acted was way out of line." Feeling like a scolded child, Derrick just looked at him, and Justin continued, "I think you should have more to say to Sam then what you just said."

With a sign of slight annoyance, Derrick blew out air, and said, "I shouldn't have blown up like that...sorry."

They shook hands and Sam told him that going forward, if he ever had something that caused him to feel like he just needed to listen in group, he could always tell him before they began. Derrick agreed and left the office still feeling angry, but realized his anger was probably directed at his situation, and not really at Sam. As he started up the stairs, relief washed over him, feeling glad he wasn't being discharged. At that moment, he suddenly realized his sobriety had become a priority.

During the next individual session, Justin revisited what happened in the group meeting and how Derrick reacted.

After a few minutes of feeling like he was being lectured, he said, "I know it wasn't right. I've been feeling…well…this whole thing is screwin' with me. Usually I would get high and that would be that… so…I'm handlin' it the best I can."

Familiar with those feelings, Justin understood what he meant because knew Derrick usually coped by using drugs. In the situation with Sam, he wasn't only reacting to what they were discussing, but also to his urge to escape reality by using. Trying to show he understood what Derrick was experiencing, Justin told him they had to work on an appropriate outlet for the feelings he was having. Admitting that the urge to use was becoming overwhelming to him at times, Derrick agreed that he needed a plan.

As they talked, they decided to hold off on the conversation about his mother for that session, and focus more on what Derrick was going through. Knowing he was always best when he had a distraction, Derrick said he needed something to focus on. Working with Calvin and Sal might help, but they didn't have too many projects for him these days. Remembering how well Derrick did when he had hands on tasks, Justin decided to speak with them and see if they could find something. Before Derrick left the office, Justin called over to maintenance and spoke to Sal. Able to just hear the one side of the call, he listened as Justin explain that if they had anything at all, it would be helpful, because Derrick needed to fill some time.

After a brief conversation, Justin hung up and explained to Derrick they wanted to paint some of the rooms in the Commons. The plan was to start in a few weeks after the fall cleanup was completed. If he didn't mind working alone, Sal said Derrick could start painting because they already had the needed supplies.

Eager for the distraction, Derrick said, "Anything will be good. I can listen to music and lose myself in the job."

Glad he was able to help, Justin told him to see Sal and he'd let him know which room to start in.

The next morning, Derrick headed out to the shed right after breakfast. On the way, as he passed the garden he would look down on from his window. He noticed the daisies had withered, and died off, with the cooler weather, and for a moment he felt sad. On the way in, he caught Calvin and asked which room in Commons he would be painting. Calvin explained that, since it was short notice, he couldn't do any of the rooms without a plan to relocate the scheduled groups. Then he was directed to start in the hallway, which would give staff a few days to make a rotation freeing up each of the meeting rooms.

Concentrating on his task, Derrick spent the day painting the hallway a very pale gray, but he couldn't escape his thoughts. As he worked, residents came and went greeting him as they passed. Due to working in the hallway, and not being confined to a room, he had to work quietly as to not disturb any of the sessions. Playing music wasn't a possibility because it would be heard by the ongoing groups. As he tried to escape in the project, his mind continued to scan the events of the last two weeks and the things he wanted to tell his mother. Derrick always did his best when he was left on his own to process things, but as he recently learned, that also worked against him when it came to letting things build up.

Later that afternoon he was meeting with Justin again. Since he was struggling, they scheduled additional individual sessions to work through what he was feeling. Midafternoon, he cleaned up for the day and headed back to the residence arriving to Justin's office right on time. Feeling fatigued, he sat in his regular chair, while letting out a big sigh.

With a smile, Justin asked, "Work hard painting today?"

Stretching and shifting to get comfortable, he nodded, and bluntly said, "I need to finish what we started."

Feeling determined, he looked at Justin, who immediately knew Derrick meant the list of things for his mother. Familiar with Derrick and his past reactions, Justin asked if he was sure, and indicated they could take a break by discussing a different topic.

Wanting to get it done, Derrick shook his head, and said, "See... now that it's started it ain't goin' away 'til I deal with it. I walk around thinkin' about it... so... it's best to get it done."

Studying him and his presentation, Justin realized that his mind was made up.

"Okay, if that's how you feel, we'll continue."

Fumbling through the file, he pulled out the notes Derrick had written, and passed them to him. Derrick scanned the pages and said they were up to the third one, *Because you were drunk all the time, I felt like I didn't have a mother.* After he read it aloud, he explained that because she was drinking and drunk all the time, she never spent any time with him and they never did anything together. Carefully, he described how she was happy to have him in the care of his nana as much as possible and when nana wasn't available, she just left him on his own to do whatever. As he spewed information, Derrick stated that she never made sure he had food or clean clothes and never even cared if he went to school.

Realizing he could continue listing things, Justin told him what he said was a fairly comprehensive list, without being so specific that it would come off like isolated incidents. Please with the items Derrick identified, Justin also validated him by saying each of them illustrated things normally done to take care of a child, so together they would show a pattern.

After Derrick wrote down his statements, Justin asked him to read it back, which he did. Needing to be sure it was comfortable, Justin asked if he felt it completely expressed what he was feeling and if he believed it would be clearly understood by his mother.

Silently he read it a few times, and said, "I think it makes sense-It's everything she didn't do, that mothers should do."

They both agreed it made the point that Derrick wanted her to know, so they moved on to the next item, *You never listened to me even when something was wrong.* Derrick rubbed his head as he thought about this one, and then decided specific examples might be best.

"I was young...'bout six I think. I fell playin' ball with the older kids and my wrist was hurt and swollen. I kept telling 'er and she just ignored me. Then, when I went to school on Monday, I couldn't pick up a book. My teacher...she sent me to the nurse. They called my mom and made 'er take me to the doctor and well...it was broken. Then she told the doctor I never told 'er I was hurt."

It was a good example, so Justin told him to write it down and asked if there was anything else that would make the point.

Chuckling slightly, Derrick said, "Lots of things!"

Then he began to talk about when he was almost twelve and some older kids in the neighborhood were pressuring him to get high. He recalled trying to tell his mother several times and she just ignored him. On one occasion, she told him he was interrupting her show which was a repeat of an old sitcom. After a few moments of thought, Derrick recalled what she said the last time he tried to tell her.

"I don't have time to worry about foolish child's play." She said with annoyance in her voice.

When Justin asked what happened, Derrick retracted his head slightly and took a breath and said, "At twelve years old I smoked my first joint, 'cause it was easier than being tormented, each day, as I walked down the street to go home." Derrick looked serious and continued, "For a long time...well... I'd get away with smoking 'bout once a week 'cause... if I stopped every now and then...then they'd let me be the other times I said no."

Leaning back and turning serious, Justin said, "Well, I'd think given the circumstances, that would be a very good example to share with your mom."

There was just one more and Justin suggested they hold off until the next session, but Derrick said he would prefer to get it done, so they continued, *I had to take care of myself even when I was really little.*

When he looked at that one, Derrick laughed, and said, "I don't ever remember my mother givin' me a meal in my entire life. When I was really little if I wasn't with my nana I'd get up in the morning and mom would be sleepin'. I'd be hungry...I remember pushin' the chair to the counter and gettin' a bowl and cereal. I'd spill the cereal...then came the milk...I'd spill that too."

"What about other meals?" Justin asked.

With a distant look in his eyes, Derrick explained he was with his grandmother frequently and a neighbor would feed him sometimes. Then he continued, by saying his grandmother would come over, collect the dirty clothes, and take them home to clean them.

"Man, I don't ever remember havin' sheets on my bed, just a blanket if I was lucky."

Seeing them as all good examples, Justin encouraged him to write them down, which Derrick did. When he was done, he read it over making a few corrections and asked about what would be next in the process.

Taking a moment to consider what they should do, Justin suggested they use the next few session to get Derrick comfortable with his examples. Then they could also decide the best way to present them to his mother. Once they both felt he was in good shape, they would take a trip to the junction.

Although somewhat apprehensive, Derrick was also enthusiastic, and said, "I just wanna get it over so I can move on to the next thing."

Knowing this part of treatment would be the most challenging, Justin explained that they also needed to prepare Derrick for the possible reactions his mother might have. He was concerned if they didn't it would sabotage his recovery. Feeling fully supported, Derrick agreed and said it made sense.

Trying to lighten the mood, Justin looked at him, winked, and then said, "Fella I always make sense, hadn't you figured that out yet."

They both laughed, and agreed to keep the extra individual sessions for a while, until they got through the daunting task of approaching Derrick's mother.

Pleased at how Derrick now seemed to be dealing with this issue better than he was just a few days prior, Justin attributed it to the explosion in group with Sam. It seemed the incident vented a good deal of his emotions and frustrations. That emotional venting was allowing him to revisit the chore, of preparing to see his mother, after a lapse of so many years and such tragic life events. If Derrick could get through the next hurdle, of actually speaking with her, the rest of his recovery was likely to be substantially smoother.

MONTH 6

—

As November approached, it was decided Derrick had prepared enough to see his mother. It had been about seventeen years, and in addition to the time that had passed, there were many obstacles faced. Some got the better of Derrick, but now he had learned how to navigate them to avoid being overwhelmed. Believing he was emotionally ready to look her in the eyes and speak his mind, he felt strong and empowered.

The day before they planned to head into the junction, Justin spent a good deal of time with Derrick. They talked about all the emotions and feelings that simply seeing her could elicit. Knowing it wasn't going to be a pleasant reunion, they also tried to prepare Derrick for the probable reaction that this type of discussion could bring about from her. Derrick knew that it wasn't going to be easy, but assured Justin he was ready to deal with whatever happened.

Midmorning the next day, they set out to the junction in search of Evelyn Bishop-Elcott. As they drove, Justin tried to make chit chat with Derrick, who just sat silently watching the scenery out the window. Having learned to read his body language, Justin could tell Derrick was pensive. Seeing that chatter wasn't easing the anxiety, Justin decided to stop trying to engage him and allow him time to contemplate being reunited with his mother.

As they arrived in the junction, Derrick began to think about the streets being his home for all those years. He saw men gathered on stoops and a few homeless in the alley next to the diner, which was one of his regular stops when looking for food. The buildings were worn, many were in need of repair, and a few rose to the level of being considered dilapidated. In some areas, trash bags were piled up and garbage cans were overflowing bring forth memories of the stench that would emanate from the refuse. While passing an empty lot, he saw an abandoned car that had been there for years. Most of the parts were stripped clean and next to it, in the middle of the lot, was an old couch. It just sat there, through all types of weather, and would often have vagrants sleeping on it or drug dealers sitting waiting for their next costumer. The visuals brought his mind to his days, not so long ago, when this was where he was most comfortable. With the depressing sights of poverty, Derrick felt sad in the memories and recognition of so much time lost.

They pulled up in front or the address for Evelyn Bishop-Elcott, and Justin said, "This is it, the door on the left. Are you sure ya want to do this today?"

Derrick just stared at the door with a deep intensity.

"I need to do this and get on with my life. I know we said I'd go in alone...but...I want ya with me...you don't need to talk...just be there."

Thinking of his encounter with Evelyn, Justin pointed out that she might remember him, but Derrick was adamant. After a few moments of discussion, they both got out and approached the door.

With a trembling hand, Derrick knocked and Justin stood behind him just off slightly to the side. After several attempts, and just as they were getting ready to turn for the car, the door opened and Evelyn was standing there. Her appearance was very similar to the day Justin spoke to her, with a gnarly expression and drink in hand. Focusing on Justin, she looked at him right through Derrick.

Then she said, "I told you, if Henry owed ya money you're shit outta luck."

Within seconds she began to close the door, never even realizing her son was standing there on the stoop. Although Derrick knew it was logical she wouldn't know him after so long, he still felt crushed by her lack of recognition.

"Mom it's me, It's Derrick," he said, before the door was fully closed. They saw it stop midpoint and then slowly creaked open.

Again Evelyn was visible, she leaned forward and studied his face, as she said, "Derrick? Really…What…What? I don't und-er-sta-nd-Just makes no makes no sense. The-the -the guy behind you was here before…said he was a bill collector."

Due to her stammering, it was apparent she was confused. Standing in the doorway, looking bewildered, she was frozen, and the smell of alcohol poured off of her. Derrick explained he was trying to find her and Justin stopped by to confirm her address as a favor.

Breaking her trance, and in a loud blunt manner, Evelyn asked, "What do you want after all these years?"

With a slight look to either side, becoming aware of the public venue, and onlookers from the neighborhood, Derrick explained he needed to talk with her and asked if they could step inside. With a non-chalant shrug of her shoulders, she agreed and walked in with them following behind. Upon entering the apartment, Derrick was immediately thrust into his childhood memories by the sights and smells that filled his senses. The odor of cigarettes and stale alcohol filled the air and the kitchen counters were cluttered with dirty dishes, empty gin bottles, and beer cans. Next to the tattered couch was an end table. On it sat an ashtray overflowing with cigarette butts and ashes so thick that the majority of the tabletop was not visible. The room was dimly lit as the curtains were drawn and the TV was running, as it did 24/7 when he was a child.

They sat, and she said, "Well, it looks like ya did pretty well for yourself."

Nervously Derrick cleared his throat, and said, "Well, I am doing better now. I'm at Conversions Recovery Center out on the other side of town. Before that…I was livin' on the streets for a long time."

Shaking her head, Evelyn laughed, and said, "So ya thought you were so much better than me…ya walked out thinkin' it was so bad in my house, but at least I got a place to live."

Justin felt sick seeing the exchange, but remained quiet. He knew his place was just to be there for Derrick, but this was a battle he had to have in order to reclaim himself and move beyond his past.

"I came by to talk about that-I-Well see-I have some things I need to say-I wrote stuff down 'cause I wasn't sure I'd remember it all."

Disinterested, Evelyn was looking at the TV and seeming to ignore him. Focused on his task, he didn't seem to notice. Derrick took his notes out of his pocket and began to read them, but it was obvious Evelyn had stopped listening. Within minutes, he realized his mother wasn't hearing a word he was saying and he became angry.

With outrage he stood up, turned off the TV, and said, "Listen old woman, I've gone through a lot a shit in my life, I see now that much of it was 'cause of you and I'm gonna say what I came to say and you're gonna listen. Then I'll be gone and you can sit in your filth and drink yourself to death."

Full of pride, Justin wanted to jump from his chair and clap, but knew he had to maintain his professionalism. With a cracking voice, standing before her, and then pacing, Derrick read his list including all the examples. When he was done, he stood looking at his mother and was slightly deflated by her reaction.

"Okay," she said.

After all that was said, all she could muster was a simple okay. A flood of confusion washed over him, and feeling puzzled he looked at her.

Realizing he wanted more, she said, "Okay...so...I was a bad mother. Who cares? I never really wanted to be a mother...it just happened. What do ya want me to tell you? I lived my life and too bad for you if you don't like it." Derrick and Justin were surprised because she was calm, and seemingly unaffected, by all that was just said to her. Then she continued, "I picked Henry over you 'cause he was my husband...I knew you'd grow up and leave...I needed to have someone for me. You should've just let it go...you made your own problems by whinin' all the time."

Stunned at first, Derrick just looked at her, then he said in a low serious voice, "You're pathetic, I wasted years lettin' the way you treated me fuck with my head. You need help...come on Justin...let's get outta here."

As they started for the door, they heard her mumbling, "Don't know who that little shit thinks he is...he wasted his life 'cause ain't nobody hugged him and he calls me pathetic."

Once in the car, Justin asked Derrick if he was okay.

"Yeah, I'm good...I'm pissed...but I'm good."

As they drove, Derrick began to spew about her and how she hadn't changed. Justin could tell he was angry, but he also knew that before long the anger would diminish and the under lying hurt would surface. Prepared to deal with that later, he just yessed him, letting him vent. With all he was saying being true, there was a value in Derrick verbalizing it, even if it was in the form of a rant.

When he seemed to be winding down, Justin said, "When you stood up, turned off the TV, and told her to listen I wanted to clap for you."

Derrick laughed, and said, "That was good wasn't it."

They returned to the center, and as they got out of the car Derrick thanked Justin for taking him.

Then in a thoughtful manner, he said, "I can't believe I let her, and her mess of a life, screw me up for all these years."

Concerned, Justin told him if his feelings started to change and he needed someone to talk to, he should come down right away. Denying it was a problem, Derrick said he felt good and would be fine, but Justin wasn't convinced that would be the case.

Before leaving for the evening, Justin alerted the staff on duty of what happened earlier between Derrick and his mother, so they would be aware in case he had a reaction. The evening passed and there didn't seem to be any backlash from the confrontation. In fact, the next week or so, Derrick seemed to be content while doing his chores, continuing the painting project in the Commons, and attending his sessions. He was pleasant and upbeat, and although Justin was glad Derrick didn't seem to be struggling, he thought the lack of an emotional reaction was suspect.

In an individual session, about two weeks after the trip to the junction, Justin asked, "Are you handling your emotions about your mom by hiding them like you usually do with things?"

Initially, Derrick denied it maintaining he was doing well, but after some conversation, Justin began to see the core of the issue.

"I can't believe she treated me that way and said those things," he said, with sadness on his face.

Justin reminded him that she had addiction issues, and had been drinking. Agreeing that was true, Derrick emphasized that it was obvious what she said was actually what she felt, because she had never been any different.

Needing him to come to terms with what transpired to move forward, Justin spoke with him about how the problem was hers and had nothing to do with him. Using examples of her behavior, he tried to reinforce the idea that it wasn't personal to Derrick, stating she would have been that way with anyone. Knowing Justin had his best interest at heart, Derrick thought about what he was saying, and even though he already knew it, it was good to hear.

Then he began to tear up, "It was terrible to want nothing more than to be loved by your mother…while feeling…feeling discarded…over…and over."

Leaning back and giving him a look of concern, Justin said, "I saw how she was and I know it was devastating to you. I wanted to stand up and defend you and tell her off, but the fact is you held your own and you did just fine. I saw a Derrick that can tackle any issue and I was impressed." Knowing Justin always spoke the truth, Derrick smiled slightly, but said nothing. Then Justin continued, "You know the problem is hers because your nana loved you and you also had a relationship with the lady of your dreams. From all you have told me, she loved you too. You have the ability to give love and be loved. Your mother, however, seems to lack that trait. The issue is hers not yours."

With those words, Derrick held his head in his hands and began crying.

After a few minutes, he looked up, and said, "I know what you said is true. Thanks man…I feel better…it helped."

Telling him he was glad to help, Justin reminded him that he knew what he needed to hold on to, in order to get through anything. Derrick reached down and took his cross and kissed it.

"Faith is all I need."

Reaching out and placing his hand on his shoulder, Justin said, "You're right, but just so you know, I am here as a backup just in case."

Skipping dinner that night, Derrick went to his room exhausted from the release of emotion and the angst over the experience with his mother. Before the sun set, he fell asleep and didn't rouse until the morning. When the alarm rang, he woke feeling renewed and invigorated, with the enlightenment that came from standing up to the demons that tortured his heart and soul for so long. Eager to embrace a fresh outlook by taking forward steps, Derrick was ready to utilize the tools and skills he was learning while inpatient. The interaction with his mother was somewhat sobering, he didn't want to end up in his sixties, alone, and a mess like her.

Towards the end of the month, just before Thanksgiving, Derrick was told he was getting a roommate. For the last few months, since PJ had completed, he had the room to himself. Although he knew eventually he would have to share it again, Derrick had become comfortable with the space being his own. Justin explained the new person was being given the same chore schedule as him, so he could help the new guy become familiar with the program. Then he was told to do what PJ did, when he arrived at CRC, and didn't know how things worked.

Two days later, he returned from his scheduled lunch duty and found Justin in the room with the newly admitted resident.

Extending his hand, Derrick said, "Hi, I'm your roommate Derrick, welcome."

Observing his new roommate to be about five and half feet tall and of slight build, when Derrick looked at him, and how thin and drawn he was, it reminded him of himself when he came in off the streets. Thinking back to his first day, he understood the stunned look the man seemed to have, as being overwhelmed by the system, just as he had been.

Shaking Derrick's hand, he answered, "Hi, I'm Randy. Justin told me that you're a great guy to have as a roommate 'cause you're doin' really well."

Derrick looked at Justin and smiled. Then he ran his hand over the hole in the wall above his bed, and said, "I'm doin' good now...thanks to Justin."

With a concerned expression, Randy looked at the, and asked, "You did that?"

Knowing it look bad, Derrick smirked, while saying, "Yup I did, but that was on day one. I'm a lot better now."

Although Randy smiled, his eyes shifted back towards the hole, and Derrick could tell he was wondering if he had a crazy man for a roommate.

Once the introductions were over, Justin left them and they talked for a while. Scheduled to attend group, Derrick told him when he came back he would give him a tour of the house. Before he left, he showed Randy which chest of drawers was his and explained the linens folded on his bed were fresh, having been left that morning. Randy said he would unpack, make up his bed, and be ready for his tour.

When Derrick returned, he saw Randy sitting on the bed reading over the paperwork given to each resident at intake. While they viewed the bathroom and shower area, Derrick explained the policies and the bin system. Then they went downstairs and toured the lounge, the dining hall, the offices, and lastly the laundry area in the basement. With so much to understand, Randy asked some questions as they went along, and Derrick was able to answer them all. Randy was also told about recreation in Commons in the evening and it was explained he could go over once he was advanced to phase two.

They came upon a group of men in the lounge. Derrick introduced Randy and then each of the men with their name, phase, and the floor they were on. After the men stepped away, he explained the reason for all the details just as PJ had done for him. Before long, it was dinner time and Derrick walked him through the dining hall rules and procedures. He also explained they would be on the same chore schedule for a while, until Randy was acclimated to the program. Then he stated they were currently scheduled for the lunch service in the dining hall, assuring Randy he would walk him through until he was comfortable.

At dinner, Derrick introduced Randy to the group he usually sat with and they all welcomed him to the program. One of the men was more nosey than the others and asked how Randy came into CRC. Looking somewhat surprised at the direct question, he explained that his case manager mandated him because he failed out of an outpatient program for testing positive three times. In usual fashion, when someone new came in, the guys gave different opinions of CRC and various aspects of the program. The majority had fairly positive things to say, with the exception of one resident, Ivan. He always seemed to be on contract for breaking the rules and being inconsiderate of the rights of the other residents.

Settling in quickly, within a week Randy was in the rhythm of chores and attending treatment. He was a quiet roommate, and spoke minimally, with just the typical small talk that would be expected when two people are sharing a small space.

As the month moved on, Thanksgiving was approaching and the residents that were permitted off grounds privileges were making plans to spend the day with family. Those that were still confined to campus were permitted to have family come and dine at CRC for a traditional holiday meal.

Feeling depressed, Derrick knew he would be permitted to leave campus, but didn't have anywhere to spend the day. If he stayed at

CRC he would be alone because he didn't have anyone to come visit him. He felt lonely at the thought, but tried to move past his feelings, knowing he was at CRC to change the things that had isolated him for so long. Working at trying to maintain a sense of positivity, Derrick was hopeful by the following year things would look differently. Perhaps by then he would have people in his life so he wouldn't have to be alone on the holidays.

The Tuesday before the Thanksgiving, while in group, each member was discussing their respective plans and the steps they each needed to take to ensure their sobriety wasn't compromised by holiday festivities. When it was his turn, Derrick said he was staying on campus and the counselor, Sam, didn't ask anything else. Being aware he had off campus privileges, he assumed Derrick didn't have any place to go and didn't want to draw attention to it in the group setting. The others all shared their plans and Derrick wasn't only sad, he felt envious. Trying to work through his feelings, he kept thinking, *next year my life will be different.* The session ended and on the way back to the residence, Phil, one of the guys Derrick often played pool with, stopped him.

"Derrick I don't know your family situation, but I'm heading to my aunt's house for a big family dinner on Thanksgiving. She's an awesome cook and they're making sure the meal is alcohol free so they won't tempt me. There will be plenty, and it would be great if you came along."

Feeling awkward, Derrick thanked him and declined, but he was persistent with his invitation. Finally, Derrick agreed to go. On the way back to his room, he stopped by Justin's office to ask that he be put on the off grounds list for Thanksgiving. Looking up from his desk, Justin gave him a sideways look because he knew Derrick didn't have family or sober friends to visit.

"Where you goin' on Thanksgiving?"

Explaining Phil's offer to join him at his aunt's, Derrick said it sounded like it would be nice so he accepted. Justin was thrilled, in part because he had been feeling bad that Derrick would be alone, but also because he saw growth in him which was evident by him going with Phil. There was a time that Derrick would have been so closed off it wouldn't have mattered what was said, he wouldn't have gone, preferring to be alone.

With a smile, he said, "Phil's family will make sure you have a nice holiday, consider it done."

Being scheduled off the rest of the week, Justin wished him a Happy Thanksgiving.

Derrick smiled, and said, "This is the first one in years that I have somethin' to be thankful for."

About noon on Thanksgiving Day, Derrick and Phil were picked up by Phil's uncle. The house was in the nice part of town and just a few minute drive from the center. When they arrived, Phil's aunt grabbed Phil while hugging and kissing him and said how great he looked. Then she welcomed Derrick, told him if he was spending the holiday with them he was family too, and gave him a big hug. Before long, the house was filled with people and the men crowded around the TV watching football, hollering, and munching on snacks.

Dinner was served about three, but since there were too many people to sit at a table it was served buffet style. Before they began eating, the TV was turned off and they all stood around the table and said grace with Phil's aunt doing the honors. During her prayer, she thanked the lord for Phil and Derrick being well enough to be there with them, causing a chill to go down Derrick's spine and choking him up. Within moments, the food was being dished out and the TV was back on. The day went well and Derrick was thankful he had been included. He ate too much, enjoyed watching the games with the guys, and felt at ease with Phil's family, but mostly he just felt like a normal person doing a normal thing. Before leaving, he thanked the hostess for the great meal and for allowing him to join them.

She kissed him on the cheek, and said, "You're a fine young man, you're welcome to come to our home anytime."

Derrick was touched, never remembering being told he was a *fine* anything. Full of emotion, he hugged her before heading towards the door.

On the drive back to CRC, Derrick thought about the day and realized it was the first real holiday celebration he was part of since the passing of his nana, other than those spent with her. He often blocked those type thoughts from the past out, because the memories made him long for more. They not only had the ability to make him feel warm, but at the same time they made him feel shattered, so he usually tried to forget. For so long the drugs helped him do just that. Now it was time to remember, time to move forward, time to reach for the things that offered warmth and comfort, and that's where CRC came in. He was more and more sure each day, that Conversions was going to help him grab hold of all he wanted and needed.

With the hum of the tires on the road as they drove, Derrick's mind began to wander to some of the holiday meals he had during his homeless years. He recalled going to one of the local churches, on the outskirts of the junction, that had a soup kitchen. On holidays they would serve a traditional meal and try to make it as festive as possible. Although Derrick would go and sit to enjoy the meal, as well as taking an opportunity to be in a heated space for a while, he felt like those working were trying to earn points by volunteering a few hours on a holiday.

They would try to make idle chatter and Derrick often felt like their tone was condescending. He realized they probably weren't aware of how they sounded, but it was difficult, because he always wanted to say, *I'm homeless not stupid.* Instead, he usually just ignored them because it was easier, and they would eventually drift off to someone else.

After they were dropped off at CRC, Derrick thanked Phil for inviting him and told him he had a great family. Derrick considered himself blessed by the positive changes occurring in his life which were giving him the motivation to go on.

MONTH 7

———

WITH DECEMBER, THE HOLIDAY BLUES came to CRC. Staff at the center did their best to create a joyous environment by decorating, and showing a different holiday movie every Friday night. In an attempt to make it special, the movies were shown in one of the rooms in Commons on a big screen with a projector. They would serve popcorn, chocolate chip cookies, and hot chocolate. Many of the residents seemed to be struggling with emotions, because although they would be able to visit with loved ones throughout the holiday season, it wouldn't be the same as being home. Tensions seemed to be running high in groups and there was a general cranky tone throughout.

In an individual session, early in the month, Justin asked how Derrick was feeling with Christmas rapidly approaching. Without hesitation, Derrick said it wasn't bothersome to him because he hadn't celebrated Christmas since the passing of his grandmother.

Justin asked, "There wasn't any celebration for Christmas since you were eleven?"

With his face turning more serious, Derrick said, "There was the year I was with her...that year I had a nice holiday."

Looking for details, Justin asked him to share a little more. He explained they spent Christmas Eve together and on Christmas morning they exchanged gifts. As he recalled the day, he remembered she gave him a few things, a sweatshirt, a couple of CD's, and in a small box was a key to her apartment.

Focused on the key, Justin asked about it, and Derrick explained, "It was her way of saying we were moving to the next level, like we were kinda serious."

Realizing it was significant, Justin explored how that made him feel, and he said, "It made me feel loved. I knew each time she did things like that how much she loved me, and how much I loved her."

Leaning back, like he always seemed to when he was about to throw out a question or statement that Derrick would react to, Justin said, "I notice when you talk about loving her, you always seem to talk about the things she did for you or how she made you feel. In your loving her, what did you give back?"

Derrick looked completely puzzled, and said, "I don't know what you mean. I told you I love her."

Justin explained that people love for different reasons. Often they feel love because of what the person brings to them in terms of caring or emotions, but the love you feel should instigate a return of caring or feeling.

Derrick just looked puzzled and was trying to understand what he meant, so Justin tried to clarify, "So she made you feel loved by the things she did for you or with you, right?" Derrick agreed. "So what did you do to show her the caring you felt? Did you do anything to make her feel she was a priority or important?"

Derrick just stuttered for a minute, "Well,...uh...we spent time together."

After agreeing that spending time together is important, he pointed out that time together offered a mutual benefit. Justin went on to state, that often when someone shows caring and the only return they get is being told they are loved, but the actions don't really support the words, they usually feel insignificant and not truly cared about.

Derrick began to think about his time with her and how she did ask him to do certain things differently. In retrospect, they were simple things. Trying to recall how he responded to her requests, he remembered he often didn't do as she asked. Suddenly, Derrick now realized how his lack of action would have sent the message that he didn't care as he claimed to.

Seeing the point clearly, Derrick told Justin he understood what he meant, and questioned, "If I wasn't usin' would I have taken the things she said serious? If I showed her I loved her, instead of just telling 'er, would things be different?"

Justin suggested that it may have been a little different, but mentioned his childhood didn't provide for any real opportunities to learn those skills. Even without the drugs there may have still been some issues. Comparing how she made sure he felt loved, and how he dismissed the things that would have made her feel loved, Derrick felt bad. Then he made a mental note, that if given the opportunity he would include something about it in his apology.

About midmonth, Phil told Derrick his aunt invited him to join them for Christmas dinner. Although Derrick initially hesitated, the memory of Thanksgiving, and how nice the family was, made him feel comfortable in accepting the invitation. Phil was glad he was coming because he considered Derrick a friend and said his family would be happy to see him again. During his next individual, he spoke to Justin about putting his name on the off grounds list for the holiday. Knowing positive connections were the foundation that would sustain him on his journey, Justin was pleased that Derrick was showing signs of developing personal relationships.

Christmas Eve at the center was interesting. CRC catered a lunch meal that consisted of many traditional holiday menu items, including a dessert table with pies, cakes, cookies, and non-alcoholic eggnog. Christmas carols were playing, the lights were dimmed, and the dining hall was filled with people talking and laughing. It was very pleasant and Derrick appreciated the thought and effort that went into making it special, even though he didn't have much hoiliday spirit.

During lunch, Derrick saw the counselors circulating amongst the residents. They were wishing them each a happy holiday while they seemed to be passing something out. As he began to wonder what was being distributed, Justin unexpectedly sat at the table across from him.

"Merry Christmas Mr. Bishop." he said, in a jovial manner, and handed him an envelope.

Somewhat surprised, Derrick thanked him and returned the wishes for a Merry Christmas. After a brief conversation about their respective holiday plans, Justin moved on to continue speaking with other residents, while Derrick held up the envelope pondering what might be inside.

Eager to see what it contained, he fumbled to open it, finding a holiday card from CRC as well a gift card for a store in town that carried a wide array of items from clothing to hardware. With a smile, Derrick thought how nice and unexpected it was to be given a gift. He wasn't sure what he'd buy and thought he might save it until there was something he really wanted. After a while, the crowd in the dining hall began to thin out and the staff at the center could be heard wishing each other Merry Christmas, from the main hallway, as they were leaving for home.

When he returned to his room, he found Randy was sitting on his bed reading. Derrick thought it odd that he hadn't joined the celebration, but since they began rooming together Randy often kept to himself. They exchanged polite greetings and Derrick put his Christmas gift in his top drawer before laying down on his bed. He was full, content, and ready for a nap, so before long he began to drift off to sleep. As he was slipping into unconsciousness, Derrick's mind was remembering the Christmas he was with her and how comforting just knowing he had her love was.

"Hurry up, I told my parents we would be there at one," she said, as she scurried around the apartment trying to get dressed.

Derrick was still lying in bed and smiling at her.

"So what if we're late. I'll just tell 'em we were busy 'cause I had to give you a Christmas gift."

She blushed a little.

"You will not either! I can't believe I let you get me into bed when I shoulda been getting ready to leave. Derrick Bishop, you're truly my kryptonite."

Feeling inflated, Derrick loved the idea that she felt so strongly about him that she considered him her kryptonite. With a quick motion, he reached out and pulled her onto the bed.

Looking into her eyes, he put his arms around her and kissed her. Then said, "Okay sexy, I'll get ready. I love you."

With a sideways look, and a smile, she said, "I love you too, now put on some pants and cover your junk."

They both laughed, and within minutes were dressed, and left for her parent's house.

After a few hours nap, Derrick woke and the memory of the Christmas with his love was fresh in his mind. Lying there, he smiled, and began to wonder what it would be like the next day with Phil's family. He imagined it would be much like Thanksgiving and was glad he accepted the invitation, because based on his last visit, he was confident that he would enjoy the holiday.

Looking at the clock, he realized it was still early, so he decided to walk downstairs and see who was around. Randy wasn't in the room and the lights were off, so he stumbled at first, but then made his way to the door. As he walked towards the stairwell, the sounds of the guys downstairs grew louder. When he hit the landing at the bottom, he could see they were all just sitting around in the lounge laughing and snacking on items left from the luncheon.

Going somewhat unnoticed, he made his way through the room and found a seat near the TV. A classic Christmas movie was playing, which could barely be heard over the chatter and periodic roar of laughter that would rise from the group. While sitting quietly, hearing the sharing of family stories and traditions, Derrick, like he so often did, felt lonely, even though he was in a crowd.

As he listened, he stared off and reached up to run his fingers over his cross, moving it back and forth between his thumb and pointer finger in an almost hypnotic motion. The cross always brought comfort when he fiddled with it, and tonight, Derrick was especially in need of comfort. Although he didn't readily admit it, he found the holiday season difficult even before coming to CRC. When he was on the streets, he was full of sadness as he'd walk, seeing the Christmas lights on the houses and the lit trees through the windows. It always left him longing to have a place to call home and people to call his family.

Continuing to stare, and manipulate the cross in his fingers, he began to think about Christmas Eve two years prior which was probably his lowest moment.

Wandering without purpose, he saw holiday excitement on the faces of people all day, as they rapidly shuffled in and out of the shops downtown. Tired of feeling deprived, Derrick decided he was going to enjoy the holiday too. He lifted a lady's unattended purse, from her wagon, when she was loading bags into the trunk of her car. After slipping away undetected, he grabbed the money out of the wallet and tossed the bag into the nearest dumpster. Pleasantly surprised with his haul, he counted the bills, and found there was more than enough to purchase a few different things he believed would make his holiday merry.

First, he stopped at the liquor store and bought a large bottle of whiskey. Then he went to the junction and bought some pot and oxy from one of TiTi's guys. One last stop at the convenience store was for rolling papers and some food, then he would be good for the next few days. As he left the store, Derrick passed a group of people and realized it was a few former schoolmates.

Trying to go unrecognized, he put his head down, but one of the guys said, "Hey, is that you? Derrick Bishop is that you?"

With hesitation, he looked back, and stopped to talk. They were all very nice, but Derrick knew they could see he was homeless, as it was obvious by his clothes and especially his smell. With awkwardness, they wished him a Merry Christmas and went on their way, but Derrick felt humiliated by the circumstances that made up the life he was living.

As he walked back to the underpass where he frequently bedded down, he saw houses with lights and knew people all over were celebrating. Consumed by regret, he laid out his blanket and rolled a joint, needing to escape his reality. As he got high, he started to feel even worse about himself, and seeing his classmates made him recognize how bad off he was.

After several hours of smoking and drinking the whiskey, Derrick decided he couldn't go on. He began the think that he lost the one woman that truly loved him, and now he didn't have any reason to continue. In an impulsive moment, Derrick took all the oxys and washed them down with the rest of the whiskey. Tears were streaming from his eyes and he prayed for forgiveness, as he believed he would soon be taking his last breath. The next day, Derrick woke up puking all over and felt terrible, with pains in his stomach, and a groggy lethargic feeling. Surrounded by vomit, he sat on the ground and thought, I guess he didn't want me to go out like that.

Never really understanding how he ended up with the life he was living, Derrick always carried with him the thought that somehow he was being punished. That belief reconcilled living on the street and being drug addicted as his pennants. As a form of validation, he believed that was why he didn't die that night.

Now things were different. Derrick saw a future, he had people that were helping him and seemed to want him to do well, and he had made some friends. It had been a slow process, but Derrick was coming to terms with the issues that effected how he lived his life, and it felt good.

With a burst of laughter from the group, Derrick was jolted back to the conversation in the lounge. Although he pretended to laugh, he had no idea what they found funny because his mind had been deep in thought. Trying to catch up in the conversation, he sat for a few more minutes before noticing the time. The hour had grown late, so he excused himself and wished them all a Merry Christmas. Derrick turned in with a heavy heart over the memory of that night, two years earlier, but he carried it, with the strength that came from his developing hope for the future.

The next morning, he rose feeling happy that he had been given the opportunity to celebrate a real Christmas. Around noon, Phil's uncle picked them up and they set out for their day. The house was decorated inside and out, and the aromas from the kitchen engulfed their senses as they stepped into the foyer. Phil's aunt gave them each a big hug, wished them a Merry Christmas, and told Derrick she was happy he was able to join them. Pleased to be there, he thanked her for including him and asked if there was anything he could do to help out.

Initially she said no, but then paused, and said, "Could you boys help move, and set up, the tables in the dining room? Phillip you know how I like it."

They agreed, and quickly completed the task as requested. Then they went to join the few family members, that had arrived before them, that were sitting in the living room.

Derrick's eyes scanned the tree and decorations. To him it looked like a scene that he'd only known in movies. Everything glistened and shined, and he felt like a child that was in awe of the spectacular presentation of it all. As his attention gravitated towards the mantle, the manger caught his attention, and his mind began to think of his Faith. Unconsciously he smiled, and then his attention returned to the conversation before him. The family members were talking about the church services they attended the prior evening, and how the choir sang silent night by candle light. Derrick felt blissful by being included in their holiday celebration, and just listened while letting his senses take it all in.

The guests continued to arrive by the car full, and before long there was standing room only. Many of them remembered him from Thanksgiving, and asked how he'd been. Enjoying the conversation, Derrick thought to himself how he was feeling like a *regular person*, and it felt good. Being included and accepted was not a familiar situation for Derrick, and he was not within his comfort zone. Phil's family was so warm and inviting, that very quicikly, the uneasiness these types of events normally brought out in him, had dissipated.

Before dining, the family stood to say grace, just as they had on Thanksgiving, and then dinner was served buffet style. Derrick enjoyed the meal, which included many of his favorites. Different family members brought dishes, so the offerings were varied, and he had to make a few trips to sample all the choices. After he was done, he was full and sleepy, so he found a seat on the couch with the men. While listening to them talk about the football games coming up on New Year's Day, he had to fight the urge to close his eyes for a short nap.

Then it was time for the gift exchange. It seemed that the family, due to being so large, did a grab bag where they picked a name, and shopped for just that one person. They began passing the gifts out and everyone crammed into the living room. Derrick got up to make room for someone that was given a gift, so they could sit as they opened it. He was going to make his way into the dining room area, so he wouldn't be in the way, when he heard his name called. As he turned around, Phil's aunt was holding a package out to him.

Stunned, Derrick asked, "For me?

With a smile, she said, "Of course it's for you. Everyone gets a gift on Christmas."

Touched by her generosity, Derrick did his best not to let his emotions show, but she could tell how he was feeling.

As she handed the gift to him, she said, "You're a nice man and we're glad to have you here with us."

To Derrick, that was more valuable than what was in the package. In his life, the times he felt like he was truly welcome somewhere, were limited to primarily when he was with her.

He smiled meekly, and said, "I'm glad to be here."

Everyone opened their gifts, and Derrick took his time with his. Once it was opened, he held it up to admire it. It was a two toned, blue, pullover sweater that looked to be just his size. After the crowd was done with the gift exchange, he found Phil's aunt in the kitchen.

"Thank you for the sweater. I really love it. You didn't have to give me anything."

She smiled, and kissed him on the cheek.

"I never give a gift because I have to, gift giving comes from the heart."

The rest of the day was filled with dessert and conversation, and although it was a long day, it was enjoyable. The group began to dwindle, and Phil's cousin drove the two back to CRC. He was passing on the way home, so it saved Phil's uncle the trip. Before leaving, Derrick was invited to join them on New Year's Day, and he eagerly accepted thanking them again for their hospitality.

They were dropped off, signed in, and processed in accordance with the rules. Both tested clean and were permitted entry, but they noticed Ivan sitting in the office, and he looked devastated. They could hear the conversation between him and the shift counselor.

"You're going to be held in the infirmary until your parole officer can be contacted. Since tomorrow is a holiday, it won't be until after that, but you can't rejoin the general population now that you've tested positive," the counselor said.

He asked, "So that means I'm going back to jail, just 'cause I drank a little to celebrate?"

The counselor could be heard responding in a firm voice, "What did you think would happen?"

Just then, another staff member saw them being nosey and told the men to move on, which they did. Wondering how it would feel, coming this far, and then sliding back because of one celebration, Derrick decided he didn't ever want to find out.

Over the week between Christmas and New Years the center was quiet. Many of the staff members had scheduled time off, and several of the residents, that were close to discharge, were permitted to be out for a few days with special off grounds passes. Derrick enjoyed the more sedate environment, as he was often most comfortable in his own company. He and Phil had become friends and spent a few evenings in Commons playing pool or video games. Having becoming comfortable with their connection, Derrick liked Phil and appreciated his reaching out to try to formulate a friendship.

In his midweek individual session with Justin, they spoke about the holiday and if there were any stressors that could have triggered a relapse if he wasn't in the program. Initially, Derrick said no, and cited that Phil's family didn't serve any alcohol to be supportive of Phil's recovery. Then Justin asked if there was anything else explaining that triggers can be more than having a substance present.

After talking a while, Derrick mentioned the memory he had of Christmas Eve two years prior, when he tried to take his own life. Justin sat and listened with a serious expression on his face, feeling slightly concerned.

When Derrick was done telling the story, Justin asked, "Why is this something you only just tell me after all these months?"

Derrick shrugged, and said, "I don't know...I didn't really think about it until now...I...I...I don't know...I guess it being Christmas and all, it came to my mind."

Never having seen suicidal tendencies in Derrick, Justin began to ask questions about having those feelings at other times, but he denied that he had.

He said, "I figure I did something bad in my life and all the time on the street, all I did and went through, was like my punishment, so he kept me around to finish it out."

Justin asked, "He?"

"God...who else?"

With a slight nod, Justin asked if he still felt punished, and Derrick said he hadn't really thought about it. He acknowledged that his life was definitely better than it used to be. Then Justin suggested that maybe God thought he had a purpose he hadn't yet fulfilled, and that's why he kept him around. Maybe he had a positive plan for him in the future.

With a big smile, Derrick said, "I didn't think about it that way. That way is better...isn't it?"

Justin laughed, and said, "Sounds better to me."

Wrapping up, they finished talking, and Justin felt comfortable that Derrick wasn't suicidal. He believed it was situational depression that he was experiencing at the time of his attempt, but still, to be safe, he had Derrick promise if he ever had feelings like that again he would speak with him, or a staff member, before trying to hurt himself.

"No worries man, I'm not gonna off myself...but if it makes ya feel better, I promise."

They looked at each other and smiled, both knew that Derrick was in a much better place than he had been two years prior. He was starting to like life again, was invested in making changes to sustain his sobriety beyond the center, and he felt like a person that mattered. As a result of embracing the tools he was being given, he was making connections with other people, by starting to let down the shields he'd put up to protect himself.

With the end of December upon them, New Year's was the next hurdle the men would face. At CRC, on New Year's Eve, most of the residents were required to stay on campus, with the exception of a few, that were scheduled to complete and discharge in the month of January. The center believed that it was a bad night to test the willpower of those living in an environment, that sheltered them from the temptations the holiday would present. In exchange for passes, they held a very nice party and each resident was permitted to invite a guest.

In the residence there was a catered buffet served in the dining hall, the lounge TV was tuned to one of the New Year's Eve broadcasts, and in Commons, the largest meeting room was set up like a dance floor with dim lights and loud music. The recreation room was open as well, for people that just wanted to hang out and play pool or cards. The part time weekend staff were all working to supervise the different areas, and at midnight they served sparkling cider to toast in the New Year.

Derrick spent most of the party with Phil, as neither of them invited a guest. They enjoyed meeting some of the wives and girlfriends of their housemates, but mostly they played pool, ate, and sat for a while watching the others dance. Just before midnight, they made their way back to the lounge. Once there they counted down with all the others, watching a massive celebration on TV, with the crowd yelling the seconds to the moment "Happy New Year" rang out. Derrick smiled, shook hands with his friends, and said happy New Year as the sound of noisemakers filled the air. Full of happiness, he realized he enjoyed his first sober New Year's Eve celebration, and he felt accomplished.

There was only one other time Derrick had attended a party on New Year's Eve. It was with her, when they went to her cousin's apartment for a get together with a bunch of friends. He recalled getting so drunk some of the guys not only carried him to the car, but met them at her place to carry him in to bed. The following morning, she was upset by what occured at the party and let him know it.

"I can't believe you got so drunk, what were you thinking?" she asked, with annoyance in her voice.

"I wasn't thinking, I was just havin' fun...Isn't that what the party was for?" he said, in a snarky tone.

She started crying, and said, "I was so embarrassed, do you even know what you said to some of those people?"

Derrick didn't really remember much past the first hour that they were at the party. Seeing her reaction, he felt bad if he said mean things, but he wasn't going to admit it, for fear of looking weak.

"So fuck 'em if they can't take it, they know I was drunk and didn't know what I was sayin'."

With that comment, she was outraged that he was demonstrating such a callous attitude.

Still crying, she said, "You acted like a shithead and embarrassed me in front of friends and family, and that's what you have to say...fuck 'em...I say fuck you."

Derrick never expected to hear that type of thing from her, she was always so caring to him.

"You don't even say you're sorry, give me a break! I'm going to my parents for dinner. Stay here and sleep it off, or go home, but I don't want to see you right now," she said, as she left.

Desperately trying to remember the events from the night before, Derrick couldn't bring up any details, but he couldn't shake her harsh words. With the way he loved her, he never thought she would turn on him. Laying there alone, he knew he had to say he was sorry, because if she was that upset, what he did was probably bad. Formulating a plan, he decided he would sleep a while and call her later after she calmed down. Still, while trying to fall back to sleep, his mind kept thinking about it and he just couldn't understand what the big deal was. New Year's Eve was for getting drunk, and that's all he did, but even if he didn't get it, Derrick reminded himself, it wasn't going to be okay until he apologized.

As the crowd at CRC began to break up, and the guests were being escorted to their cars, Derrick's mind was pulled back to the center to say goodnight to a few of the visitors he met earlier. The group was down to a few and he decided to head up to his room for some rest. The next day would be a long one, as he would be visiting with Phil's family.

Upon entering the room, he found Randy sitting alone and reading.

"Hey, I didn't see you at the party, you all right?"

Barely looking up from his book, he said, "I didn't want to celebrate, it's too soon. New Year's was always a big night for me with the partying, and I felt like just being in a crowd would make me wanna use. I just stayed up here and all was well."

Derrick congratulated him on knowing how to predict what would trigger his urges, then he turned in. It was late and within minutes he was asleep.

The next day, as planned, he went with Phil to see his family. The get together was much of what he expected, consisting of food, football, men by the TV, and ladies chatting at the table. There were far less people than the other times he visited, but with all the whooping and hollering over the games, it was far louder. They had a nice day that was relaxed and comfortable, time passed quickly, and before they knew it they were back at CRC and a new year was upon them.

As Derrick walked towards the residence, he looked around at the buildings and grounds. He stopped and thought for a minute, *this time next year is going to be all good, no more looking back, just moving forward.* Phil was ahead of him and looked back to see him just standing there.

"Hey you okay?"

Derrick looked at him and smiled.

"Yeah...for the first time, I think I am."

MONTH 8

———

THE FINISHING OF THE HOLIDAYS seemed to bring about a mundane spell that made Derrick feel like he had cabin fever. After having the celebrations with Phil's family to look forward to, and getting a taste of spending time with people in a non-treatment setting, Derrick was eager to utilize off grounds passes whenever he was eligible. Since he didn't have any real support, Justin monitored his passes very closely. He didn't want him just wandering the streets, for fear that Derrick might come upon an old acquaintance, and fall to temptation, because he had nothing better planned.

January 10th being Derrick's birthday, he wanted to spend time off grounds. It was a chore free day and he would be excused from group if he had plans, so he asked Justin to put him in for a pass. Hesitating, Jusitn took a deep breath, as he was filled with apprehension. Although Derrick was eligible, he was concerned that a day wandering town, especially on his birthday, could lead him back to choices that were self-destructive.

"Tell me what you're planning to do on your birthday?" he asked.

Derrick shrugged, and said, "Not sure exactly, just need to feel like I'm making progress…going out…being able to do normal things. I've been here for a long time. I just wanna be able to do stuff."

Understanding what he was saying, and not wanting him to feel stagnate, Justin suggested they try to come up with a plan. The truth was, Derrick had made substantial progress in many areas, and Justin believed he should be permitted to go off grounds. Although that was the next step on the journey, he just didn't think he should be wandering aimlessly downtown. Agreeing, Derrick sat down and they talked about a few options, but each required money, which Derrick didn't have. Then he remembered the gift card from Christmas.

"I'd like to use my gift card that I got for Christmas and buy myself somethin'. I could shop…then maybe stop by the library for a bit which is right near there…then come back. I'd probably be gone just a few hours."

Convinced it would be a good experience, Justin explained to Derrick making plans, especially when taking new steps, would help prevent him from slipping backwards. He agreed to put him in for a pass and said he would also requisition bus tokens for him. Thrilled with his chance to feel *normal* on his birthday, Derrick thanked Justin for helping him figure it out.

"You're right, if I was just wandering around, I might've felt like a loser on my birthday with nothin' to do."

Smiling, Justin emphasized a plan would always get him through the roughest times.

The morning of his birthday, Derrick slept late and caught breakfast just before they were shutting down the dining hall. He took his time and read the morning paper that was left behind, probably be a staff member. As he meandered through his meal, he thought how fortunate he was that he was celebrating another year. With many of the choices he made in his life, he was often surprised he'd gotten this far.

When he finished up, he stopped by Justin's office. Justin wished him a happy birthday and told him to have a nice day. Smiling, he nodded and thanked him, as he headed out. It was a long walk down the drive to the road, but the bus stopped right at the entrance to Conversions, so once he reached the end, it would just be a matter of waiting for the next one. With a bounce in his stride, Derrick didn't really mind the walk, because it was a feeling of being free and it felt good.

The bus arrived a few minutes later and on the way to town he watched out the window taking it all in. His stop was about a block away from the store he would be shopping in, and he would pass the library as he walked. He decided to shop first and then hit the library on the way back.

Stepping into the store, without worrying the manager was going to chase him, like they did when he homeless, felt odd at first. Almost on instinct, Derrick kept looking over his shoulder, expecting to see someone following him around to make sure he wasn't stealing anything. This time there wasn't anyone there, he was just like all the other shoppers going about their business.

Unsure what he would buy, Derrick figured when he saw it, he would know it was what he wanted. He made his way up and down the aisles, picking things up and looking at prices. Then he entered the men's clothing department, and was shuffling through the racks when he saw it. It was a sweatshirt, very similar to the one she had given him way back when. He held it up and looked at it, and thought, *although it isn't the same, it's really close.* Knowing funds were limited, he looked at the price and saw it was on clearance, so his gift card would just cover it with a few dollars to spare. Derrick knew he couldn't replace the one she'd given him because that was from her, but having one that reminded him was the next best thing.

Enjoying his outing, he continued to look about the store, even though he was sure he had found what he wanted. After he was convinced he had seen all they had to offer, Derrick made his way to the checkout. While waiting in line, he picked up a soda from the small cooler by the register, and calculated that gift card would cover both. The items were rung up and he had just enough to cover them, with just a few cents left over.

Next on his agenda was the library. As he neared it, he opened his soda and sat on the bench under a shade tree out in front. Although the air was crisp, he didn't mind because he was feeling free. Fully relaxed, Derrick studied those passing. Mothers with young children, young adults that were probably there to work on a school projects, and a few elderly ladies that seemed to be traveling as a group all walked by without even noticing him. Having been cooped up at the center for so many months, he was enjoying watching the people, and thought about each of them, speculating on what type of life they had.

Finishing up, he tossed the empty bottle in the trash can and went inside. Derrick had lived in the same town his entire life, but didn't remember ever being in the public library. When he was in high school they lived in the junction, which was clear on the other side of town, so trips to the library weren't easy. He recalled using the school library for projects and research. Back then, he dreamed of going to college and tried to be as diligent as possible about his schoolwork, within the boundaries dictated by the life he had.

Upon entering the library, he just looked around soaking in the atmosphere. Straight back he could see a computer room with a large glass window separating it from the reading area. To his left were tables, a few couches, and upholstered chairs, while on his right was a doorway with a sign above it saying children's room. Then in the back portion, next to the computer area, there were stairs and two levels of books. The library was brightly lit and uncomfortably quiet, with an unidentifiable fresh smell which he couldn't quite place. The smell hit him immediately as he entered, giving him a feeling of having possibilities, and he stood still inhaling a long deep breath, just trying to soak it in.

Derrick decided to walk around and see where the different isles led him. Feeling like he was on an adventure, and discovering something unfamiliar, was exhilarating. As he explored, he walked through the reference section, the fiction area, poked his head into the children's room, and then wandered over to the area with the couches. On the wall there was a magazine rack, which had magazines in plastic binders and in the center was a holder with newspapers attached to long wooden poles. Derrick decided to select a magazine and read for a while.

Immediately, a sports magazine caught his eye and he took a seat by the window. Before settling in, he looked at the clock and checked the bus schedule. There was a bus going back to CRC, which was leaving in about an hour and ten minutes. Derrick thought that would be the best one, because the one after that was two and a half hours later, which was far more time than he needed to read a magazine. Enjoying the relaxation of reading, his concentration was broken from time to time to look up and glance at a passerby.

With an interest in sports, the magazine he selected was a perfect choice, containing articles on various sports topics. First, he read a segment about basketball and some featured players. After that, he went on to one about football and the playoffs. Finishing up and smiling, Derrick Bishop was appreciating things he considered to be activities of so called *normal* people, and it gave him a feeling of being content.

On the way back to the bus, it was cold as the wind picked up, but Derrick didn't care. He was enjoying the feeling on his face, unlike when he was on the streets and the cold would be an added complication to his life. Finding protected shelter didn't come easily in those days. Now, the cold on his face reminded him he was alive, and it gave him the desire to retreat to his home. Even though it was an inpatient rehab, he had a bed, a roof, and food to eat. Boarding the bus was a good feeling, and the ride back gave Derrick a sense of security to be returning to a place he belonged. Security was a feeling that had escaped Derrick for so much of his life, but now he knew he never wanted to be without it again.

Walking down the drive to the center, he was happy to have it in his sights. It was midafternoon, and he carried his bag with pride as he entered the main hallway. In accordance with the rules, Derrick reported to the front office to be processed for admittance. As always, when returning from an off grounds pass, he was tested and signed in. Within a few minutes, he was cleared and admitted without incident.

Justin saw him walk by, and hollered, "How was your day?"

Beaming, Derrick stepped back, and stuck his head into the office.

"It was nice. I loved just spendin' time feeling...well...feeling normal."

Pleased to see him happy, Justin smiled, and told him he was glad it was a good day.

Derrick went to his room, took the sweatshirt out of the bag, and held it up. As his eyes scanned up and down, it was obvious he was pleased with his choice. Then he folded it and put it away, with gentle handling that would normally be reserved for a person's most prized possession. There was just enough time for a nap before dinner, and since most of the guys were in groups or doing chores, the hallway was relatively quiet. He set the alarm for five and closed over the door. While lying in bed, before falling to sleep, he thought that he had a nice birthday, it was the best in years, and one, among only a few, that he could classify as good.

That evening at dinner, there was a cake for Derrick as the center did for any resident celebrating their birthday. They didn't sing, but the cake was on the table and had his name on it. Several of the other guys wished him a happy birthday as they went by, and Derrick smiled while thanking them. It felt a bit odd for him to be getting so much attention, but he knew CRC was a very supportive environment, not just by the staff, but the residents as well. During dinner, he began to realize it was probably because they were all in the same situation, and the supportive mentality was promoted in the groups they were all required to attend.

Later in the week, Parole Officer Randolph came by to check on Derrick's progress. While meeting with Derrick and Justin, he stated he was pleased with the reports he'd been given. As they conversed, Derrick was open about how he was feeling and some of the things he learned about himself while at Conversions. His insights impressed his parole officer, especially since he was aware how resistant Derrick was the day they arrived. Then PO Randolph talked about the next few months and what was needed to satisfy his sentence. They discussed a report being given to the court at the eleventh month mark, even though he was mandated for a year. That would allow the judge time to review it before the end of Derrick's mandated term.

Derrick was told the report would explain if he was progressing towards the discharge goals that he and Justin were going to work on over the next few months. The goals were required to include employment and self-help. Seeing an end within his sights, Derrick said he understood and was eager to take on the next challenge. PO Randolph reminded him that he'd be keeping close tabs on him for the next couple of months, so the needed paperwork could be prepared and filed. Before leaving, the parole office shook his hand and told him to keep up the good work, reassuring Derrick he was satisfied with his progress.

Justin asked Derrick to stay behind to discuss any questions he had about what would be required to successfully complete the program. Shaking his head, Derrick said he felt he understood everything, but shared he was a little nervous about trying to get a job, because it had been so long since he worked. Understanding his apprehension, Justin told him not to be concerned, because by the time he was facing a job search he would be completely prepared.

Having never explored his work history, Justin asked about his last job and Derrick mentioned he was fired because he was getting high all the time and making mistakes. Thinking back, he recalled he would use in the morning and then again at lunch.

"I was making mistakes on the repairs and forgetting to do things. A few times trucks broke down on the road after I had them in, and when they looked at what I'd done, they realized the breakdown was kinda my fault." Derrick explained he'd worked there a long time, and they were the people that taught him how to work on engines, so they gave him several chances. "The boss even asked me if I was usin' a few times and told me he would hold my job when I went inpatient. I denied it, and said I just had things on my mind, like I always did when she asked me what was wrong. Then I made a bad mistake...the brakes on one of the trucks...I forgot to hook up the air line. The truck crashed into the fence at the yard...it was lucky it didn't happen on the road at a higher speed. They told me they liked me, but my mistakes could leave someone unsafe and they couldn't have that."

As he often did when remembering painful things, Derrick looked off in the distance and the expression on his face showed the regret he was feeling. Then he looked down and clenched his fists.

"They fired me on the spot and everythin' went down from there! I'd already broken up with her...now I had no job. I spent the little money I had on food and drugs. I didn't pay my bills, so I was behind in my rent and car payments. First, the repo guy came and took my truck, and then the next thing I knew, the sheriff was servin' me with eviction papers...but...I still didn't realize I needed help...I kept sayin' it wasn't my fault...I convinced myself it was just a string of bad luck."

Listening carefully, Justin let Derrick just blurt out his stream of thought. He continued explaining, how before long, they came and put him and his things in the street, and from then on he had no home of his own. Recalling that he bounced from friend to friend for a while, he admitted he would steal from them to buy drugs, so one after one, the friends that were willing to let him crash with them, stopped bothering with him all together.

"Ya think I would've figured it out, but I just started to accept it and adapt. I watched the others on the street to learn, and as I met more of them, I saw they have their own little subculture."

Since Derrick seemed to want to talk, Justin asked, "Did you ever think about trying to stop using and returning to the mainstream?"

Derrick looked sincere, and said, "It's weird, but no...it never even crossed my mind." They looked at each other a minute, and then Derrick asked, "Isn't that strange? I mean...I had nothing...it just seemed like how it should be. I never even thought about doin' somethin' to make it different."

Giving it consideration, Justin thought for a minute.

"Well, maybe it was just easier to accept the circumstances, because you didn't have to think about what you were doing, you just lived it. If you made the choice to come off the street, it would have taken a lot of effort that you didn't want to make. Remember how hard it was, to be here in the beginning, even though it kept you out of jail?"

Derrick agreed, and looked to be deep in thought, just sitting and not saying anything.

Trying to explore as much as possible, Justin asked if there was anything else he wanted to share. Feeling comfortable with the conversation, Derrick said he was just feeling regret for how he had lived, and the time he wasted.

"Spendin' my birthday doing normal things...things I would have dismissed before...made me see it. It used to be, even before I was on the street, that when it was my birthday, if I didn't get wasted, it wasn't a good birthday." Pausing he looked at Justin. "I would set out to get ossified, sayin' things like, it was such a great birthday, and I got so drunk I don't even remember how I got home."

Thinking of his own past, Justin said he could relate, because he had done things like that as well.

Looking very serious, Derrick said, "Man...that shit is fucked up. What was wrong with me, I was actin' like a child...adults don't set out to get wasted."

Seeing the turmoil on his face, Justin reminded Derrick he was probably in the early stages of addiction and agreed, that although adults can get drunk, it isn't usually the goal. They both recognized the behavior of purposely getting drunk is usually reserved for teens and young adults, but understandood that those struggling with addiction often mask it with the justification of having fun while partying.

Derrick got up, and thanked Justin for talking, even though they weren't scheduled for a session, then he said, "Believe it or not, I'm sorta glad I got picked up by the cops, 'cause this all got me to see what an ass I was."

Feeling encouraged, Justin told him anytime he wanted to talk to come by, and if there wasn't anyone scheduled, he'd make time for him. Every disclosure was a sign of growth, so Justin was pleased to see Derrick begin to mature by understanding how his behaviors had been juvenile. Although addiction was not an excuse, it was a reason for some of the things that happened, and Derrick needed to come to terms with that as well.

The rest of the month was relatively routine, Derrick attended group and individual sessions in which he began to talk and talk. In his

Wednesday group, the topic of failed relationships came up and Derrick actually spoke about her. This unexpected openness was new, because prior to that, he hadn't really discussed her in great detail with anyone other than Justin. This time he talked about how she wanted nothing but to be there for him, and how he hurt her with his actions. In full disclosure, he mentioned how he would blame her for not accepting the issues he was having, even though he would never discuss what they were with her. In his sharing, he also detailed how she began to assume he was cheating, and that he stopped caring about her. In owning his choices, Derrick began to verbalized an understanding of how his actions would have sent that message.

Several of the other guys had similar stories about their wives or girlfriends, but in those situations their secret was eventually revealed to their ladies. Derrick carried a guilt that she was left thinking, the way he acted, was somehow a reflection on her or how he felt about her, but he didn't share those feelings with the group. All the disclosures brought up more and more memories, making him thinking about that time with her, when he was getting bad and doing his best to conceal his drug involvement.

"Derrick, if you're seeing someone else be decent enough to just tell me," she said, as she began to cry.

Derrick just looked at her for a minute.

"You're overthinkin' things again, you know that's ridiculous and just your way to try and pressure me into tellin' you what I'm goin' through."

She was flitting around the apartment, crying, and randomly straightening things.

"Well...no...that isn't why I said it, but if what you're going through affects me, then...well...then I deserve some information. I shouldn't be expected to just suck it up."

Having been so invested in his position, Derrick recalled he never even considered how she might have been feeling. He became annoyed and defensive, kissed her on the cheek, and walked out.

"You feel any way you want...I gotta go."

Without looking back, Derrick left her standing there, alone and crying. Of course he headed to his buddy's house to get high, and spent the evening telling his friend how his girlfriend wanted to be in his business so much, that she was trying to manipulate him by accusing him of fooling around.

"Hey Derrick, group's over," the voice of his counselor, Sam, rang out, and broke into his train of thought.

He was startled and then laughed.

"Sorry, I musta been daydreamin'."

Knowing Derrick had been going through an emotional time, Sam asked if anything was wrong. He said all was well and mentioned he was just remembering his ex-girlfriend. With a smile, Sam offered to talk with him if he ever felt the need. As always, Derrick appreciated the willingness of the staff at CRC to be helpful, so he was polite and thanked him, but truth be told, if he needed to just talk, he would always look for Justin.

Derrick headed back to the residence and had the chore of preparing dinner, so he washed up and went to the kitchen. The head cook was a staff member and he oversaw the work of the residents. Always enjoying the feeling of being productive, Derrick didn't mind any of the chores, but the kitchen was his least favorite. In most of the others chores, they would just tell you what to do and you would do it, but when preparing meals, the chef would keep coming around and looking to make sure you were doing it right. Also, each night the meal was different, so there were different instructions each day. Derrick felt he worked best in situations that required minimal supervision because he enjoyed the solitude of getting lost in a task, but meal prep didn't permit him to do so.

After eating, he decided to see if the computer in the lounge was available, so he could fiddle online for a while before heading over to Commons. Most of the guys were still in the dining hall, so getting on the computer wasn't a problem. He started out by looking up some sports scores, and then he began to wonder what he would find if he plugged her name into the search engine. With a quick entry of her name, he hit search, and a list of web results came up. Clicking on the first in the list, he saw it was a site that had addresses for people, including household members and phone numbers. The address was the same as it was when they were together, so he had no way to determine if it was current or just an old listing.

Returning to the search results, he clicked on the next one. It was a link to the website for the local newspaper. As it loaded, he took a quick breath, it was a picture of her and a few kids from her class. As a science teacher at the middle school, she was standing with one of her students that won first place, for their age group, in the county science fair. He studied her picture for a long time, looking at each feature in her face. The image of her was just as the one his mind had carried throughout the years they were apart. She looked happy and her name was still the same, so he assumed it was likely that she wasn't married. Quickly, his eyes jumped to the top corner to see the date, and he noted the article was from just two months prior.

After a long time, Derrick decided to print the article so he would have her picture, and then he clicked back to the search results. With a scan of the list, to see if there was anything else that might be of interest, he opened a runner's website, and saw her name listed on the results for several different runs in the last year. When she came to mind, he often wondered if she was still running because he knew how much she loved it. Thinking about her love of running triggered another memory from the first time he spent a Saturday night at her place.

When he woke Sunday morning she was gone. Her car was in the drive but she was nowhere to be found. Not knowing what to think, he felt somewhat panicked. It was like something from a movie where the woman was abducted when her partner was asleep.

Pacing about, and looking anywhere he could think, his heart was racing. He was about to start making calls, to her family and friends, when he heard the door open. With a quick turn, he watched as she came in. Still with her ear buds in, and all sweaty from running, she gave him a big smile until she saw his face.

"Honey, what's wrong?" she asked, with concern in her voice.

Having been filled with fear, Derrick sounded short with her.

"I was worried...I didn't know where you were...your car was here..."

Apologizing, she said she never thought about him being worried, and explained she would go out running early most Sunday mornings, because it was quiet and less crowded on the roads. With a sense of relief, Derrick just hugged her, and held on tight. At that moment, he realized just how much he cared about her. Being overwhelmed with emotion, while holding her in his arms, he could feel himself shaking. Derrick thought about it later that day, he couldn't think of a time, in his entore life, he felt worried about anyone else like that.

A few men had filtered in from the dining hall, and he got the impression one of them wanted to use the computer. He closed out the browser, collected his article off the printer, and left the lounge for the recreation hall with hopes of finding Phil for a game or two of pool before closing out the night. When he arrived, Phil was playing Texas Hold 'em for chewing gum, so Derrick just watched for a while, then decided to head back to the residence.

His mind wasn't really on the recreation hall anyway, he was thinking of her face, and the picture he was holding tightly in his hand. After returning to his room, Derrick opened his top drawer and placed the article under the sweatshirt he purchased on his birthday. Slowly, he was trying to replace those things he lost along the way, things that made him feel connected to her, connected to normalcy, connected to Derrick Bishop the person, that for so long, had been lost. As he carefully covered the picture with the sweatshirt, he thought she would be safe there, almost like he was tucking her in for the night. With a smile, he climbed into bed feeling content with the changes he was making towards reclaiming a life worth living.

As the month closed, there was a snowfall and the grounds of the center presented like a picture postcard. The wooded area that surrounded the property was snow covered, and quite scenic to look at. With the distraction of the weather, the residents were like kids looking out the window instead of focusing on the group session. A few of them even had a snowball fight on the way back from group, running and chasing each other like boys in a school yard. This was the first snowfall of the year, and likely the last. Accumulating snow was a rare occurrence in their area, which is why, even the adults, enjoyed seeing and playing in it.

After years of living on the streets, Derrick didn't like the snow because it created problems for him when he was homeless. When snow came down, even if it wasn't measurable, it made things more difficult. Finding a place to ride out the storm could prove to be challenging, with the few spots that were relatively warm being in high demand. Evading the police also became more difficult. In bad weather they would often come by the areas that the homeless flocked to in a storm, to try and round them up for placement in shelters. When the weather was harsh, the authorities would make efforts to get the homeless off the streets to protect them from freezing to death. Yet, regardless of the attempts to protect them, each year there was at least one homeless person found dead after a cold spell. Now Derrick watched the snow, and thought how blessed he was to have a warm bed, a front porch to stand on, and even some friends that were giddy like children, as they hit each other with snowballs.

MONTH 9

As FEBRUARY BEGAN, IT WAS a challenge for Derrick to continue his motivation in treatment. He knew he was doing well in the program and close to completing phase two, but like for many, the lull that came after the New Year made him feel down. The effects of winter were obvious in the world around them. The trees were bare, the flowers were long gone, and everything seemed to cast a grey hue. The odd jobs with Calvin and Sal were at a minimum because the outdoor activities were put on hold until the weather improved. Derrick felt like he was going through the motions and was beginning to feel restless in his setting.

Early in the month, after an identifying triggers group, Justin asked Derrick to stop by the office before the end of the day. Not giving the request much thought, he agreed, and he walked over to the residence after talking a few minutes with a several of the guys from group. Before going to the dining hall, to work the dinner shift, he stopped by Justin's office.

When he arrived, Justin asked him to come in and close the door behind him.

"I just wanted to take a minute and talk to you about your phase advancement. You would be due in about two weeks, but it isn't going to happen then."

Feeling annoyed, Derrick started to argue the point, when Justin laughed.

"Because it is gonna happen today, congratulations."

Shaking his head, and letting out a sigh, he said, "Man you're an ass! I was gettin' ready to fight with you."

Justin just laughed, they had become comfortable enough with each other that they didn't have to stand on formality.

"Why's it comin' early?" Derrick asked, in a skeptical tone.

Assuring him it was a positive move, Justin explained that job placement heard about an opening at a bus company for a diesel mechanic. Since he was qualified for the position, the decision was made to advance him two weeks early, so he could get set up with job placement and apply for the position. Feeling like he was caught in a whirlwind, Derrick was happy and overwhelmed at the same time.

"You mean I could be workin' soon?"

With a nod, Justin confirmed that it was possible if he got the job, but he could tell, by the look on Derrick's face, that he wasn't processing the idea very well.

"Aren't you happy?" he asked.

Nodding with a shrug, Derrick made a few expressions, before saying, "I guess...I just wasn't prepared...I guess I'm not use to the idea."

Trying to reassure him, Justin explained the job placement department would prepare him before anything actually happened. Then he instructed Derrick to meet with them the following day at 10:30 a.m. to find out all the details. Full of conflicting feelings, Derrick thanked him, and Justin reached out and shook his hand.

"I know you'll do fine, no worries. If I didn't think you were ready, I wouldn't let you move forward."

After looking down for a minute, considering what was said, Derrick looked up, and said, "It just seems so close...real life I mean. It's exciting, but a little scary...I don't wanna fuck it up again."

Putting his hand on the back of Derrick's neck, Justin opened the door, and said "Friend, we all felt that way...you're no different. You'll be fine."

The next morning, Derrick felt a flutter in his stomach when he was at breakfast. He told himself his feelings were silly, he was just meeting with the job placement department, and it wasn't like he was going on an interview. Although he felt anxious, he was able to eat most of what he had on his plate and finish his coffee. Then, on the way out of the dining hall, he saw Leo, another resident that had given him a hard time early on during groups. Leo had returned to work about a month earlier, so Derrick decided to stop and talk with him, to see if he could offer anything that would settle his mind.

"Hey Leo, you got a minute?" Derrick asked, as he sat down at the table across from him.

With an expression of annoyance, Leo looked up from his plate.

Once he saw it was Derrick, he seemed to relax slightly, and said, "Hey Derrick, I haven't seen you in a while. How's everything going?"

Derrick said things were well and asked the same of Leo, but the conversation felt awkward because they'd never really been friendly. For Derrick to stop, just to sit and chat, was out of character, so with discomfort he cleared his throat.

Realizing it was out of the ordinary, Leo asked, "You have something on your mind?"

With a deep sigh, derrick paused, because it was so difficult for him to talk to people about something he was struggling with. One thing he had learned, in his time at CRC, was that holding things in contributed to his self-destructive tendencies, so he forced himself to continue.

"I know you've been workin' for a while. I'm starting with job placement today. They have a lead on a job that I'm qualified for and...well...I don't know how to feel about it."

Leo smiled, and said, "You're excited, but scared shitless at the same time."

With an uncomfortable chuckle, Derrick said, "Somethin' like that."

"I was scared to get back to work too. I didn't know if I could do it, work and stay sober I mean. I knew working meant I would soon be out there dealing with everything on my own."

Shaking his head in acknowledgment of Leo's statement, Derrick said, "That's how I feel...what did you do? How'd ya get past it?"

"I didn't, each day is a challenge, but now I realize, the minute I stop questioning the challenges I face…the day I stop trying to overcome them…that's the day I run the risk of returning to my old habits."

Pondering what was said, Derrick was still for a moment and just looked at him, until Leo began talking again.

"I never wanna be too comfortable in my belief that I can maintain my sobriety. I have the tools, but I know I have to keep questioning if I'm using them properly. If it isn't the challenge of the job, then it will be something else."

Feeling better, Derrick smiled, and said, "I'm glad I stopped to talk to you."

When Derrick stood to leave, Leo looked up, and said, "Be honest in your interview, don't hide where you're coming from. Take responsibility for your past and share what you've learned to make you a better man. If they don't want you 'cause you're in recovery, then you don't wanna work there, but the job placement people will tell you all that."

Thanking him again, Derrick smiled, and as he walked away he thought about how helpful talking to Leo was. The old Derrick wouldn't have reached out for advice, but by doing so, he realized his apprehension wasn't unique to him.

At 10:30 a.m. he reported to job placement, which was in the Admin. building. His appointment was with Emily, and she told him she would be his employment skills coach during the process of finding a job. They spoke for some time about Derrick's work history and the skills he had to offer an employer. Then she explained that the job placement department at the center was often approached by companies looking to fill positions, and recently they got a call from a bus company looking for a diesel mechanic. As per normal procedure, they canvassed the counselors to see if any of the residents, that were nearing phase three, would be qualified for the job and Justin submitted his name.

Eager to know about the position, Derrick mentioned Justin only told him it was as a mechanic, but he didn't know the details. Then he expressed he was interested and would like to know more specific information about available job. Emily was able to tell him about the company, where it was located, and the work hours that would be required.

Derrick smiled, and said, "Sounds perfect, but I'll be honest...I'm a little nervous. It's been a long time and...a lot has happened."

Reassuring him, Emily explained that the supervisor was aware that anyone at the center would be coming with a history, but he was willing to work with a motivated person.

She gave Derrick a job application to fill out, and told him to ask for help if he wasn't sure how to answer any of the questions. After finding him a place to sit, Emily returned to her desk and worked on her computer, while he completed the paperwork. A few minutes later, he was done and Emily took the form and reviewed it. With a scan of both sides, she said it seemed complete to her, and told him he'd done a good job. As it was being faxed to the company, she explained he was already scheduled for an interview that Friday at 3:00 p.m.

Raising his eyebrows, and Derrick asked, "How do I have an interview when I just completed the application?"

With a smile, Emily said that based on what she told the supervisor, an interview was scheduled with the application to follow.

Derrick grimaced, "I don't even know what to say in an interview, it's been such a long time."

Comforting him, Emily assured him that over the next couple of days she would meet with him and practice interviewing skills. They set a daily appointment for 9:30 a.m. and she also mentioned she'd drive him to the interview and back.

After he thanked her Derrick started to leave, but she stopped him and told him Justin should bring him to the wardrobe closet to choose clothes to wear.

Derrick asked, "Wardrobe closet?"

As that reaction was not uncommon, Emily pointed out that most residents don't have interview clothes, so the center has a closet containing slacks, suits, button down shirts, and ties in various sizes, which are loaned for the purpose of attending job interviews. She told him he wouldn't need a full suit for this type of position, but indicated he should wear slacks, a button down shirt, and a tie. Although Derrick thought the tie was a bit much, he agreed to follow her suggestion.

The next morning, he got up and went down to the dining hall early with the plan of stopping by Justin's office, before meeting with Emily, to ask about the wardrobe closet. At breakfast, he sat with his usual crowd and listened as they talked about their plans for the day. Not having much to say, Derrick often just seemed to blend in when with a group. He presented as friendly, laughed at jokes, and paid close attention to the things his friends said, but was always much more content to be an observer as opposed to a participant.

Finishing up, Derrick set out to find Justin and stumbled upon him in route to the office.

"Hey, I was coming to see you, can you take me to the wardrobe closet before Friday? I have an interview on Friday afternoon."

Feeling proud that Derrick had come so far, Justin smiled.

"You have an individual today, we can go before or after...whatever you prefer."

Thinking about it, Derrick decided that going after his session would be better. His assigned monthly chore was housekeeping, which was basically done midday, so he would probably finish just in time for his individual.

As he walked across the parking lot to the Admin. building, the wind was whipping, so Derrick pulled his arms in tight and tilted his head downward as he felt the cold air blowing against his face. He arrived right on time to find Emily waiting for him. After she got him settled, they began to talk about possible questions that could be asked during the interview.

Wanting to be successfully with his answers, Derrick expressed he wasn't sure how much about his addiction and recovery he should disclose.

"You need to be honest without disgusting your potential employer."

Derrick laughed, and asked, "So umm... I'm disgusting?"

Realizing that what she said might have sounded harsh, Emily explained that most people that end up in long term inpatient programs have an extensive history, which includes many incidents and behaviors that could be upsetting to the average person. Then she used an example of a behavior often associated with being homeless.

"When you lived on the streets what did you eat?"

Without hesitation, Derrick said, "Anything I could get my hands on."

With a nod of her head, she continued and asked if that sometimes included items from the trash. Thinking back, Derrick agreed that he would often rummage through dumpsters and garbage cans for discarded food. Clearly emphasizing the original point, Emily explained if he shared that with just anyone, they would be turned off. With immediate understanding, Derrick knew what she meant, and for a moment felt sad about the life he once lived.

Although his potential employer knew his history was not always conventional, Emily stated he should think of creative ways to present the information. She told him to find a positive in the situation, offering to practice with sample questions and answers.

Then she asked, "Do you believe your drug history and recovery would affect your work in any way?"

Hesitating at first, Derrick said, "I don't think so...I...I feel confident in my ability to maintain my sobriety."

Complimenting him on his answer, Emily smiled, and offered an alternative, "You could also say, yes I believe it will make me a better employee. I've overcome a difficult challenge and learned that I have an ability to achieve any goal I put my mind too."

With a big smile, Derrick said, "You make it sound like sobriety is a good opportunity."

Emily shrugged, "Isn't it? It seems that it gives people a chance to face things that haunt them and learn to move beyond the trouble they've encountered."

Feeling enlightened by what she said, Derrick admitted he hadn't thought about it in that way. Seeing that he understood, Emily suggested he give it some thought and pull out positives. Then when being interviewed, he would be able answer with a demonstration that he is not only clean, but has morphed into a person that would not repeat the mistakes of the past. They finished for the day, and Derrick thanked her for the time and suggestions.

Later that afternoon, after his chores, Derrick met with Justin for his individual session. They focused on the apprehension Derrick was feeling about moving into the next segment of reclaiming his life, and Derrick told Justin about the conversation with Leo.

Thrilled, Justin pointed at him, and said, "That is a man demonstrating growth right there."

Slightly embarrassed, Derrick laughed, and squirmed in his chair. Seeing the changes in him since entering CRC, Justin pointed out that in the past he would have never disclosed what he was feeling to someone that easily.

Knowing he was right, Derrick explained that it was far from easy. He admitted after the conversation he felt better, knowing he wasn't the only one that had feelings of apprehension about rejoining society.

He said, "I was surprised to hear Leo say he was scared too, 'cause he always tried to come off like a bad ass, so I didn't expect it."

Appreciating how the conversation was growth for both men, Justin pointed out that sharing with others is a way to connect with their in feelings and common experiences. Then, he reiterated when a person resists sharing, they often feel isolated while dealing with problems or emotions. In full agreement, Derrick mentioned he had to force himself to talk to Leo, but acknowledged he now saw it was a choice that was better than bottling up his feelings.

After the session, they walked down to the wardrobe closet, which was entered through the main office by a door located in the far corner. It was a walk in closet and had the clothing items separated by category.

The suits, slacks, shirts, and ties were each in a different area. There were even dress shoes, and the items were all clean and neatly pressed.

Sharing what Emily said, Derrick told Justin what he should wear, and said, "I don't know why she thinks I need a tie, mechanics don't wear ties."

Explaining that an interview is where you sell yourself to a potential employer, Justin said, "You should always dress slightly better than you would for the daily work."

With a selection of black slacks, a light blue shirt, and a tie that was blue with black and white stripes, Derrick was pleased. He felt like his clothes would make a good first impression. Then he perused the shoe rack and picked up a pair of black dress shoes. Justin told him before the interview he would be given a new pair of black socks. Then he asked if Derrick had a belt, and with a shake of his head, he indicated he didn't. They found one, from a few that were hanging on hooks on the back wall, and his outfit was complete.

Mentioning he should try the items on before Friday, Justin stated if for some reason they didn't fit they would come back and trade them for a replacement. Being aware that the clothing in hand shouldn't be run through the basement laundry, Derrick asked what he should do with them when he was done. It was explained that the clothes would be sent to the cleaners, then returned to the closet for another resident to use on an interview. To ensure they made it to the cleaners, Justin instructed him to dropped them in his office after the interview.

Derrick thanked him for his help, and Justin said, "No need to thank me. I'm proud to see how far you've come, and I look forward to seeing you continue to make progress and complete."

With a long exhale and a deep sigh, Derrick gave a cockeyed smile, which showed the nervousness that was brimming below the surface.

The rest of the week, Derrick continued to meet with Emily while learning to find the positive answer to any and all of the questions she posed to him. The clothes he selected from the closet fit perfectly, and he decided to log on to the computer in the lounge and refresh his memory with regard to diesel engines. Utilizing his free time, he went online a few hours a day and was pleased to see the amount he remembered.

On Friday he was excused from his chores, which he appreciated because he was far too nervous to focus on anything. After lunch, he paced while waiting to get ready. Watching the clock, he wished the appointment had been scheduled for the morning so he wouldn't have had all the hours of waiting and thinking. Knowing this was a difficult step, Justin found him to give him a pep talk and tried to calm him down. Feeling unsure about what was happening on many levels, Derrick felt like he could jump out of his skin.

After he spoke with Justin, he went upstairs to shaved and take a shower. He dressed and looked at himself in the mirror. While he studied his image, he thought to himself, *Derrick you have come a long way in the last nine months.* Being pleased with his appearance, he decided he didn't want to sit until he had to, for fear of creasing his pants, so he stood and paced.

About 2:15 p.m., Derrick went downstairs so he would be on time for Emily who planned to meet him out front at 2:30 p.m. As he hit the bottom step, a few of his friends, that were coming in the front door, whistled and clapped.

"Lookin' good Bishop. You clean up nice!"

Feeling a flush on his face, Derrick laughed as he continued on to Justin's office. The door was closed, and he would usually never interrupt, but this time was different.

He knocked and heard, "Come in."

As he opened the door, he saw Justin was with Phil, and he apologized for interrupting. Derrick explained he was leaving for his interview soon and wanted to make sure he looked alright. They both told him he looked fine, wished him good luck, and then Justin asked him stop by on the way back to talk about how it went.

Right on schedule, Emily pulled up out front with her own car, which was a baby blue sedan that was relatively new.

"I thought you'd be usin' the center van," Derrick said, in a questioning tone as he got it.

"Well, I figured if you get the job you don't need to be labeled the CRC guy by all of your coworkers. That information is yours to share, only when you're comfortable."

Impressed by her thoughtfulness, Derrick expressed that it was hard enough rejoining the work force without complicating the matter, so being discrete about his circumstances was appreciated.

On the drive to the bus company, Emily reminded him of some of the key points to try to remember when answering, and Derrick admitted he was nervous. She told him everyone gets nervous for job interviews, and if he wasn't that would be unusual. They arrived a few minutes before three and parked in view of the door. Before he stepped out, Emily wished him luck, reminded him to think about he was going to say, and to be sure he was answering the question that was being asked.

While approaching the building, he reached under his shirt, pulled out his cross, and kissed it. Then he dropped it back under his collar and opened the door. Upon entering the office, he told the receptionist he was there for an interview. With a motion of her hand towards a group of chairs, she told him he could have a seat. Before he sat, the woman pointed to a coat rack and suggested he hang up his jacket, which he did. A minute or two later, an older man stepped out from behind the counter and approached him. As expected, he reached out his hand while introducing himself as Joe, the shop supervisor. As he shook his hand, Derrick thanked him for having him in for an interview. Then Derrick was led behind the counter and into Joe's office.

The office was small and the desk was cluttered with piles of paperwork. A bulletin board hung behind his desk, where a calendar, and what looked like lists of phone numbers, were posted. On the sidewall, a collection of labeled clipboards hung and each seemed to track a maintenance schedule of one type or another. After they sat down, Joe explained the job, the salary, and the hours. Then he looked at the application that was faxed to him by Emily, and began to talk to Derrick about his past experience as a mechanic. With detail, Derrick explained the work he did while at the trucking company and the responsibilities he was given in mentoring some of the less experienced mechanics. Joe had his fingers laced together and his elbows on the desk with his hands by his chin. His pointer fingers were extended in front of his lips, and he listened intently as Derrick spoke.

Next, he asked Derrick if he felt his time out of the field would prevent him from being able to repair engines. Initially feeling a flutter in his stomach, he paused, then Derrick remembered that Emily said he should be honest.

He said, "I know it's been a while, but I've been refreshing my memory by readin' articles and publications online. Most of what I've read, are things I remembered prior to readin' anything. I understand I might need guidance if I come up against somethin' I don't remember-But-Well-I think the more I do, the more comfortable I'll be in tacklin' the needed repairs."

With a smile, Joe nodded, and Derrick felt reassured by his gestures.

Before ending the interview, Derrick was given the opportunity to ask questions. Feeling eager, he inquired as to when they were looking to fill the position. Joe noted that he wanted the new man to come on board in two weeks, and asked if Derrick would be available to begin then.

Unsure of what was meant, Derrick said, "If I get the job I'll start wheneva you want."

With a slight laugh, Joe said, "Son you got the job. I was asking if you could start in two weeks."

Filled with glee, Derrick shook Joe's hand, and smiled from ear to ear.

"Yes sir, thank you for the opportunity. I won't let you down, you'll see, I'll work hard."

Joe told him that he didn't have to convince him, he already had the job. They agreed Derrick would begin two weeks from that coming Monday, and Joe walked him out to the receptionist to introduced him as the new mechanic. After welcoming him, she asked Joe when Derrick would be starting. Looking at the wall calendar, Joe noted the start date, and asked her for a new hire packet. The paperwork was given to Derrick and he was asked to bring it back completed on his first day. Before leaving, Derrick shook Joe's hand again and thanked him one last time.

While walking towards the car, where Emily was waiting, he had to resist the urge to run. It had been so long since Derrick felt so excited, he couldn't wait to share his news with anyone he could.

While getting into the car, he said with enthusiasm, "I got it! He hired me on the spot, I start two weeks from Monday."

After congratulating him, Emily said she wasn't surprised, because he seemed to be just what the supervisor said he was looking for. On the ride back to the center, Derrick found it difficult to contain his excitement, squirming and shifting in his seat. He couldn't wait to tell Justin the good news.

After appropriately thanking Emily, he rushed into the house, and barreled into Justin's office. Startled at first, Justin looked up and saw the happiness on his face.

"Did you get it?"

Trying to maintain the suspense, Derrick just smiled.

Justin jumped up, and said, "Congrats man, I knew you would get it." and he high fived him.

The two sat down and Derrick detailed the interview, question by question, while Justin just listened with an occasional okay and nod. After talking for about a half hour, Derrick said he was going to head upstairs, change clothes, and find some of the guys to boast to a little.

The rest of the evening, Derrick was consumed with thoughts about his new job. He imagined the garage, and wondered about the other people that worked there. Then he thought about how it would be to actually have money in his pocket. With that, thoughts about saving towards a place of his own ran through his mind. Even though he was excited, Derrick was also leery of allowing himself to become too comfortable in the belief of normalcy. He referenced the conversation with Leo in his mind and reminded himself that he needed to be mindful of his recovery before anything else.

Eager for progress, the weeks following the interview were torturous for Derrick. Full of anticipation, he was beginning to feel caged in at the center, as the thought of being out every day fueled his desire to taste the world again.

Derrick tried to distract himself with his groups, individual sessions, and chores. With the new job, a transition back to work group was added to his schedule. It was designed to assist with the challenges a resident might face beginning employment after being out of the work force for a long period of time. Additionally, Justin took time in the individual sessions to address Derrick's feelings. A good deal of their time was spent reinforcing the point that, even though he was going to be out every day, Derrick was still a resident at the center and expected to follow all the rules, even when off campus.

"I know...I'm not gonna do anything stupid," he would say, when Justin began to emphasize the importance of remembering he was still in recovery.

The Saturday before he was scheduled to begin at the garage, Derrick was in his room putting away laundry and getting things ready for the work week when Justin knocked on his door.

"I won't be here tomorrow, so I brought you somethin'." he said, as he handed him a gift bag. "My wife made me wrap it, I was just gonna give it to you."

Not being accustomed to getting gifts, Derrick always felt slightly uncomfortable when someone gave him something.

"Thanks...umm...you didn't have to give me anything." he said, as he fumbled around reaching into the bag.

With a smile, Justin said, "It isn't anything big, just a small somethin' to start the new job."

As Derrick pulled out a navy blue insulated lunch bag, Justin explained that the kitchen would give him a sack lunch each day.

"Walking in with your lunch in a brown bag is kinda cheesy in my mind, so I thought you could use this instead."

Feeling like everything was somewhat of a blur, because it was slightly overwhelming, Derrick reached out and shook Justin's hand while thanking him. Knowing he was nervous, Justin reassured Derrick, by telling him he was going to do fine and he had no reason to worry. After Justin left, and he was alone, Derrick sat thinking about the turnaround he had undergone in the last year.

With that, his mind wandered through the time on the street. Remembering the challenges, he recalled digging in dumpsters behind fast food restaurants to have something to eat. Feeling internally outraged at the way he had lived, Derrick remembered sometimes being so out of it, that days would go by and he wouldn't eat, or even think about eating, because the drugs were the priority. Then he began to think about all the men and women still living that life, and how it was the time of year that they would have to battle the cold.

Hating the cold months while on the street, Derrick recalled breaking into a used clothing collection bin when he didn't have warm clothes and the temperature had dropped. Rummaging through the bags, he found a sweatshirt, sweatpants, and even a hat and scarf. With his memory came thoughts about how ridiculous he must have looked, but at the time it didn't matter as long as it was warm. In a moment of levity, he chuckled thinking about the hat and scarf that were bright pink. Then he remembered sleeping in that same bin for few nights.

Looking for something to wear, he realized it was somewhat warmer inside the donation bin, so he pulled the clothes out of the bags and laid on them, half propped up against the wall. Then covering himself, he used some as blankets and althought the space was small, it was fairly comfortable. It was one of the only times he had a soft surface to sleep on during the years he was homeless and the bin itself kept him sheltered from the wind. Derrick closed the door over so no one even knew he was inside, until one morning when an employee of the store where the bin was locate saw him coming out and chased him away.

For fear of being picked up by the cops, Derrick didn't return, but when the wind whipped and the temperature dropped, he would sometimes find himself wishing had the shelter of the clothing bin. Slightly emotional from the memories, Derrick began to think *I didn't even have food to eat, and now, not only do I have food, I have a special bag to carry it in.* With that thought, he knew he never wanted things to be as they were before, and he began to feel pressure to do everything right. Catching the alarm clock in the corner of his eye, he saw it was time to head over to his new group, Transitioning Back to Work. It was his first session with them, and Derrick thought how the timing was perfect because he could talk about the stress he was feeling.

Upon entering the meeting room, Derrick was surprised to see Emily in addition to the counselor Michael. He greeted her and she explained the group was assigned co-leaders, to address the different issues that might come up, each with their own specialty. Emily would assist with the employment and job related things, while Michael was there for the recovery and maintaining sobriety issues. The group began and Derrick noticed it was small group, having only three others besides him. In the opening Michael told the group Derrick would be starting a new job that coming Monday. With a round of applause and congratulations, Derrick felt slightly embarrassed and shifted in his chair.

In an organized fashion, each of the men were asked about any challenges they faced over the last week or feelings they were having about work. Each of the men were able to articulate at least one issue, just small situations that made them uncomfortable enough to feel the need to talk about them. Michael and Emily allowed the group to offer guidance, and only commented after the members shared their thoughts. Since the other members were already working, Derrick found it interesting to listen to the conversation. Playing the situations out in his mind as he listened, he wondered if he might be faced with some of the same things his friends were already dealing with.

Then it was his turn, and Michael said, "Derrick, I know you haven't started work just yet, but do you want to share how you're feeling about it?"

Without hesitation, Derrick told them that he had been thinking about how he use to live his life and how different things were now. In an open disclosure, he continued and told them how he felt pressure to make sure he did everything perfectly so he wouldn't end up back where he had come from.

Almost in unison, the men said, "You'll never do everything perfect."

Then the group tried to help him see that expectations of perfection would be toxic because the first time things weren't just so, he would feel like he failed. Different men spoke up and explained that he had to prioritize his sobriety by making sure he didn't lose sight of it. The key to being successful wasn't about being perfect, it was about being able to handle things when they were less than perfect. Feeling a sense of relief with their words, Derrick listened to them carefully. To him, what they said made a lot of sense and it was reassuring. As the group ended, they all wished Derrick good luck on his first day and he thanked them. Pleased he had shared his feelings, he was feeling more confident than he was when the group began.

MONTH 10

———

HE HADN'T BEEN SO APPREHENSIVE since he was a kid on the first day of school, so Derrick scrambled around his room getting dressed with nervous energy. He hurried downstairs to be in the dining hall when they started serving at the stroke of seven. Feeling at home at CRC, he laid his things at his usual seat, and then went up for coffee and some cereal. He ate quickly, and kept checking the clock. Finishing up in record time, he was ready to head out to where the bus stopped. Although he knew he would be early, he decided he would feel better waiting there, so he cleared his dishes and stopped by the kitchen to pick up his sack lunch. The with a deep breath, Derrick set out for the first day of his new life.

Rapidly walking towards the bus stop, Derrick was nervous, excited, and a little anxious all at the same time, but kept telling himself if he wasn't ready Justin would tell him. Knowing it was a long time since he had worked on an engine, thoughts of doubt kept creeping in. Feeling concerned, he was worried they may not keep him on if he forgot things and wasn't any good at it anymore. Trying to keep those thoughts in check, he told himself Joe knew he was away from it for a long time and hired him anyway. About half way down the drive to the road, he saw Justin driving in and felt comforted with the sight of his car. Slowing down, Justin stopped and rolled down the window.

"Glad I caught ya. You're early aren't you?"

Knowing he was right, Derrick said he just felt better heading to the bus stop. Having seen many men with the first day jitters, Justin understood. With a big smile, he wished him good luck and told him he would be fine. Before driving off, Justin asked him to stop by the office when he got back to let him know how the day went. Having already planned to do so, Derrick agreed.

As he pulled away, Justin yelled out the car window, "Nothing to worry about, you got this!"

With a smile, Derrick continued on to the bus stop and thought about how he was lucky to have been assigned Justin as his primary counselor.

While waiting, he paced until a few others from the center arrived. With idle small talk, they began discussing the weather. They knew it was Derrick's first day, so a few asked him about the garage where he would be working. Feeling unsure, he told them the little he knew, and said he would find out more details once he was there.

Arriving at the bus company about twenty minutes early, Derrick headed directly to the office. There was a different woman at the desk, and she was on the phone, so he patiently waited to give his name. As he watched her, he noticed she had a butterfly tattoo on the inside of her wrist. He was intrigued by it and he tried not to stare.

It was similar to the one she had on the left portion of her chest, right over her heart. His face flushed slightly as he remembered seeing it peek out of her blouse on occasion. Even though he had seen it in full many times, the presentation of the smallest of portion would be exciting to him, and always made him want to see more. Standing there smiling, he heard the woman hang up, and ask if she could help him pulling his mind back from the memories of his love.

"Hi, I'm Derrick Bishop. I start work here today."

With a welcoming smile, she said they were expecting him and after looking at the assignment log, told him he would be working with Luis who would be arriving shortly. Then she collected his new hire paperwork, looked it over, gave him a time card, and showed him the time clock. She explained each morning he would punch in, then out and in at lunch, and then again at the end of day. Derrick punched his card and placed it in the holder, which brought about a flash of pride that almost made him shutter.

As he was waiting, he saw the boss, Joe, come in. When he saw Derrick he stopped and welcomed him with a handshake. Taking a minute to help get Derrick settled, he explained Luis was their top mechanic. Then he stated Derrick would be working with him for a few weeks until he was back in the swing of things and could work independently. Like a weight was lifted, he felt slightly relieved that he wasn't expected to just jump in.

He was nervous about being out of the field for so long, especially with the circumstances that ended his last job and the mistakes he made. In proper form, he thanked Joe for the opportunity, and just then Luis arrived and they were introduced. After a standard welcome, Luis punched in and they headed out to the bay they would be working in.

Luis seemed friendly and while showing him around the garage he explained where the different tools were kept. Without any details of what he knew or didn't know, he mentioned he was told Derrick had been out of the field for a few years. Then he reassured Derrick that he would fall back into it quickly once he got started. As they worked on the first bus, Luis took the lead and let Derrick assist. A few times Derrick saw him looking at the work he was doing and it was uncomfortable, but he understood why he needed to keep a watchful eye.

As the day went on, he felt more and more comfortable tinkering in the engines. He remembered more than he thought and was enjoying working with his hands. As they worked, he and Luis talked and he learned Luis was the father of two boys. His wife worked at the power company in the evening so one of them was always available for childcare. As the head mechanic, Luis explained he'd been working for the bus company for about seven years, and felt the company, and Joe specifically, were great to work for.

Hoping he found a long term position, Derrick felt encouraged by Luis' positive feelings about the job. Derrick disclosed a little about himself, explaining that he was a resident at CRC, and was nearing completion. Never really having to tell people he was in recovery before, Derrick felt somewhat uncomfortable disclosing his personal information, but realized it was who he was and it would be part of him forever. He knew that owning it was a big part in maintaining it. Luis went about his work and seemed unaffected by Derrick's life circumstances.

"My wife's cousin was out there for a while, and it did great for him."

While they continued with the work and talked about different topics, Derrick's fear that he might be treated differently because of his past, was immediately erased from his mind.

The day finished, he punched out, and walked to the corner for the bus. Once he sat down he realized how tired he was. Feeling somewhat relieved day one was behind him, he had a sense of satisfaction for having worked a full day back in the field in which he was skilled. Hurting from head to toe, because it had been a long time since he worked eight hours while standing, bending, and laying under a vehicle, he just wanted to get back to CRC. With each twinge of muscle soreness, Derrick felt content in knowing he had worked hard, and he was reminded he had something to offer.

Once back at the center, the walk down the drive to the residence felt like it was lasting an eternity. As promised, he stopped by Justin's office after being processed by the main office.

"It was great, they have me working with the head mechanic until I get back in the swing of things. He was nice but...BOY AM I TIRED."

Pleased with the Derrick he saw before him, Justin smiled, and said, "Welcome to the world of the working man."

Then he told Derrick to get some dinner and rest up because tomorrow was another day.

After a slow climb up the stairs, Derrick took a long hot shower, and was able to get back to the dining hall just before the end of the dinner service. Only a few guys were left eating and he decided to take a seat by the window instead of joining them. He hadn't really been alone all day and enjoyed the solitude, which he missed when he didn't have it. Eating in silence, he looked out the window, which overlooked the parking area. He could see staff leaving and men walking over to the Commons for the recreation hall. For a moment he thought about joining them to talk about his day, but decided he was a tired man and would be better off resting up.

Upon returning to his room, he got his things ready for the next morning so he could just get up and go. Then he laid down and turned out the light. Randy wasn't in the room and he was concerned he might wake when he returned, but he couldn't keep his eyes open and before he knew it he was asleep. That night he dreamed of her, and the night they took their relationship to the next level, with the images vivid in his mind.

They were in her apartment and had been out on several dates. He was shy about making a move, because he really liked her, and he didn't want her to feel like he was rushing things.

As he began to say goodnight, she said, "I was hoping our night didn't have to end here."

Feeling turned on, he smiled, put his arms around her, and passionately kissed her with a probing tongue. In an almost automatic motion, she took Derrick by the hand, and led him into the bedroom. They began kissing and he pulled off her shirt. As he kissed down her neck, he was surprised when he came across her tattoo, which ignited his passion even more. His hands moved up and down her back.

Beep! Beep! Beep!

Derrick jumped awake, looked at the clock, and took a deep sigh. Feeling disappointed, he stood up with a stretch, and turned off the alarm. *Damn clock couldn't have waited five more minutes*, he thought to himself. He put on his sweats and headed down the hallway to the bathroom. In a robotic manner, he quickly got himself ready and down to the dining hall for breakfast. Although he wasn't nearly as nervous as he'd been the day before, he still wanted to get out to the bus stop early. Without wasting time he finished, cleared his dishes, picked up his lunch, and headed out.

On his way to the bus stop he saw Justin driving in, just as he had the day before, but this time he didn't stop.

Waving out the window, he yelled, "Have a great day."

This caused Derrick to smile as he walked along. The other men showed up a few minutes later and they made small talk while they waited, just as they had the day before. During the ride to work, Derrick smiled as he daydreamed about her tattoo and his dream, and before he knew it he was at the bus company punching in.

Unsure if he should wait for Luis in the office, he decided to walk out to the first bay and found he was already there.

"Good morning Derrick, I guess we didn't scare you off yesterday."

Admitting the day tired him out, he laughed, and said he enjoyed getting his hands dirty again and was glad to be back. Luis began to work on the bus they started the day before.

"I can see you have really good skills, before long you'll be back to your old self...like second nature."

Derrick felt relieved by the compliment. He thought he'd done okay and had hoped Luis was of the same opinion. Now his mind was free to focus and not second guess the work he was doing. As they began to tackle the work of the day, Derrick was glad he was mandated to CRC and working, but most of all he was glad he was reclaiming his life.

The morning went quickly and at lunch he met some of the other mechanics. Being the newbie, he listened when they spoke about sports, girlfriends, and their kids. In typical Derrick fashion, he was more comfortable to listen instead of being the center of attention. In fact, he could remember always considering himself a person that had many friends, but truth be told, very few of them actually knew stuff about him. He always took a more passive role in the relationship because he didn't like being vulnerable. By blending in, and allowing others to take the lead, was a good way to stay safe.

After work he attended an individual session with Justin, they spoke about the job for a while and Derrick mentioned his dream. Justin just sat and let him talk for most of the session.

"Justin I miss her. I didn't realize what I had when I had it…she cared about me so differently than anyone else ever had."

Justin could see tears building up in Derrick's eyes. There had been times in the past that he thought Derrick was emotional about her, but up to now, tears had only been seen when childhood memories were discussed.

He let Derrick sit for a minute, then said, "I know you miss her, but why is it so strong now?"

Derrick thought for a moment.

"I think …well…..it's what is goin' on. I have this new job, I'm close to completin' here, and I have all good things happenin'…and…I don't have anyone to share it with." Now the tears were running down his face. While sitting quietly, Justin handed him a tissue. Derrick continued, "I've loved her always, and missed her everyday, but… before this I had in my mind that I couldn't let her see the drugs, or…I didn't deserve her, or…I had nothing to offer. Things are different now, the drugs are gone and I have a future. I'm not lookin' at how much I love her, now I see how much she loved me."

He leaned forward and covered his face.

"I didn't see how valuable that was, until I started to see myself alone in the future without havin' someone to celebrate these big steps with. I listened to the guys at work talkin' about their lives…wives… girlfriends…kids."

Derrick cleared his throat, sat up, and looked at Justin with an almost pleading look, like he was waiting for him offer a solution.

Justin nodded, shrugged, and said, "So what's the answer, what are you going to do about it?"

He felt slightly irritated by the nonchalant manner.

"I guess I'm gonna be alone," he said.

Then Justin asked, "Is that what you want?"

Now a little pissed off, Derrick said, "I just sat here cryin', what do you think?"

Telling him to calm down, Justin pointed out that something is only a problem if he lets it be one. Then he talked to Derrick about making choices that would allow him to share his life, and positive moments with someone special, either her or another.

A few minutes passed, Derrick calmed down, and said he understood. They talked about the positive choices Derrick made so far and some things he could try to do going forward.

Still feeling lonely by his newly developing life, Derrick thanked Justin and said, "I guess what's getting' me is, I didn't realize how special it was to have someone that cared about me. I've had many people in and out of my life, but truly carin' for someone is rare. I'm mad I didn't see the value when I had the chance."

Seeing the discouragement he was feeling, Justin reassured Derrick that if he made the right choices he would find it again.

As he stood to leave, Justin asked him, "Hey, what do you need to make it all happen?"

Derrick smiled, and without hesitation reached for his cross, kissed it, and said, "Faith."

As usual, Justin winked with a smiled, and Derrick felt comforted in the regularity of his actions.

Over the next few weeks, Derrick fell into the routine of getting up each weekday morning and getting out to work at the bus company. Then he returned home each evening, showered, and ate dinner, just like a typical working man. Once a week Derrick had an individual session with Justin. Weekly he had the relapse prevention group as well as the transition back to work group. On the weekends he was assigned one chore per day and occasionally, if he wanted a project to fill the time, he would ask Sal or Calvin if they had anything he could work on. Most evenings he skipped recreation so he wouldn't be too tired to get up in the morning, but made a regular appearance on Fridays. Derrick felt content with how things were going and enjoyed feeling like he was gaining control over his life. It was a feeling that had eluded him for so long.

After he was working with Luis about three weeks, Joe showed up in the bay to speak with Derrick and his heart began to race. Although he couldn't imagine what he had done, he was sure he'd made a mistake and just knew he was going to be fired. All at once, he felt his hands begin to tremble as he walked towards Joe.

They stepped out of the bay, and Joe said, "Luis tells me you're a good mechanic, you're getting quicker, and seem more comfortable working on the engines."

Derrick felt proud and smiled, as relief washed over him.

"Thank you, I've enjoyed getting back to it and Luis has been great to work with."

Then Derrick was surprised at what came next.

"Starting tomorrow you are going to have your own bay, if you feel ready that is?"

Resisting the urge to jump up and down, Derrick said, "Yeah, of course I feel ready. I appreciate you being confident in my abilities."

Knowing Derrick's history, Joe was pleased he could tell him he was doing so well. Then Luis came outside, and Joe explained they were putting Derrick in the bay next to him in case he had a question or needed help.

Then he shook Derrick's hand, and said, "We are glad to have you with us, keep up the good work."

That evening, Derrick felt like a kid rushing home from school to report a special event. He bounded up the stairs, into the house, and down the hall, as he made a sprint for Justin's office. The door was closed, which meant someone was in there, so he went to the main office to be processed in and then back to Justin. This time his door was open and Justin could be seen sitting at his desk.

"Hey, guess what happened 'cause I can't believe it."

Derrick was talking really fast, smiling, and pacing side to side. Justin looked at him and decided to mess with him a little.

"Hmm...well... let me see, did you win the lottery?" he asked, with a giggle.

"No man, stop messing with me, they gave me my own bay...they said I'm a good mechanic...they think I'm good enough to work alone."

Justin was happy. He liked Derrick and often saw himself in him. Sometimes he felt a little parental where Derrick was concerned and was invested in him maintaining his sobriety and being successful. Having worked in the field of addiction for many years, he knew the more positive experiences a recovering addict had, the better off he would be in the long term.

Shaking his hand, Justin said, "I'm not surprised, you're a good worker and care about the work you do. Congrats!"

Feeling restless with the excitement of being seen as a valued employee, Derrick took a shower and grabbed a quick bite because he was eager to get to Commons. Since he started working, he hadn't gone for recreation during the week, but this was different. He wanted to boast just a little, so he walked over to hang with the guys for a while. When he came in, the fellas teased him about being *out on a school night*. Derrick handled it well and just laughed. Then he put his name on the list to play pool and walked over to the area where a few of his friends were sitting. They greeted him, asking what brought him over on a work night.

Careful not to appear to be bragging, Derrick said he had a good day at work and just felt like walking over for a while. With instant curiosity they asked what happened, and he was proud to share that the boss told him he was a good mechanic and that he was getting his own bay. They all congratulated him and asked what it meant to have a bay. Excited to talk about it, Derrick explained he would basically be working independently while repairing the buses. He also shared that it was an expression of their confidence in his abilities as a mechanic.

Before long, it was his turn on the pool table, so he played a few games of singles until he lost, and then he headed back to his room. After getting everything ready for the next day, Derrick decided to read before turning in. The prior weekend he selected a book from the shelf in the recreation hall. Derrick enjoyed reading when he was younger, but got out of the habit when the drugs dominated his life. Recently he began to think about how much he used to enjoy it, and since he rarely sat in the lounge to watch TV, it gave him something to do in his room in the evening.

The next morning, he rose with a cheery disposition while going about the normal routine, and before he knew it he was at work. After he punched in, he walked to his bay. Before entering, he stuck his head in to Luis' bay and said good morning. Already working on the brakes they started the day prior, Luis told him to get settled, check the bench, and make sure he had all the basic tools. Once he was organized he would be given a job. Often mechanics were required to have their own tools, and although most of the guys at the bus company did, there was an ample supply of shop tools available.

A few minutes later, Derrick reported he was settled and organized. He was told he would be working on bus #1549, which was reported to be having low power issues.

Before handing him the work slip, Luis asked, "What do you think it might be?"

Derrick smiled, "It could be the fuel filter, a leaky gasket, or loose throttle linkage. I'll check the filter first of course."

In an almost cheering tone, Luis nodded, and said, "You got it!"

On the way out to get the bus, Derrick almost had a strut about him as he walked across the parking lot, full of pride and enjoying the feeling of being productive.

It turned out it was only a dirty fuel filter, so bus #1549 was completed relatively quickly. Derrick logged the repair and asked Luis what needed to be done next. He was told that brakes needed to be done on one of the mini buses, #920. After grabbing the keys and the work slip, Derrick drove out the first bus and pulled in the next. As the day went on, he completed one job after the next with confidence. Every once in a while Luis would step in and make small talk, but Derrick suspected he wanted to make sure all was going smoothly.

Finishing his first day of autonomy at work, Derrick felt good. That evening he had an individual session with Justin. Feeling proud, Derrick was happy to start their session by talking about his day and how well it went. Justin asked him how he was feeling with regards to his recovery, pointing out that many times when people have things go well they want to celebrate. Since celebrations are often connect that with drinking or getting high, learning to enjoy things sober can sometimes be a challenge.

Without hesitation, Derrick shook his head, and said, "Nope, I haven't even thought about it. I wish I could call her and share my good news, but using hasn't even been a thought."

Justin asked about how he used to celebrate special things before his addiction took hold. In thinking about the past, Derrick admitted that growing up they rarely had celebration moments. Then he drifted in his thoughts, and began to speak of an incident when he was with her.

"She was given an award at work and called to tell me. I stopped at the store on the way home and picked up her favorite wine and flowers. Then I ordered dinner from the Italian restaurant and got to her apartment before her to set the table with candles. After I turned on music, I set place cards on the table. Hers had her name, followed by winner of whatever the name of the award was that she won...I can't remember what it was called." Derrick was smiling as he recalled the evening. "She was so surprised and happy. We had a nice dinner, finished the wine, and then made love in the living room by candle light." Drawing in a big breath and sighing it out, Derrick looked sad for a moment. "I had anything I could have ever wanted when I had her."

Refocusing him on the celebration, Justin asked, "So if that happened today, what would you do differently?"

He just looked at him blankly for a second.

Then Derrick said, "Wow, I never thought of it like that, I guess... huh...I wouldn't have the wine."

Then Justin asked if that would change things and he could see that Derrick was really thinking about it.

With hesitation in his voice, he said, "I don't know...it...it might."

So Justin continued, "How would it change things for you?"

Stammering for a minute or two, Derrick said, "It feels like it would lose some of the romance without the wine." Then he shifted in his seat. "What if she wanted wine? How would I do it, kissin' her and tasting it?"

Glad to see him thinking, Justin explained those are the types of situations that aren't a reality until after leaving CRC. He explained that to be prepared, he had to start thinking about those possibilities. Looking serious, Derrick agreed that he was starting to see how life would be different than he remembered, and how his recovery would be a lifelong challenge.

Before leaving, he said, "I guess thinkin' about that situation, I need a lady that supports my recovery and is invested in my success. I don't think I could have the wine as part of that type of night and not drink any." Justin felt good about his insight and gave a nod of acknowledgment. "I have to learn how to find the specialness in the moments and the people, not the substances."

Looking up in a flash, Justin said, "You know what, you're one hell of a smart man. You're gonna do fine as long as you keep thinking before you act."

Feeling pleased with Justin's reaction, Derrick smiled, and thanked him.

As the month wrapped up, Derrick felt closer to what he called *real life* with each passing day. Spring was around the corner and just as the world was starting to emerge with a rebirth, he felt the same was happening to him. In the months at CRC, Derrick had gained an insight into himself that allowed him to see his strengths and his shortcomings. He learned how his poor choices led him to his lowest moments and how they left him missing the one person in his life that whole heartedly believed he was amazing. Over the months that had passed, he broke free of his juvenile attitudes and behaviors, and now he wasn't just seeing himself as a man. Feeling confident, Derrick was pleased about the things happening in his life and was proud of the person he had become.

MONTH 11

———

TIME WAS PASSING QUICKLY AND Derrick couldn't believe he only had two months left at CRC. He'd been working for about a month, and it felt good to get out of the center every day. His routine included riding the bus to and from work, chores at the center on Saturday and Sunday, and recreation with friends on non-work nights. With the tasks that many would call humdrum, he was starting for feel *normal* again. Missing the work with Sal and Calvin, he would sometimes try to catch them when he got in at night. A few times, he asked if they had anything for him to work on over the weekend, when they were off. Knowing he was a good worker, and appreciating the help, they would leave him a small task to complete.

Nearing completion, his treatment schedule now consisted of the independence group and the relapse prevention group. Each group met once a week in the evenings and he also had one individual session with Justin each week. Parole Officer Randolph was still coming by monthly, and both he and Justin would always comment on how far Derrick had come. They would laugh about how, at the onset, neither thought he would last the first week.

Just when Derrick was comfortable with his routine of work and responsibilities at CRC, Justin surprised him in an individual session,

"Okay, so it is time you connect to self-support outside of the center, and find a home group and a sponsor."

Appreciating his relatively new state of stability, Derrick wasn't fond of change.

"Can't that wait til I get out?" he asked.

Shaking his head no, Justin explained it was important to connect before his discharge so he would already have a network.

As Derrick was visibly uncomfortable with the idea, Justin asked what was concerning to him. Unsure, he was quiet for a minute trying to find the words to describe his thoughts.

"I feel like...like...well, it's like starting over."

Already understanding, Justin knew what that meant, but wanted Derrick to work through it.

"Starting over how? You still have all your sober time."

Derrick stuttered a little, then said, "Well...you already know me, what I've been through...you get me? If I get a sponsor, I'll have to go through all that again."

Trying to get him to buy in to the need for self-help, Justin asked, "Isn't it better to do that when you still have me and CRC?"

Shifting his eyes downward, Derrick nodded, and said, "I guess it is."

They looked at the schedule of self-help groups in town, finding two that weren't far from Derrick's job, that also lined up with his work schedule. Trying to ease the transition, Justin pointed out that he would be able to get to them right after work. As the buses didn't run to the more remote area of town that housed CRC, after a certain time in the evening, Justin told him if he arranged it ahead of time a staff member from the center would pick him up from the meetings. Agreeing to start the following week, Derrick asked for a little time to get use to the idea. Knowing Derrick would shut down if pushed, Justin told him that would be fine, but emphasized he would need to pick a start day and stick to his plan.

Then he asked, "You remember what you need to get through?"

Derrick laughed, and said, "I remember."

That wasn't good enough for Justin.

"You need to say it friend."

With a roll of his eyes, Derrick just shook his head.

"I need Faith."

Knowing spirituality was an anchor that got so many men through the hardest times in recovery, Justin always got happy when he was given the answer he wanted.

This time was no different, so he raised his hands, and said, "AMEN!" and they both just laughed.

The next week, while Derrick worked, he thought about his uneasiness regarding going to meetings and finding a sponsor. Realizing he wasn't very happy about taking this step, and unsure how to even go about having someone become his sponsor, Derrick knew he needed guidance from Justin before attending a meeting.

Knowing he didn't like to open himself up to people, and getting a sponsor meant sharing his thoughts and feelings with yet another person, he wanted to try and make the process as simplified as possible. Feeling this was so far outside of his comfort zone, Derrick knew in the past he would have naturally tried to avoid it. Now, having travelled as far as he had on his journey of sobriety, he realized that staying in his comfort zone was what made his life fall apart in the first place.

During his individual session at the end of the week, Derrick said to Justin, "I've been thinking about the self-help meetings."

Hearing the tone of hesitation is his voice, Justin said, "Nope, it is not optional."

With a laugh, Derrick said, "Hey I know, I'm goin'…I just need your help. I don't know how to act when I go there…or…what to say…or…how to even get a sponsor."

Feeling relieved that they weren't going to debate, Justin smiled, and explained that he should just follow what everyone else does. He stated that they would realize he's was new and walk him through it. As for a sponsor, he mentioned that when the meeting breaks there is usually coffee, and people stand around and talk, so he would get aquainted with the members. Relieving some of the pressure, Justin explained that

Derrick didn't have to get a sponsor at the first meeting. He was told that he would eventually find someone, through the social portion of the meetings, that he'd feel comfortable talking with. Once that happened, he said Derrick could ask them to sponsor him, or they might even offer. Feeling more comfortable to begin self-help, he agreed to start the following Monday. The group he choose was scheduled to begin a half hour after work and it was at the church around the corner from the job. Justin reminded him to stop at transportation and arrange a ride home from the meeting, and Derrick agreed.

With the completion of a successful week, he earned an off grounds pass which he used on Saturday. Knowing the importance of a plan, he and few other phase three guys headed into town to see a movie and grab a bite to eat. They decided on an action flick which started at about two. Then they would eat before heading back to the center. On the bus into town, they talked about work and their plans after they completed the program. One of the men was married and anxious to return to his wife, while the other was young and planning on living with his parents and going back to school. Then they asked Derrick what he wanted for his post Conversions life.

For the first time outside of a treatment session or group, he spoke of her.

"I lost the love of my life a few years ago when my addiction took hold of me. I want to find her and explain and…if I'm lucky…she'll listen."

The guys asked about her and Derrick described her as he always did, stating that she was beautiful, kind, and loving.

Then one of them asked, "Hey, what's your lady's name?"

Derrick just looked out the window.

"I keep that to me."

The men looked at each other and shrugged, but they didn't press the matter.

Enjoying a fairly nice afternoon, complete with a movie that was your typical shoot 'em up flick followed by a walked across the street to the best burger place in town, Derrick was content. Sitting in a booth near the back wall, they were laughing, talking, and enjoying the food, when he looked up and saw her cousin Lindsay. Feeling his heart sink, Derrick didn't know what to say or even if he should say anything.

Just then she walked over to the table.

"Hi Derrick, how are you?"

Feeling embarrassed, he stuttered slightly, and said, "Hey Lindsay, things are good and you?"

In an uncomfortable manner, she said she was doing fine, and then they both hesitated. He wanted to ask Lindsay about her, but stopped himself, feeling like he shouldn't. Lindsay wanted to tell him off for how he hurt her cousin, but thought better of it because she didn't want to make a scene. They looked at each other for a minute and then said their goodbyes.

While walking away, Lindsay looked over her shoulder, and said, "She's doing really good without you."

She didn't miss a step and kept moving towards the door.

The guys immediately began to tease him a little, but could tell, by the look on his face, he wasn't going to have any part of it. For the rest of the meal and the bus ride back Derrick was quiet. Upon returning to CRC, he headed right up to his room when they got back and did't even stop by the office to be cleared to re-enter. A few minutes later, Justin appeared in his doorway.

"The guys told me you ran into someone you know and it seemed to upset you." he said, as he entered the room.

Sitting on Randy's bed, Justin explained he was heading home when the group stopped him on the porch.

Derrick looked up and explained it was her cousin. Then he told Justin what she said, as he jumped to his feet and paced the length of the room. Full of emotion, he picked up a lamp like he was going to smash it to the floor, but stopped himself before he did.

"Why'd ya stop?" Justin asked, and Derrick shrugged, saying he didn't know but it just didn't seem like it would make him feel better.

They talked for a while, and Derrick said that Lindsay's words made him feel sick when he heard them.

"I know...after all this time...she wouldn't be still cryin' over me, but...I didn't need to hear how good she's doin'."

Seeing his pain, Justin reminded him that all this time he didn't know what he could encounter when he found her. Running into her cousin, and hearing those uncomfortable words, was probably a good way to prepare him. Derrick saw his point, and thanked him for coming back in to talk him through it, even though it didn't really seem to offer any comfort.

After Justin left, he laid there thinking about the time he spent with her and her cousin. The two were close like sisters, so they often did things with Lindsay and her boyfriend, Nick. He also began to wonder, *Did Lindsay tell her she ran into me? What did she say? Did she ask Lindsay any questions about me? Did she even care?*

Trying to distract himself, he got up and began to straighten up the room. Then he stopped for a moment to look out the window towards the garden below, which wasn't blooming just yet. Feeling anxious, he put music on the clock radio to fill the silence. Derrick felt lonely. He was lonely for her, for the times they shared, and for the life they could have had.

As he cleaned, he began to think about a night they spent with Lindsay and Nick when they went to a carnival. He smiled remembering how she was so excited to get on the rides and play the games.

"Win me a big stuffed cat," she said, and made a pretend baby pout face.

Teasing her Derrick smiled, and said, "I don't know if you deserve a big stuffed cat."

With a laugh, she tickled his ear.

"Pleeease."

Squirming from being tickled, he put his arms around her, and said, "Since you put it that way, I'll try."

Nick just rolled his eyes and shook his head.

"Guy, you're making me look bad."

To Derrick it didn't matter what Nick thought.

He shrugged, and said, "I can't tell her no."

Then he spent forty dollars to win the big stuffed cat, because of course you don't win the big prize right away, you have to keep trading up. Thrilled with their bounty, she giggled and hugged the silly thing, then hugged him. It was unexplainable to him, but Derrick remembered feeling almost as happy as she was, just by seeing her so excited.

Walking through the carnival, he toted the cat as she held his hand and he remembered feeling the contentment of pure bliss. Lindsay teased them a little about how cute a couple they were, and although he acted macho and told her to stop, he secretly enjoyed thinking they were a cute couple. At that moment, he felt at home in the idea of being with her the rest of his life.

Suddenly his thoughts were shifted to the here and now, and just then he started to think about how she was doing just fine without him. Unexpectedly, Derrick started to hurt inside. Accepting what Lindsay said, he knew it was probably all true. Truth be told, Derrick knew he hadn't done just fine without her, so it made him feel even more alone. After an evening of beating himself up inside, he decided he wasn't going to let himself think about her anymore. He would complete CRC because he needed to, but as for the thoughts of finding her, he decided he would push those away until they weren't even a consideration.

Without even realizing it, he fiddled with the cross Justin had given him. He hadn't taken it off since that day he put it on, many months earlier, and would often find himself holding it in his hands when he felt challenged. It was his anchor and this time was no different. With a headache from thinking, and over thinking, he turned off the light and rolled over, determined to keep all thoughts of her at bay.

Monday came and that meant his first self-help meeting. Before catching the bus, Derrick stopped in the office and confirmed they would have someone pick him up when the meeting was over. Although he was nervous about this next step, he knew it was the right thing to do. Making a connection between what happened with Lindsay, and how talking it out with Justin seemed to help bring understanding, Derrick realized he would need someone to talk to when things come up after leaving CRC. He knew that eventually a sponsor would fill that role. Regardless if he tried to find her or not, he felt he hadn't come as far as he had, to let it all slip away. Derrick wanted to give himself every advantage in maintaining his sobriety and self-help was the next step.

Work was relatively uneventful, and the time seemed to pass very slowly as he was full of nervous anticipation. Monday was always the most difficult day in the week, but since he couldn't help but be fixated on his upcoming meeting, it seemed to drag more than usual. After work, he washed up in the men's room and changed into a fresh tee shirt he brought with him. Since he wore coveralls and his clothes usually stayed relatively clean, going out straight from work wasn't too problematic, but a fresh shirt made him feel better.

In almost slow motion, he walked around the corner to the church and entered through the front door. In the vestibule was a sign for a meeting room with an arrow pointing down the stairs. Consumed by nerves, he sheepishly approach the door with shaky legs, so he paused and stood for a moment before entering. Then he took a deep breath and stepped in.

The room was a basic meeting room with chairs in rows facing the a podium that stood in the front. In the back was a table with coffee and some donuts where a few men were gathered. They all looked towards the door as he entered and Derrick gave a half grin. Slightly early, he looked uncomfortable enough for one of the men to notice and walk over to him.

"Hi, I'm Shawn. I haven't seen you here before, is it your first time?"

Derrick nodded, and said, "Yup, I'm a newbie."

They sat about midway between the front and back of the room, and Shawn tried to make him feel welcomed by saying it was a really nice group of regulars. Motioning towards the back of the room with his head, he told Derrick the coffee and donuts were free. Then he pointed to a rack on the side, saying there were flyers and pamphlets about each part of self-help. He elaborated by explaining they outlined what the meetings were about, different steps to take, and how to work the program.

Derrick thanked him, and said, "I've been clean almost eleven months already."

"Why is this your first meeting if you're clean that long?" Shawn asked, in a questioning tone.

Feeling comfortable sharing what he had been doing, Derrick explained being inpatient at CRC and how self-help is part of the transition to completion. Having been in recovery for some time, Shawn said he was familiar with the program at CRC and knew some others that had also gone there.

He added, "Everyone I know that comes out of Conversions always has a really good foundation." Then he stood up, and said, "I'm gonna to get some coffee before the meeting starts, you want somethin'?"

With a nervous stomach, Derrick said he didn't. He just wanted to get through the meeting and get back to the comfort of CRC. A few minutes later, Shawn returned to the seat next to Derrick and startled him as he sat.

"If you have any questions, I'll be happy to answer them."

Already much more comfortable than he expected, Derrick thanked him, and was very appreciative of Shawn's friendly nature.

"Do I have to speak if I don't want too?" Derrick asked.

Shaking his head no, Shawn explained he didn't have to do anything until he was ready.

The room had filled up and it seemed they were getting ready to begin. At the start of the meeting, an older man went up front and opened it by going through the formalities of welcoming everyone, introducing himself, and stating he'd been clean for ten years. Everyone clapped, which was unexpected to Derrick, so he jumped slightly at the onset.

About that time, he was already feeling bored and began to look at the floor. Next the leader stated there was a special speaker that requested to come in and then everyone clapped again. The special speaker took the podium, and suddenly Derrick began paying attention because he couldn't believe what he heard.

"My name is Justin and I've been clean for twenty three years." The crowd clapped, Derrick's head shot up, and his eyes were locked on Justin. "Thank you for letting me speak this evening. It's a special night for me, it's my wedding anniversary, and I'll be heading home after this to spend it with my wife." He looked at Derrick and continued, "I wanted to speak on my anniversary, because if it wasn't for the help I was given in my program, and the support I was given through self-help, I wouldn't be celebrating my twenty fifth year with my lovely wife." Looking almost as if he could cry, Justin paused a moment, and then continued, "I was married just under two years, when my cocaine use grew out of control. I was hurting my wife and eventually she moved back to her mother's house. A friend told me it was my fault and they were very blunt about it. After the anger wore off, I decided, if I wanted the woman I loved, I had to reclaim my life and be the man she fell in love with." Justin took a breath and paused again. "It was difficult to swallow my pride and admit, even if it was unintentional, that my actions were hurtful to her. I told her I knew I was wrong, and she deserved to be treated the way I treated her before my addiction grabbed hold of me."

Looking to the back of the room, past the crowd, Justin smiled at someone. Derrick turned slightly and saw a pretty woman smiling back.

Then he continued, "I vowed to be the best I could be at protecting her feelings. I told her I had learned when you love someone, it's important to listen when they tell you that what you're doing hurts them. Then going forward, you have to try and do it differently. It's a give and take. I knew I didn't see all the bad when it was happening and I let her know." Looking very emotional, Justin shook his head before continuing, "It wasn't really about what I wanted, what I thought, or how I felt...it was about how I chose to do certain things that made someone I love hurt. If I kept making those choices, I'd be sending the message that my selfishness was more important than her or the love I felt for her. I couldn't let that happen."

He went on to say, meetings and his treatment program helped him keep his promise to be the best he could be, without additional hurtful actions. Looking towards the back again, Justin said after he proved himself his wife returned to him, as he motioned to the woman in the back of the room.

"I speak on my anniversary every year, with my lovely wife looking on, to renew my vow to her that I will not let selfish choices make her feel bad ever again." Blowing a kiss, he said, "I love you baby."

Everyone clapped and Justin joined her, but winked at Derrick as he walked by.

The meeting continued with a few people standing at their seats and speaking about challenges or milestones. Now mindful of the value in the meetings, Derrick listened, hearing bits and pieces of himself in their comments. As the they wrapped up, Shawn asked him if he had any questions, but Derrick didn't, as it seemed relatively straight forward. They shook hands and Shawn told him he hoped to see him again.

Eager to catch Justin before he left, Derrick walked up, and said, "I was surprised to see you, you didn't mention comin'."

Justin smiled and introduced him to his wife, then said, "I don't usually come to this group, but I knew you were uneasy about your first meeting and I was going to speak tonight anyway, so I asked if I could speak here."

With a pat on the shoulder, he asked what Derrick thought of the program. They talked for a few minutes about how he met Shawn, who seemed really nice and had been helpful. Realizing the time, Derrick said he better get outside for his ride, but Justin stopped him.

"I'm your ride. I told them we would drop you back, I have to pass it anyway."

On the ride back, Justin's wife, Denise, was very friendly. She spoke to Derrick about his recovery and the center, and before he knew it they were in the lot at CRC. He thanked them for the ride and wished them a happy anniversary. On the way in, he stopped by the office to be processed and then headed upstairs. With a quick shower and he was in his room for the night, but his mind kept running Justin's earlier sharing over and over.

Thinking of the topic Justin discussed, Derrick wondered if he had come to the meeting to give him some subtle direction about her. Since he talked about salvaging his relationship, and knew Derrick had been upset thinking that she was doing so well without him, maybe Justin was trying to get him to think about what to do. Derrick had decided to give up his dream of reconnecting with her, but now he wasn't convinced that would be the right choice. Justin was able to make amends and maybe he could too. Seeing her wouldn't be immediate, and now, feeling conflicted, he was glad he had a time to consider all the options.

The next night, after work, Derrick had his weekly individual session and asked if Justin was trying to send a message to him with his own story.

With a wink and a smile, Justin said, "Well, there are some similarities and I wanted you to see certain things. Did you learn anything?"

Derrick thought for a moment.

"Yeah, I guess what I took from it…umm…I think what it told me, is that it doesn't matter what it is. If it hurts someone you love, it's not in any way about you or what you want or think. If you love someone, you don't make a choice you know will hurt them."

Content that Derrick picked up the key points, Justin smiled, and said, "That is the simplest rule, but will keep you out of the most complicated relationship issues."

Taking it one step further, Justin explained he'd been seeing Derrick fixating on finding her to satisfy his own wants and desires, but maybe the focus needed to be her. He thought Derrick should start to see the purpose of a reconnect as making a mends so she could feel better. If anything else came of it, then it would be a bonus. Before moving on, he emphasized, the focus should be her feelings and owning what happened between them. With those words came clarity, and Derrick agreed. He realized he had lost sight of her feelings, having been so determined to find the happiness he was missing since they parted.

The evening seemed to dwindle and Derrick didn't know where the time went. His mind was full of so many things, including thoughts of her, the self-help meetings, work, Justin's story, getting a sponsor, running into Lindsay, and the need to find a place to live soon. With a whirlwind of concerns swirling about him, the hours just slipped away. The various topics all needing attention, and he was feeling a little overwhelmed. He decided he should make a list of things that had to be done. Then he could mark them off as they were completed.

* *Get a self-help sponsor*
* *Save each week towards the apartment*
* *Find an apartment*
* *Buy furniture*
* *Buy household items*
* *Find her and explain and apologize*

With the list being relatively short, he finished it up quickly, read it over, and decided it was a good start. He placed it on his nightstand, so it would be available if anything else came to mind. Oddly, his tension seemed to release once his thoughts were on paper. They weren't quite as overwhelming as they were when they were all muddled up with the emotions he was dealing with. Now, on paper, they were just the tasks he had to complete.

As usual, he got things ready for the next morning and reached to turn out the light, but hesitated. Picking up the list, Derrick added an another item that came to mind. Before placing the page back, next to the lamp, he underlined his addition and studied it for a moment.

* *Make choices that are mindful of the feelings of those I love!*

Derrick decided that one would stay on his list and never be marked off, because it needed to be a regular occurrence. It wasn't something that could be completed with just one or two decisions.

Confident in what was going to get him through, he kissed his cross and whispered, "Faith." Then he turned out the light.

That night he dreamed of Justin's story, but instead of Justin and his wife, it was Derrick and her in their place. When he woke, the dream had him feeling both happy and sad, at the same time. The thought of being married to her, for twenty five years, was joyful, but the truth of knowing she wasn't his brought remorse to the surface.

At the end of the week, Derrick planned to attended his second self-help meeting. He decided to go back to the one at the church and try it for a while before sampling the other. In the pamphlets it said the recommendation was to find a home group. He thought going to the same one several times would give him a good idea if it was a good fit. Arriving much like he did the first time, feeling substaintially less nervous, he noticed men gathered by the snack table. Almost immediately, he was greeted by Shawn.

"Hi Derrick, glad you came back," he said, as Derrick entered the meeting room.

With a wave, Derrick answered, "Thanks, this meeting fits well with my work schedule. I decided to try it a while and see if it's a good fit for a home group."

Shawn asked where he worked and he told him which opened a conversation about both their jobs.

After explaining he was a refrigeration and heating repairman, Shawn asked, "Do you have a sponsor?"

Derrick explained he didn't, so Shawn made an offer, by saying he would be happy to sponsor him if he wanted. Already feeling somewhat comfortable, Derrick liked Shawn and what he had seen of him in their two meetings. Without much thought, he thanked him and accepted his offer feeling slightly relieved that he wouldn't have to search for a sponsor.

Shawn gave him his number and told him that he usually attended meetings on Monday, Wednesday, and Friday with the occasional week-end group, depending on what he had going on. Knowing the weekday meetings would work well for him, Derrick thanked him and said he'd try to make those as well. Then he explained that he just needed to set up transportation back to CRC, so as long as he had a ride he would be there.

Thinking back to his own past, and remembering how difficult it was to depend on others for rides sometimes, Shawn said, "I pass that place on the way home. I can drop you...no need to arrange a ride."

With an offer so unexpected, Derrick felt slightly uncomfortable and asked him if he was sure. Assuring him that it wouldn't be a problem, Shawn said he wouldn't have it any other way.

The meeting was much like the last. Derrick listened and heard things that resonated with him, because he had done, or said them, at one time or another. Part of him wanted to speak, but he still wasn't comfortable enough. Knowing he could take things at a pace that was right for him, he decided he would speak at the next meeting for sure. Right on schedule, his ride picked him up and he went about the normal evening routine. As he completed his evening tasks, he smiled thinking *I have a routine.* There was a time he never expected to have a routine, a job, or a life again, so the regularity gave him a sense of peace.

Over the weekend he did his chores and stayed on campus. After what happened the last time he ventured out on a weekend, he needed to feel the safety of the center.

While passing Justin in the hallway, he told him that he had a sponsor who would be giving him a ride home from the meetings. Understanding what a big step that was for Derrick, Justin congratulated him and patted him on the back. Although he knew it was silly, Derrick liked when Justin validated his progress because it felt good to have his approval.

That week, during his relapse prevention group, his mind drifted and although he was very comfortable at the center, he was starting to feel like he needed more. Politely he sat, but felt like he was hearing the same things over and over. The others members were frequently complaining, worrying, or speculating. It was becoming apparent to him that he wanted to feel like he was doing something and not just sitting around. Even though meetings would always be part of his world with the self-help program, he now wanted it to be on his terms. That week-end, Derrick realized he was outgrowing the center and was starting to feel ready to strike out on his own.

MONTH 12

———

STARTING HIS THIRD MONTH AT the bus company, Derrick felt comfortable getting back into the routine of working. After years of not working, the beginning was rough, but Justin kept him encouraged and motivated. The people there were nice and the work was perfect for him, because as a mechanic, he was given solitude. Although he had changed in many of his ways, Derrick still preferred solitude, and probably always would.

Derrick always had friends, but after all of his months in treatment, he learned that those, he always considered friends, weren't true friends. They would hang, get high, and bullshit the hours away, but they really didn't know him. Having dissected his past in his session with Justin, Derrick now saw that he liked it that way. She was the one that knew the most about him, and he even hid so much of himself from her. Knowing she would disapprove, he didn't want her to see the drug involved portion of his life. When they first got together, he tried to hide all of himself, like he did with others, but she had a genuineness that allowed him to feel comfortable.

He recalled saying to her one time, *"You really do care about me."*
She smiled, and said, "Of course I do, in my eyes you're amazing."
He had never felt loved like that before. As time went, on her love was consistent, so he began to open up and show her some of his true self.

Each time he disclosed something new, he expected her to turn tale and run, but it seemed her love for him grew even more. Once he asked her how she could love him, even knowing some of his ways.

She smiled with a look of caring, and said, "I love every part of you and when you show me more, I feel more and more loved by you. Then my love for you grows."

It made sense to him, but more importantly it made him feel accepted. That acceptance gave his a safe zone and he was able to open up and leave himself somewhat vulnerable.

It was Friday, which was payday, and that was always good. Derrick had been saving as much as possible and was finally in a position to start looking for an apartment. With his completion just weeks away, he and Justin were supposed to start the process of searching for a place that weekend. CRC had connections in the real estate field that worked with the residents getting ready to complete, in finding a place to live.

On the way out that morning, Justin stopped him. and said Lorna, the real estate agent, had four potential places in his price range and they were scheduled to see each of them the following day. Although Derrick was excited, he was also nervous. He knew once he left CRC, maintaining his sobriety was completely up to him and the choices he would make. He'd done well in the past eleven months, but he realized that, on some level, it was a forced sobriety.

The day was relatively uneventful and thinking about apartment search made it seem to drag even more. Longing for independence, he felt excited like a kid the day before a holiday. Joe, his supervisor, came in about midday to check on him and his work. As usual, he was pleased at what he saw and complimented him.

"Derrick you're doing a great job."

Derrick felt good, smile, and thanked him.

Then Joe said, "A bunch of us are going to grab a beer later, why don't you come."

That was the first time Derrick had been confronted with a choice that could affect his sobriety.

"I can't, but thanks for thinkin' of me."

Joe looked embarrassed, and then said, "Hey, I'm sorry, I forgot."

Understanding he meant well, Derrick told him not to worry about it, and Joe went on his way. As he continued to work, he kept running his talk with Joe over in his mind. Derrick was pleased with himself because he didn't even hesitate in his decision. He had changed, he now knew what was important, and he hadn't come this far to ruin it for a beer. Then he thought, *my heart and soul are full of Faith and it will keep me going.*

As he finished up the day, he punched out, and collected his paycheck. A quick wait on the corner for the bus and he was on his way home. Since it was Friday, he would have usually attended self-help with Shawn, but knowing he was going to be apartment searching in the morning, he wanted to get back to the center early. Arriving at CRC just in time for the end of the dinner service, he grabbed something and headed upstairs for a shower. Getting everything ready for the morning, he thought he would cash his check when he and Justin went out to meet Lorna. Embarking on a new chapter, Derrick spent most of the evening thinking about what he hoped to find in an apartment.

The apartment he had before he let his addiction take control wasn't what he pictured as ideal. It was small, and a mess all the time, and he remembered how she would clean up or do laundry when she'd come over.

She would sound wifely by saying things like, "What would you do without me? I think you wouldn't even have any clean clothes."

It would make him smile. He enjoyed the feeling of being slightly nagged because it reminded him that she cared.

Derrick wanted an apartment that wouldn't be too far from work and in a decent area. He knew that if he wanted drugs he could find them, but he didn't want to be facing it on every street corner. Also he decided he would like something that had windows and in an area that wasn't too noisy.

Wanting to be rested for the next day, he turned in early. His roommate, Randy, was always quietly reading in the evening, so falling asleep when he was there was never a challenge. As he drifted off, his mind was thinking of her. That night, he dreamed about an apartment that was neat and clean, and having her come over.

She teased him about how it was clean and how he didn't need her anymore. Then he put his arms around her, and said, "I will always need you, but I need you for so much more than cleanin' up after me."

While he getting dressed in the morning, he smiled when remembering the dream. Then he thought, *if only that dream came true, I would have all I ever really needed.* Before he left the room, he stopped and paused to look out the window. The daisies were blooming again and he gave them a moment, reflecting on his dream.

Breakfast smelled good. Saturday was French toast and bacon which was one of his favorite meals. Entering the dining hall, he found a seat by a group of guys that he'd socialize with during recreation time. Then he went to make a plate and grabbed a cup of coffee. During breakfast, he talked about his plans for the day and they all wished him good luck with the apartment search.

Derrick finished up quickly and headed over to Justin's office. The office was empty when he arrived so he stood and waited in the hallway for him.

A few minutes later, he heard, "Hey there trouble maker, are you ready to find your next home?"

Slightly nervous, Derrick turned, and smiled.

"I guess we'll find out,"

Justin said before they left he wanted to have a mini session, so they stepped into the office, and he closed the door.

Heading for his regular seat, Derrick sat down, and Justin asked, "How do you feel about finding an apartment?"

Conflicted in his feelings, he shrugged, and said, "I don't really know...it's...it's what I'm supposed to do."

Trying to focus him, Justin asked some question. Derrick admitted he was scared about doing it, knowing he would be all on his own. Continuing on, he admitted he worried about relapsing once he was out. Having been through this with many residents, Justin reminded him that he had a home group and a sponsor. If he stayed connected, he wouldn't be doing it all on his own.

Looking up, Derrick said, "I never thought about it like that."

After discussing what Derrick was hoping to find in an apartment, they set out to meet Lorna at the first address.

When they pulled up, they saw she was standing outside waiting for them. Before going in, she explained it was a two family house and the apartment they were going to look at was on the second floor.

They entered the front door into a small foyer and they saw two doors. The one on the right was what they wanted, as it opened into a small landing at the bottom of a staircase. As they reached the top, they saw the stairwell emptied directly into the combination living room dining room area. On the right was a doorway into the kitchen, which was a small galley type, being very long and narrow. Off the living room was a short hallway, which led to the bathroom and a large bedroom. They took their time walking around and it looked appealing to Derrick. There were several large windows, with vertical blinds on them, and it was all painted neutral beige with mocha colored carpeting.

Although he liked the look, there were other things to consider, so he asked Lorna about the price. It was right in the middle of his range, making it a very good possibility. The bus stopped a block away which would allow for an easy commute to work.

Then he asked about the neighbors in the downstairs apartment and Lorna said it was a couple that worked at the hospital. Familiar with the listing, she was aware they usually worked the evening shift, so she shared that as well. Derrick immediately thought, *with them at work it'll be quiet when I'm home.*

The neighborhood was a decent working class area, which was also appealing. Very pleased with this first listing, he reminded himself that he needed to see the others before deciding.

The next stop was an apartment building. As they approached, he saw several kids playing in the courtyard area. This apartment was on the ground level and it was also a one bedroom. As they perused the rooms, Derrick observed the living space comparable to the first one they had looked at. The bus was a block or so away, and the price was about a hundred more a month, than the first.

As they walked out, Justin asked, "So far which do you prefer?"

Without hesitation, Derrick said the first. Both Justin and Lorna agreed, with the concensus of the group being it was the better of the two.

The third stop was just a block away. It was a converted garage space set up as a large studio type apartment being all one room, with the exception of a small bathroom. It had a large window in the front, which faced the street, and a small window in the back, which faced the yard. They walked around the small space and looked at each other, not knowing exactly what to think.

Finally, breaking the awkwardness, Derrick said, "I don't know what you think, but this place is a hole."

In unison, they all laughed, and agreed.

Number four on the apartment tour was in a two family house and was also on the second level. It was very similar to the first they saw in regard to space and price. Derrick liked it, but it was close to the drug traffic in town, and the trip to work would require a bus transfer. Lorna told them she would give them a minute to discuss the choices and she stepped outside.

"I think this apartment is nice, but it would be harder to get to work and...well." He hesitated, but Justin told him to just say it. "Well, it's kinda close to the things I wanna stay away from."

Smiling, Justin put his hand on Derrick's shoulder.

"Friend, I'm proud of you. You've come a very long way."

Liking the feeling of having the approval of his counselor, Derrick smiled. So the choice was made, he would rent the the first one they looked at. Meeting Lorna by the cars, they shared Derrick's choice, and agreed to head back at the real estate office to draw up the paperwork. On the way, they stopped by the bank to deposit Derrick's paycheck so he could cover the cost of securing the apartment.

Sitting at the desk reading over the rental agreement, Derrick felt butterflies in his stomach. He knew, that taking this huge step, signified the commitment he made to a sober lifestyle. Without hesitation, he signed and wrote out a check for the deposit. Confirming his move in date of June 1st, Lorna stated she spoke with the landlord about allowing him to have the key a week earlier. Since the apartment was empty, Derrick could start moving things in so he would already be set up when he was discharged from CRC. They both thanked Lorna for her help and Derrick was given copies of the lease.

The car ride back was quiet with Derrick just staring out the window.

Always trying to keep him from isolating, Justin asked what he was thinking, and he said, "I was thinking about her, just wondering if she's with anyone. I was wondering if I have a chance with 'er."

He sounded so serious, and Justin could tell that Derrick was thinking of his future, feeling lonely at the thought of not sharing it with the woman he loved.

"What would you say to her if you found her?" he asked.

"Well...hmmm...I don't know, I guess I would say I was sorry...I would tell her I love 'er...I would ask her to forgive me."

Understanding his feelings, Justin told him that would be a good start, and even if she didn't take him back, he would probably feel better because he told her he was sorry.

"Maybe," he said, as he continued to stare out the window.

They pulled into the lot at CRC and Derrick said he had to run. He had dinner detail and had to get to the kitchen. Before jumping out of the car, he thanked Justin for helping him.

Committed to Derrick's success, Justin said, "I was happy to do it. You deserve to have all you want, I am glad to be a part of it with you."

With surprise, Derrick did a double take towards Justin when he heard what he said. Even after all this time, it was hard for him to believe he deserved anything good. They said their goodbyes for the day and Derrick set out to get to his work.

May seemed to be flying by with work, chores, groups, and his individual sessions with Justin. Derrick felt like the 1st of June was closing in, and he worried he wouldn't be ready. He wanted to start the next chapter of his life in good standing. After all, he would have enough to focus on with maintaining his sobriety and trying to find her to win her back, so he didn't want to be starting out in a hole.

During the individual sessions with Justin, they talked about his feelings of self-doubt and Justin was always able to make him feel better. He just always seemed to say what Derrick needed to hear. Reassuring him, he reminded him of all that he'd done over the past year, and all the tools he now had that he didn't have in the past. Even though he knew Justin was right, and he would try to remind himself of those things, when his mind got to worrying, it was hard to remember.

They also spent a great deal of time discussing her because Justin knew he was somewhat fixated on finding her. Still in love, he had a desire to see if they might reconcile and Justin was worried that Derrick would be disappointed. They talked about different possible scenarios to prepare him for whatever he might find, and whenever Justin would try to talk about her being with someone else, Derrick would become visibly uncomfortable.

Finally he said, "I know it's possible...I even know it's probable, but I just don't wanna talk about it. If I find that, I'll accept it, but...I don't know why we need to talk about her being with someone else now."

Concerned Derrick was leaving himself open to be crushed, Justin tried to explain that if Derrick wasn't prepared for any possibility, it could trigger a relapse.

"If I find out she's with someone else I'll call you...or Shawn...so... can we stop talkin' about it now."

Seeing he was frustrated, Justin agreed to let it go.

About mid-May, Derrick began collecting items for the apartment. He went to a thrift store, with a voucher provided to him by CRC, and picked out some gently used furniture which was enough to give him a good start. He was able to get a sofa, one end table, and a coffee table for the living room as well, as a small dining table that came with two chairs.

The bedroom proved to be a little trickier. They had dressers and night stands, but no beds. After looking at all the choices, he decided on a dark wood dresser and night stand. The bed would have to purchased elsewhere out of the money he had saved. The store agreed to deliver the items to the apartment the following weekend, when he would have the key and could start setting up.

On the way out, he decided to take a quick gander at the small household items they had for sale. In need of just about everything, he found dishes, glasses, and a few pots. They would be perfect, at least for now. Remebering the colors in the apartment, he liked the dishes he picked out, and thought they would be a good match. They were beige with an orange and brown geometric pattern. Autumn colors had always been his preference, so he felt satisfied with his selection.

After leaving the thrift store, he crossed the road to a dollar store. Everything they had was ten dollars or less and he hoped to find some of the items he still needed. It felt good shopping. He found some towels, a set of sheets, utensils, an alarm clock, and a pillow. On the bus ride home, he began to think about how the items he was carrying were more than he had actually owned in the last four, or five years, and his mind began to drift to an incident from his time on the street.

Walking in the dark, getting ready to bunker down for the night, to his regular place under the highway overpass he was tired. Climbing up high, to just under the road, where it was relatively well protected from the elements, provided a cloaked existence. He knew the cops couldn't see him, unless they got out and climbed up there, which they rarely did.

Approaching the area, he saw TiTi, a guy in the neighborhood that was in the business of selling anything an addict would want. Derrick had "found" a wallet earlier in the day, so he had a few bills on him. He stopped, made a buy, and went to set up camp. A little further down was a guy he didn't recognize, but he paid him no mind as he sat down and fiddled around in his things getting himself situated. Then he smoked what he bought, spread out his blanket, and laid down.

The next morning when he woke, his pack was gone. The only things left were what he was wearing and the blanket he was laying on. Instantly his stomach sank. He didn't have much, and most of it didn't matter, but all he had left of her was in that bag. The sweatshirt she had given him for his birthday was gone. The few letters she'd written him, that he would read when he felt lonely, were gone. Most upsetting, was that her picture, that helped him get through the most difficult of times, was also gone. Derrick just sat there crying. He felt like he'd lost part of his heart and hit rock bottom.

As he looked around, he saw he was alone and realized the unknown man, that had been bunkered down a few yards away, must have taken his things. At that moment, Derrick Bishop hated himself and what had become of his life.

Just then the driver, who recognized Derrick from his frequent rides, broke in and said, "Hey pal this is you."

Looking up, he saw they were at the entrance of CRC. Having quite a bit to carry, he collected his bags and stepped off while thanking the driver. As he walked down the long drive, he thought about that first trip, many months earlier, with his parole officer, and how much had happened since arriving at the center. Derrick was truly grateful he had been given the opportunity to change all the things that were working against him. With his appreciation, he knew he would do his best to make sure he didn't fall victim to his bad choices, or addiction, again.

As he entered the main hall of the house, he heard Justin call him.

"Derrick, you got a minute?"

When he turned and stepped into the office, he saw Parole Officer Randolph sitting, talking with Justin.

"Hey Bishop, been talking to Justin and hear you're getting everything together to get out of here."

Not feeling scared of his parole officer anymore, because he knew he'd done well, Derrick smiled, and then said, "Yup, I've been out shoppin' all day."

His parole officer reached out to shake his hand.

"I am happy to tell you, your term of probation is over as of today."

Shaking his head, Derrick said, "I knew it was comin' up, but I didn't know it was today."

Parole Officer Randolph signed a form and had Derrick sign as well. They were each were given a copy, and one was also handed to Justin to be placed into Derrick's file.

"Now you are officially a free man. Don't let me see you again!"

Pleasantly surprised, Derrick nodded, and said, "That's the plan."

After his PO left, Justin asked, "How does it feel to be done with probation?"

Derrick didn't know how to feel.

"I don't know, good I guess…I'm just surprised."

Justin and Derrick quickly discussed the finds of the day and what was still needed. Then, Justin offered to go with him the following Saturday to get the apartment ready and be there when the furniture was delivered.

When he returned to his room, Derrick dropped the bags on the bed and looked at the clock. There wasn't much time to get to the main building. His chore of the day was to work the reception desk on the afternoon shift. Quickly, he stopped in the bathroom, freshened up, and jogged across the lot. Arriving right on schedule, he was just in time to relieved Lisa, a part-time staff member that was always trying to get him to flirt.

Derrick thought Lisa was pretty. However, since he never stopped loving her, and as long as he was keeping some hope alive of rekindling, he didn't think of other women romantically. After a few minutes of idle chatter, Lisa gave up and left. That afternoon, as Derrick visualized living in his own place, he answered the phones and signed in a few visitors while directing them to their destination.

The following Saturday, Derrick and Justin loaded up the car and pulled out early to set up the apartment. They stopped at the store to buy some basic cleaning supplies and then went to Lorna's office to pick up the key. When they arrived at the house, they saw a couple on the porch that turned out to be Derrick's downstairs neighbors. He stopped to introduced himself and learned their names were Stan and Heather. They seemed nice, and just as Lorna had told him, they worked the evening shift at the hospital.

Motivated to get the apartment set up, he and Justin unloaded the car and decided to clean as much as they could while they were waiting for the furniture. Derrick started in the bathroom and Justin worked in the kitchen. Before they knew it all was done and just in time for the delivery.

The men arranged the furniture and it looked just as he had picture it would. Scanning each of the rooms and feeling proud, he thought, *It looks good. I have a placed to live. A place that's mine, that I paid for...I set it up and I'll keep it up.*

Watching Derrick, Justin saw the excitement and happiness on his face.

"Hey, let me buy you lunch to celebrate," he said.

With a big smile, Derrick agreed, and they decided on pizza.

"I'll run to the place on the corner," Justin said. "be back in a few."

Being all alone in his place, it felt weird to Derrick. For the first few minutes, he wandered from room to room just taking it all in. Studying each area, he was thinking of what could be added as he saved up. Right now, he had a few dollars left that was put aside to buy a TV. Still missing a bed, he would sleep on the couch until his next paycheck, when he could afford to buy a mattress and a frame.

About thirty minutes later, Justin returned with a pizza, a bottle of cola, paper cups, and plates.

"My first meal in my apartment, thanks Justin."

Relishing in his joy, Justin told him he was glad to do it. In fact, he was very happy to be part of this step with Derrick because he felt they shared a connection. To him, the pride he felt over Derrick's success at CRC, was similar to how he might feel towards his own child. During those first days with Derrick, Justin had his doubts. With time, and some struggles along the way, Derrick eventually rose to the challenges he faced. As they worked on what needed to be done to put the shattered

Derrick back together, a bond fostered between them that grew with each obstacle they conquered.

Finishing up, they cleaned up the lunch mess and carried out the trash. When they returned to CRC, Derrick felt a little sad realizing he was starting his final week at the facility. Although it was what he worked so hard for, the end was somewhat bitter sweet. Once he got back, he cleaned up and ran over to the main building for his last Saturday shift at reception.

The last week at Conversions was typical and uneventful. As usual, he got up each day and headed to work. Each evening, if he wasn't attending a self-help meeting in town with his sponsor, he would return straight from work and go about his weeknight routine.

Shawn was working with him on transitioning, and would talk with him after the meetings to focus on any reactions that could sabotage his sobriety. This week Derrick was unusually quiet, and Shawn could tell he was pensive about the changes. While they talked about how Derrick was feeling, Shawn learned he was mostly worried about what would be discovered when he reconnected with her. They agreed that Derrick should focus on living outside of CRC and would know when the time right to seek her out. Telling him not to rush, Shawn stated that perhaps an opportunity would present itself.

That Friday after dinner, they had a last night celebration for Derrick in the dining hall, with a cake that said good luck. The residents had the chance to wish him well and he had a hard time not getting choked up. Never having had anything like that done for him before, and although he had been a part of the goodbye ritual for others, he didn't anticipate how he'd feel to be the recipient of such attention. The evening was nice, but he was glad when it wrapped up and he could return to his room. Full of apprehension, he started to empty his drawers and placed his clothes into his bag. As he worked, he paused by the window and looked down at the daisies in the garden below.

"Soon," he said to himself, turning to return to his packing.

While he was giving everything one last check, he caught a glimpse of the hole in the wall above his bed and he reached out to run his hand over it. Then looked down at his fist and remembered the anger he felt that first night. Thinking back, he was astonished at how he hadn't seen his life back then as a mess. With that, Derrick said a prayer and kissed the cross he wore around his neck. Exhaling a deep sigh, he laid down and snuggled into bed for the last time as a resident of CRC.

EMERGES A MAN OF HUMILITY

———

DERRICK STOPPED AT THE FRONT desk and looked out into the parking lot. It was hard to believe he had walked into the center one year ago, so full of anger, and resentful of all the problems he had encounter in his life. At the time, he was totally unaware of just how much of the turmoil he had created himself.

Standing by the door, he was lost in thought about what would come next, and thinking about her. Knowing it was a longshot, he still couldn't help wondering if she'd want to see him. Although fearful of how he might be received, Derrick was still determined to find out out if there was anything salvageable between them.

Full of ambivalence about being on his own, he was very worried that he might not be able to maintain his sobriety, even though he'd done all the right things. He had a job, saved a little money, and rented an apartment. For the last few months he had attended meetings in the community and found a sponsor. Even though on paper he was ready, and all the plans were in place, Derrick was scared and knew it. Mindful that he had only began this journey to stay out of jail, he came to understand that he needed to finished it because of all he had lost along the way. That insight gave him a desire to try to get it all back, but he was concerned he would relapse when presented with independent life's first challenge. Fighting off his self doubt, Derrick told himself it was time to move forward.

"Well trouble maker, are you ready to reclaim your life?" Justin asked, as he walked up from behind.

As Derrick turned, and gave a half smile. Justin could see the apprehension on his face.

He put his hand on Derrick's shoulder, and said, "I know you'll be fine, you are no longer who you were when you arrived here a year ago. You have faced your demons, and gained a maturity that will help you tackle whatever life brings to you. My Friend, you have done well and should be proud."

Feeling a little sad, Derrick nodded, and agreed. He asked if he could call Justin if he needed to talk. After reminding him that had a sponsor to turn to, Justin told Derrick he would always be there if he needed anything.

"I know, but you know me better than Shawn does."

Feeling flattered, Justin smiled, and said, "You are probably right on that one, so call me anytime, and we can talk."

They walked outside and shook hands. Then with a sigh, Derrick began to get into the cab that was waiting when he stopped and looked back at Justin.

"I got up early this morning because there was something I needed to do before I left." Curious, Justin looked at him in an inquisitive manner. With a smirk, Derrick paused, then said, "When ya move out, you always have to leave the place as you found it. I did some redecorating when I moved in and needed to change it back, besides...It wasn't really to my likin' anymore anyway."

With a hug, Justin said, "Derrick Bishop, you are quite a man."

As he got into the cab, they both had tears in their eyes. Knowing they had grown very close over the past year, it was apparent the transition would be an adjustment for the both of them. As the taxi drove through the parking lot, towards the road, Derrick couldn't help but think, that even though he was in his thirties when he stepped into Conversions Recovery Center, at the time he wasn't really grown.

While escaping his past, he was also escaping responsibility and hadn't been living an adult life. Looking inward, he found the man he was always meant to be, and as a man, he knew he needed to take ownership of his past. That was especially important to him with regard to the hurt he had caused her. *Maybe she'll be glad to see me,* he thought to himself. It was wishful thinking, and he needed to plan how he would go about it, because without a plan he didn't have a chance. Although he understood it was somewhat of a dream, it gave Derrick something to aim for.

Arriving at the apartment felt odd even though he had been there several times with Justin while setting up and moving in his things. This time was different, this time he was staying and starting the next chapter in his life, While it was a new beginning, it was also an end to the life he had learned to embrace at CRC. He paid the driver, made his way upstairs, and dropped his keys on the table.

With a quick look around, Derrick felt empty. Being aware that he was starting over, without anyone to love, made he feel like he somewhat lost and aimless. He had traveled a long way on his journey, but still had miles to go to make his life all that he wanted, and hoped, it would become.

The evening included dinner for one in front of the TV while watching basketball, a hot shower, and getting things ready for work in the morning. He considered himself fortunate because he had skills as a mechanic, which made securing employment at the bus company relatively easy. The pay was good and the bus ran just two blocks away from the garage, which made getting there fairly simple.

Over the next week, he spent his evenings settling in and getting comfortable in his new home, with a routine to match. Saturday was set aside for laundry, cleaning, and a trip to the market. If he followed his plan, he'd be able to take Sunday as a day of rest.

Leaving the market that weekend, he noticed a sign for the local marathon which ran every June. It was scheduled for the following day and his heart fluttered slightly when he saw it. If she was still running, that is where he would find her, so it was time to make a plan.

The afternoon was spent thinking, and re-thinking, about what he would say. He decided to stand near the finish line, to run into her *accidentally*, and then start up a conversation. He knew he would have to apologize for how he had acted four years earlier, and admit his poor treatment of her was a result of his drug abuse. Dreading the conversation, Derrick knew it needed to be done if he wanted a chance with her.

Sunday morning came, but Derrick was awake before the sun came up. He was excited, scared, and worried all at once, but mostly he was full of hope. Knowing he loved her every minute, since their first kissed, his heart ached to see her again. What he did to her was wrong and just thinking of it made his insides feel jittery. Accepting that he wasn't right, due to the drugs, when it was happening, didn't take away the responsibility for his poor behavior. Derrick knew this could be his one, do over, chance and he had to do his best to make that happen.

Now appreciative of what they had shared, he was aware that he never loved anyone else like he loved her. He also saw that she loved him unlike anyone else ever had. Truth be told, she loved all of him, good and bad. With that type of love seeming to be extraordinary, he was afraid he would never find it again with anyone else. Since he had been too foolish to see it when it mattered, he needed to let her know just how much he regretted all that he had done.

Standing near the finish line, as the runners came in Derrick started to shift from foot to foot. He stretched his neck out beyond the crowd hoping he would spot her as she approached. Even though he wasn't sure she was still running, he was confident he would find her there, because when he knew her she had run the marathon every year since she had been sixteen. Knowing her love of running, he believed he had good reason to expect she would be in it again.

Just then, he saw her as she passed and he was momentarily paralyzed standing like a statue and holding his breath. She was exquisite. Derrick always remembered how she looked and knew she was beautiful, yet somehow his memory failed to remember that her beauty seemed to sparkle in her eyes and shine in her smile. As she finished, she high fived several of the runners standing nearby that had crossed before her and she simply glowed.

Mesmerized, he couldn't take his eyes off her. Rendered powerless to what he was feeling, his heart was racing and his hands were sweating. As he eagerly made his way through the crowd to get into her general vicinity, he was suddenly stalled by reality. A tall, lean man walked up and she threw her arms around him. In one quick swoop he lifted her, twirled around, and they kissed. Derrick knew he had no right to put a claim on her or her affections, but his heart was breaking nonetheless. The thought of holding her again, and feeling the safety of her love, moved him forward for the last year, but now, in one split second, that hope and dream died right before his eyes. With his emotions crashing in on him, he knew he was going to cry and had to get out of the crowd as quickly as he could. Aware of his vulnerability, he needed to call his sponsor before his hard work died right along with his hope.

Sitting in the corner booth at the diner with a cup of coffee, he stared out the window feeling disconnected to everything around him. Derrick didn't even hear Shawn walk up and jumped slightly when he sat across from him.

"I came as quickly as I could," he said, "What happened?"

Derrick just looked at him with tears in his eyes and couldn't talk at first.

Then in barely a mumble, he said, "She's with someone else. I knew it was possible, but...I never wanted to think about it...she's moved on."

Shawn took a deep breath and sighed. He knew from experience, that one of the biggest blows to a guy's ego was the realization that the woman he loved had moved on to love another.

Motioning to the waitress to bring coffee for the two of them, Shawn began to say the things that would help Derrick stay sober. Understanding that there was nothing he could say that would soften the feelings of loss, his focus was to help Derrick from losing himself at the same time. They sat for hours, speaking about all the hard work Derrick put in and how this was the first challenge, of many, in his sober life.

It had grown late and Shawn offered to drive him home. When they parted, Derrick felt like he was beyond the risk of relapsing, but to be supportive Shawn told him to call him in the morning before heading to work. Comfortable with Shawn, Derrick agreed, but then was shocked at what came next.

Shawn said, "You realize to move past this, you still should see her and apologize for what happened between the two of you."

Even though the thought of that conversation made every muscle in his body clench, Derrick knew his sponsor was right.

"When you're ready Derrick, no rush, but you need to face it."

Without comment, Derrick nodded, and said goodnight.

For hours, he sat in the quiet of his apartment thinking about how he pushed her away. The closer she got, the more things he did to try and get her to back off. Of course at the time he blamed her, telling her there was nothing different about him and nothing had changed. He realized she felt dismissed and rejected at times, even when it was happening he knew. Recalling the bickering that ensued, he recalled having a somewhat satisfied feeling when something he did upset her. His satisfaction didn't come from a place of malice, but from his need to maintain a level of secrecy with regard to the activities she would disapprove of. When she became upset, she would retreat a little, and his secret would be safe for a while longer. The drugs were the priority and getting high was his focus. Missed dates, unreturned calls, and the lack of interest in conversations, sometimes deliberate and sometimes unintentional, were all symptoms of his addiction. They all generated conflict, they all kept her at arm's length, and they all led to their break up.

Feeling guilty for how he had treated her, Derrick knew she played no part in their failure. He also knew Shawn was right. Even if she had moved on, he owed her an explanation and an apology, so Derrick needed to find her and make a new plan. As he turned out the light, he realized the hardest part of his sobriety journey was just beginning. Up to that day, he assumed being inpatient was the hardest segment, but in retrospect, he saw that the sheltered environment of the recovery center, was just the catalyst to prepare him to move him forward on the path.

Over the next few days, Derrick tried to come to terms with seeing her in the arms of another man. He would find himself withdrawing slightly, while internalizing his self imposed criticism. Each time he found his mind wandering to those destructive thoughts, he would use some of the activities he learned in recovery to talk himself back to a place of understanding. Now he wondered how he could have ever thought she would be available and waiting, after all, she was wonderful and had no reason to think she would ever see him again. Derrick needed to mentally prepare himself before he stood to face her. If he didn't, he wouldn't be able to get through all that had to be said without breaking down.

Over the summer, Derrick thought about her and the impending conversation. Each time he thought he was ready to see her, he would suddenly find a reason not to. He and Shawn spoke every couple of days, met for coffee about once a week, and sometimes they attended the same sober support meeting. When they spoke, they always went over maintaining sobriety, stressors, and relapse triggers. Often, the discussion found its way back to her and Derrick's need have the dreaded conversation so he could move on. In his heart, he knew apologizing was the right thing to do, but he was finding it difficult to motivate himself to take that step. After all, there was a finality that came with that conversation, and although in his mind he knew it was over, his heart hadn't accepted it just yet.

Work was going well and Derrick found his routine to include home responsibilities, self-help groups, and work. Buying just the necessities, he'd been successful in saving each week, and by the beginning of September he was able to buy a reliable used car. It was nothing fancy, just a midsized sedan, but the miles were low and the engine was clean. The body was free of dents, scratches, and rust, so Derrick's days of riding the bus were over and he knew it was time to try and find her. Feeling scared and full of avoidance, he was struggling to make it happen. After a few failed beginnings, he decided to call Justin.

With trepidation, he dialed the number. When the phone was answered by the front desk, his stomach knotted, and he took a deep breath.

"Hi, can I please speak with Justin?" he asked.

Then, in standard CRC fashion, he was asked his name and put on hold.

A minute later, the familiar voice of Justin came on with a questioning tone, and asked, "Derrick, is everything alright?"

He hadn't heard from Derrick since his discharge, and was concerned that a call, so many months later, was due to a relapse.

"Everything's fine. I'm just strugglin' with somethin'. You always seemed to know what to say when things weren't comin' easily for me."

Derrick explained what happened when he saw her at the marathon. He also explained how he and Shawn had repeatedly discussed the need to clear the air and own what he did. They both knew that was what had to happen, so he could begin to heal, and move on.

As expected, Justin confirmed that he also believed that was the best plan.

Almost crying, Derrick said, "I know once I have that conversation, it's over forever...the thought of that hurts and scares me."

Understanding what he was feeling, Justin knew thoughts of her were what got him through, even when he was living on the street in his lowest moments. Back then it was her picture that kept him going, and later is was the fond memories and feelings of love that Derrick carried in his heart. Then, what Justin said was direct and had a sobering effect on Derrick's mind.

"Do you hear yourself? You need to talk to her and apologize for the pain you brought to her, but you can't get it done 'cause you're afraid of it hurting you. What's wrong with that thought pattern?"

Derrick was quiet for a moment, knowing that it sounded ridiculous, selfish, and cowardly.

Then he breathed out a heavy sigh, and said, "I knew if I called you it would be put into perspective."

Appreciative of the advice, he thanked Justinm and said he would try and see her that Saturday. Before hanging up, he agreed to call back and let Justin know how it turned out.

Knowing it was a long shot, Derrick decided to drive past the apartment she lived in when they were dating. Saturday morning, he got in the car and headed to the other side of town. As he turned onto the street where she lived, his mind ran through their dates and driving with her in the passenger seat. She would love to sing along with the radio and often bop with silly movements. When he would shoot her a questioning look, she would giggle and laugh. He smiled at the memory and stopped a few doors down from the apartment. Sitting there, he didn't really know what to do. He wondered if he should he get out and knock, or just wait and see if she came out. While trying to pump himself up with courage, by running positive thoughts through his mind, he saw the door of her old apartment open.

His heart pounded, and he thought, *Maybe I should jump out, but what if it isn't her?* Just then he saw a man step out. It was the man from the marathon and he was talking to someone behind him. In a split second there she was in his sights. She stepped out, stopped, and turned to lock the door. The two were engaged in conversation, and then they began to laugh, when the man moved closer and slid his arm around her shoulders.

Derrick felt his stomach jump, but immediately began to remind himself that he had no claim. Fixated on the couple, he stared at her and her beauty, and felt love wash over him. Seeing her there with him, he knew he couldn't talk with her while her current love was standing there looking on. Somehwat disappointed and somewhat relieved, he accepted it would have to wait until another day.

Mourning the loss of his long term dream, Derrick hung his head and began to cry. Always so guarded, he hated to cry. Having developed insight and skills, he learned, over the last year, that letting the emotions out when he felt them would prevent problems later on. If they were suppressed, they would likely come out later in a destructive form.

Watching as they drove off, Derrick dried his eyes and called Shawn. While he explained what happened, he remembered that she would love to run in the early morning, especially on Sunday. She found it offered peace that wasn't always the case during the week. Determined to achieve his goal, Derrick decided he'd go back in the morning and hoped she still ran alone each Sunday.

That night he had a very restless sleep and was up earlier then needed. On the way over to her apartment, he picked up the Sunday paper and a large coffee. Upon arrival, he parked in the same spot as the day before. Sitting, while reading the paper and feeling nervous, part of him was wishing she wouldn't appear.

Almost on schedule, the door opened and she stepped out. As expected, she was dressed for a run. She closed the door behind her, leaving him confident she was going to be alone, and he said a prayer while kissing the cross he wore around his neck. Then he stepped out and began walking towards her. He could hear his heart beating as he watched her stretching on the front lawn.

When he was within steps of her, she looked up and saw him. In disbelief, the look on her face was one of shock. Tears instantaneously welled up in her eyes and began to trickle down her face. Franticly, she began to wipe them as she reached up and removed the ear buds.

"Oh my God, Derrick, I can't believe it's you." she said, and then he saw her draw in a deep breath.

Derrick just looked at her for a minute with a long gaze. Having a difficult time not reaching out, putting his arms around her, and pulling her close, he was eventually able to muster up a small smile.

"Hi there sexy, you're still beautiful."

Not exactly knowing how to act, she smiled and shrugged.

"What are you doing here?" she asked, completely overwhelmed by his appearance.

Sensing how she was feeling, he knew she didn't know how to act or what to say, and in that moment neither did he. All he'd mentally rehearsed, and all he thought he needed to say, rushed out of his mind the moment her eyes caught his. Overwhelmed by her presence, he felt his thoughts spiraling.

As emotions rushed through him, Derrick looked at the ground, and tilted his head slightly. Then with a shake of his head, jolting him back to his purpose, he began to speak.

"I'm here 'cause I need to say some things to you, but I don't know how to exactly begin. I thought I did, but seein' you made me lose my plan."

Then he looked up and saw her smiling. Looking into her eyes, he still sensed caring in them, which make his heart ache even worse.

Reminding himself she was with someone else now, he continued, "I wanna apologize to you for the way I treated you when we were together. I was havin' some problems at the time that I didn't tell you about. I know you felt like I lost interest in you...or stopped loving you...or was seeing someone else, but it wasn't anything like that."

Listening intently, she stared him, and he could tell by the look on her face that she was starting to feel a little bad. It was probably due to the memories he was eliciting. Not wanting to lose his momentum, he continued on before she had a chance to ask any questions.

"I was usin' drugs...smokin' pot all the time and takin' oxy every day. I couldn't tell ya 'cause I knew it wasn't right. I didn't wanna admit I had a problem." Derrick was holding back tears and unable to look her in the face. "I wanted you to know nothin' that happened was your fault...it was all me...I'm sorry for any pain I brought you 'cause of my problem."

With the admission out of the way, he explained he had completed inpatient rehab and was now clean, but had always carried guilt for the things he did while they were together.

Not sure what, if anything, to say next, he stood looking at the ground and had tears in the corners of his eyes. Realizing he was done, she started to talk and then stop for a minute.

Now she was crying too, and said, "You could've trusted me to be there for you and to help. You could have let me in. I would've stood by you."

As he looked up, he saw her tears and how she looked at him in a loving way, even after the passing of time and all that had happened.

Seeing her pain first hand when he looked into her eyes, his voice cracked when he said, "I understand that now, but I couldn't see it then."

Then, what she said next hit his heart like the stab of a dagger.

"You were my kryptonite. I would've done anything for you." She paused to wipe away tears, then continued, "I walked around with a broken heart for over a year and I didn't even know why, blaming myself for the unknown thing I did. I waited, hoping you'd come back, but you never did."

Smacked with the guilt her words brought forth, Derrick drew in a deep breath and narrowed his brow.

"I know how bad it was. I loved you more than I ever loved anyone, but the drugs took hold of me. I never stopped lovin' you. I know you've lived your life since me, but I wanted you to know it was never anything you did. It was all me and my addiction."

As she cinched her lips together, he could tell she was holding back a full cry. Tears streamed down her face, and she reached out, and took his hand. The touch was unexpected, and it was almost electric to him, feeling his gut tighten and shoulders pull back slightly.

"Thank you for coming here and telling me this, I know it wasn't easy. I'm glad to hear all you said and to just know you're alright. Over the years, I would wonder about you and I often included you in my prayers."

Next she gave his hand a squeeze and a gentle shake, and then she let it go. With a sense of relief, his tension released slightly, and he gave her a smile feeling grateful that she treated him in such a kind manner.

Motioned to the road, she said she should get started on her run, and he thanked her for listening. As she began to walk away, she stepped back, and gave him an awkward hug.

"I hope everything continues to go well for you Derrick."

He thanked her and wished her the same.

"Thanks," she said smiling. "I am getting married in two weeks, so I'll take all the well wishes I can get right now."

She saw the shock on his face and he sounded somewhat nervous.

"Oh…married…two weeks…that's great, congrats."

Although he tried to sound enthusiastic, she could tell it bothered him. Then they awkwardly discussed the details of where and when, as he pretended to be interested and glad for her. In reality he wasn't glad, his mind immediately began to think about ways to disrupt the wedding and reclaim her love. Before she walked away, she put two fingers to her lips, kissed them, and then placed them on his.

"I will always love you " she said, as they parted ways.

Unable to drive until he calmed down, Derrick sat in the car watching her as she began her run and disappeared out of sight.

Over the next two weeks, he kept picturing her walking down the aisle to *that guy*, which was what Derrick labeled him. He knew nothing of the man or who he was, nothing of his positive points or how he treated her, but he didn't like him and wouldn't like him. Even though he knew she seemed to be happy with him, Derrick couldn't get past the *that guy* reference, because in his mind he was *that guy* who stoled her away.

Shawn knew Derrick was in a high risk cycle for relapse. Wanting to ensure he stayed clean, he called Derrick every morning and met with him every evening while attending meetings together. They would continue with that plan until after the wedding, and possibly beyond, depending on how Derrick was presenting. Realizing having Shawn as a support was the only thing holding him to his sobriety, Derrick was thankful for the dedication of his sponsor.

The morning of the wedding was upon him and Derrick felt like his heart was breaking. Every day for over five years he had loved her. They were together a year, but his love lived on through the four plus that had followed. Now his love couldn't simply stop because she was marrying another man. Feeling like this was somehow a punishment for the heartbreak he caused her, he now understood, first hand, just how bad it was for her. Wandering about his apartment as an emotional mess, he was filled with remorse all over again.

Without much thought, he decided he had to see her get married to make it final in his mind. At first he considered sitting in the back of church, but knew that wouldn't be appropriate. With a flash, he suddenly remembered there used to be a donut shop across the street, that they had gone to a few times when they attended services with her family. Knowing it was a clear view to the door, he decided he'd sit by the window and watch her come out as the happy bride. Then his mind, and heart, would know for sure it was over, and he might be able to move on.

About 1:15 pm he arrived at the donut shop. The ceremony was scheduled to begin at 1:00 pm, so he was sure she would be inside before he got there. Fearful he wouldn't be able to stop himself from running out and trying to stop her, he was avoiding being there while she entered. Having skipped breakfast, he got coffee, his favorite donut, and found a seat by the window with a direct view of the church steps. As he waited, his phone rang, and he looked down and saw it was Shawn. Not wanting to hear a sobriety speech, Derrick silenced it, and continued to look out the window. As a last minute decision, he hadn't told Shawn of his plan, because he was sure that he wouldn't agree. If Derrick insisted, he would have likely shown up to sit with him.

Appreciating Shawn and his help, he was grateful for the support, but felt he needed to do this on his own. He would call him after she and the groom left, but for this part he needed to confront the reality of her being married to another man in solitude.

Derrick left his things at the table and stepped away for a minute to add cream and sugar to his coffee. When he returned he was struck by her standing near the limo. She was more beautiful than he had ever seen, but he wondered how it could be over so quickly. Then he became angry with himself for making a mistake with the time. Standing at the window, looking at her, and hoping to see something that would give him the finality he needed to move on, Derrick was motionless.

Unexpectedly, he felt deflated. She was married, but he stepped away and missed what he had come to see. It was the image of her and her groom, leaving the church to depart for their life together, that he had been in seeking. Now all he got to see was her, but he missed them as they emerged from the church a newly married couple. Knowing she would never again be his, Derrick couldn't help but feel isolated by his own past indiscretions.

Taking a deep breath, he leaned closer to the window just as she looked up and saw him. Catching sight of her glance, and the expression on her face that switch to a brief moment of pain as she closed her eyes, he was sure his presence was noticed. Then in an instant she was in the limo and out of sight. The cars began to pull away, and he stepped out and started to walk in the opposite direction.

Suddenly, he heard the screech of brakes followed by a loud crash and the sound of crushing metal. Dread washed over him, and he turned running in the direction of the limo expecting to see it had been in in accident. Scanning the road, his heart stopped momentarily when he saw a small car had smashed into a pole just past the church. The limos were stopped in the middle of the street and she was standing behind them looking at him.

Derrick caught his breath, and said, "What are you doing?"

She crinkled her forehead, while saying, "You hurt me."

He nodded, took a step towards her, and said, "I know...I'm sorry."

Shaking her head slowly side to side, and looking at him with a pleading look, she said, "I had a broken heart for a really long time and didn't know why."

Holding back tears, he nodded again, "If I could undo it I would. I know how I made you feel. It hurts me to know I did that to you."

The guests that had gathered in front of the church, stood in awe of what was happening right in the middle of Main Street, while people in stopped cars rolled down their windows to listen. On the sidewalk stood the bridal party, that had emptied from the limo, looking on in shock.

"What if you hurt me again?" she said, with tears building up.

Derrick took another step, "No, no, no, I am not that person anymore. I say that as a promise to you."

They were standing face to face and looking into each other's eyes. His heart was pounding and he wondered if this truly happening. He thought, *Could it be real?*, as he stood inches away from the woman of his dreams.

Then she said, in a soft meek voice, "Okay."

Unsure what was meant by her okay, his head retracted slightly, and he asked in a questioning tone, "Okay?"

"You're still my kryptonite," she murmured, as her lips made a natural pout and tears hung in the corners of her eyes.

Overwhelmed by her words, he couldn't believe she was coming back to him. Derrick was consumed by the love they shared, and was hit with the realization if he had been open to seeing the value of that love four years prior, they both might have been spared a great deal of heartache. Now it seemed he was being given a chance to do it over, to do it the right way.

Studying her every expression, he leaned in to kiss her, but hesitated and asked, "What about your husband?"

With a sparkle in her eyes, she smiled slightly, then said, "I don't have a husband." Derrick felt confused and she could see it on his face. "I couldn't go through with it. After seeing you, I realized I would never feel for him, what I feel for you."

His heart fluttered in his chest and he was at a loss for words. Pulling her close, Derrick put his arms around her, and they kissed. Again he looked into her eyes and felt the warmth of the love they once shared.

"I have always loved you Faith."

Faith smiled, gazed at him, and said, "I will love you forever."

Finally feeling he was back where he was always meant to be, Derrick was hit with the realization that in all those months of facing the past, he was actually finding the future.

www.ingramcontent.com/pod-product-compliance
Lightning Source LLC
Chambersburg PA
CBHW070824180626

46818CB00001B/385